A VISION OF FIRE

GILLIAN ANDERSON

& JEFF ROVIN

A VISION OF FIRE

BOOK ONE OF *THE EARTHEND SAGA*

**SIMON &
SCHUSTER**

London · New York · Sydney · Toronto · New Delhi

A CBS COMPANY

First published by Simon451, an imprint of Simon & Schuster Inc., 2014
This edition first published in Great Britain by Simon & Schuster UK Ltd, 2014
A CBS COMPANY

1 3 5 7 9 10 8 6 4 2

Simon & Schuster UK Ltd
1st Floor
222 Gray's Inn Road
London WC1X 8HB

www.simonandschuster.co.uk

Simon & Schuster Australia, Sydney
Simon & Schuster India, New Delhi

A CIP catalogue record for this book is available
from the British Library

HB ISBN: 978-1-47113-770-9
TPB ISBN: 978-1-47113-771-6
EBOOK ISBN: 978-1-47113-773-0

Printed and bound by CPI Group (UK) Ltd, Croydon, CR0 4YY

A VISION OF FIRE

PROLOGUE

Rocking gently under the full moon, the Falkland Advanced Petroleum survey ship rested in the harbor at Stanley. Its hull was weather-beaten after three weeks at sea, its sensitive below-deck sensors were rattled by the relentless waves, and its chief geologist was exhausted.

But as he bent over the tiny lab table in his forward cabin, Dr. Sam Story could not stop staring at a rock the remote-controlled Deep Sea Grab Vehicle had pulled from a ledge on their last day in the South Atlantic. The silvery stone fit in his palm and was roughly the shape and thickness of a playing card. He had been studying it for more than an hour through a magnifying glass, slowly moving the lens up and down and side to side; the fifty-three-year-old geologist was finding it difficult to accept what he was seeing.

Finally, the man sat upright on the stool, blinked his tired eyes, and thumbed on a small audio recorder.

"Specimen E–thirty-three," he intoned cautiously, "definitely appears to be a pallasite meteor fragment. And it is my observation that chipping marks on the back indicate it was hewn from the parent stone by hand. However . . ."

He gently set the stone on a cotton swath he'd placed on the table and pulled off his latex gloves. The relic had been washed by frigid waters for centuries, perhaps millennia, and rough surfaces and body oils might cause further damage.

Dr. Story looked down at the stone again and studied the symbol that gently shone from it. "On the anterior façade is a carving of four triangular shapes arranged in a pyramid," he recorded. "Each triangle is formed by three interlocking crescents, with small, extended crescents at the three corners. More of a claw or talon shape, actually, those small ones. No claws at the corners of the center triangle. I cannot begin to guess at the meaning or function of this."

He bent low, peering at the stone. "Regarding process, the width and depth of the markings suggest they were carved by a smaller, finer tool than that which made the relic itself. While there existed any number of local tribes that could have cut these figures, the edges of the markings themselves are a real mystery."

Picking up the magnifying glass again, he murmured, "Every side of every etching has a rounded perimeter that suggests eons of erosion. Yet these edges are not worn down uniformly but are built up, like blisters. Blisters like these could only be generated by intense heat, Class D at a minimum, and ancient peoples did not have the wherewithal to generate twenty-one hundred degrees Fahrenheit."

Dr. Story sat upright, picked up the recorder, and grinned. The modern device felt strange and inconsequential in his hand. This relatively sophisticated by-product of human invention was dramatically less interesting than a simple stone pulled by chance from the ocean.

No, he corrected himself, *this is not simple.* Volcanic magma could reach that level of heat, but even that was uncommon. By the time lava reached the surface, it was closer to fifteen hundred degrees Fahrenheit. He had only seen this kind of melting and hardening on meteoric rocks that softened and bubbled during their flaming passage through the atmosphere and hardened when they reached the cooler surface, free of friction.

"But that doesn't explain how the carvings melted," he mumbled into the recorder. "*They* couldn't have come through the atmosphere. That would mean they had to originate in . . ."

Dr. Story was tired. He had been awake for nearly forty-eight hours. Before he considered the implications that the evidence suggested, he needed rest.

Turning off the desk lamp, he fell into the small bed that folded down from the wall. The gentle rocking in the harbor was a balm after twenty-one days at sea. Despite a sudden thumping on the hull beneath the water—possibly a pilot whale; the cetaceans had shown a surprising tendency to beach themselves of late—the scientist was asleep within moments.

The door opened and a figure entered the room. He moved quietly, cautiously. The rocking of the boat was unpredictable and he did not want to fall against the desk or the bed.

The man laid an empty camera case on the floor. Guided by the light of the moon through a porthole, he quickly gathered up the tablet and the audio recorder. He swaddled the small piece of rock in its cotton wrap and placed it in the camera case.

And then he was gone, headed away from the public jetty. Dropping the two electronic devices into the water, he watched their gurgling descent in the ivory moonlight, then continued toward the Malvina House Hotel.

PART ONE

CHAPTER 1

It was an unseasonably warm October morning, better suited for a stroll than a stride, but Ganak Pawar and his daughter maintained their usual quick pace up the east side of Manhattan. The permanent representative of India to the United Nations, veteran of thirty years as a foreign-service officer, wore a practiced expression of tolerance. Sixteen-year-old Maanik seemed especially energized by the blanket of sunlight that spilled across York Avenue.

"Papa, your presentation last night was amazing!" Maanik said. "I couldn't get to sleep for hours, my brain was alive with so many ideas."

"That is gratifying," her father replied.

"It's time for people to think differently about Kashmir and you made that point with the General Assembly," she said. "I'm glad CNN covered it, it was totally inspiring."

"I am glad you feel so. I am not being universally thanked for it."

"Papa, you got in their faces. That took courage!"

Ganak smiled. "I 'got in their faces,' did I?"

"You know what I mean," his daughter said, grinning. "Anyway, don't be so modest, especially now. Now is the time for a determined follow-up."

Ganak wasn't sure if it was courage or desperation that had compelled him to show the video of a Kashmiri mother immolating herself over her dead son. Tensions occurred in Kashmir every few years but this time it felt different. Thirty-two people had died in two days, and Pakistan and India were once again rattling their nuclear sabers. Perhaps that familiar, tired bragging had driven Ganak to suggest they make Kashmir a UN protectorate. If the UN temporarily governed the region, as it had in Kosovo for nine years, that could buy time for the populace to choose whether to join one country or the other, or to opt for independence . . .

"Papa?"

"Yes?"

"I want to be part of that follow-up," Maanik said, bouncing in her stride with excitement. "You should hear my ideas."

He smiled as he regarded her. She looked so mature in her brown faux leather jacket over a dark blue dress. Her leggings were orange and gold, one leg striped horizontally, the other swirling in a feather pattern. She had sewn the disparate halves together herself and matched them with an orange and gold scarf. He noticed with surprise that she had begun to pluck her eyebrows, and though her black hair had always been strong and thick, the way she arranged it over her shoulder was a recent development.

She is so unlike her mother, he thought. When the Pawar family had moved from New Delhi to Manhattan two years ago and Maanik started at Eleanor Roosevelt High School, the girl immediately began to change. Where her mother, Hansa, was reflective, Maanik did her thinking aloud. Where Hansa planned, Maanik improvised. Hansa embraced tradition but Maanik liked to Rollerblade on the sly with the son of the Canadian ambassador. The Pawars' American bodyguard, Daniel—who was walking a few paces behind them—was charged with clandestinely keeping an eye on the young lady when she was not at home.

Ganak couldn't decide whether he was concerned at her shrugging off the old ways or if he was proud that she lived her own life. Hansa did not like it but Ganak was not sure, and his diplomatic skills were sometimes tested at home in ways that could rival the current crisis in Kashmir.

Thinking of India and Pakistan pulled down the edges of his smile. These days, walking Maanik to school was one of his only refuges.

"Maanik, I want to hear your ideas but I must caution you, sometimes it is wise to pause after a push."

"How can that be wise?" she asked. "If something is moving, why not keep it in motion?"

"I read the reports from home before we left this morning. India and Pakistan are both infuriated even while the rest of the world applauds the idea of a protectorate."

"That's my point," Maanik said, undaunted. "Now you need to convince India and Pakistan."

"Ah. It is that simple?"

"Maybe not *so* simple, but my ideas can help with that. I've been thinking up op-eds for you, press releases, but especially"—she turned and walked backward, facing him and glowing—"what if you let me interview you on video, talking about the situation? Networks would eat that up, parents would watch it with their children, it would be casual and nonthreatening but with our hearts in it, you know? We could get people used to your proposal through conversation instead of arguments. If we get it just right, maybe it could go viral."

Ganak was impressed. Maanik had prepared a presentation of her own. This revelation about his daughter was one of the reasons that, even in the middle of a crisis, he insisted on maintaining their half-hour, no-cell-phones walk to school.

"Those are very creative ideas, Maanik."

"Okay! So the next step is, I take a break from school and get an internship with you at United Nations headquarters. Actually, school will probably count that as a class—"

Ganak interrupted. "Interns at the headquarters must be in graduate school. High school students are out of the question."

"But, Bapu"—she softened him with the Hindi word for "Daddy"—"I have the intelligence and the desire and right now my help is crucial."

"I appreciate your interest, but every member of the staff is well-credentialed, not just well-intentioned."

"An exception can be made—"

"Exceptions are the exceptions," he said.

Maanik frowned. "I don't even understand that."

"It means no. I'm sorry, Maanik."

She turned and walked forward again, visibly frustrated. "So I am supposed to just waste my days thinking up ideas and never making any of them happen?"

"You are a very exceptional young lady—"

"And I am telling you, I am wasting time at school."

"You are learning about other lives, other times."

"While I ignore the fact that our homeland could erupt into war? I am trapped in irrelevance, Bapu. I want to help."

"Your books are not irrelevant."

"Really? And what if one crazy officer in one of the armies actually prepares to launch a warhead this time? What would you do, talk to him about a novel you read? Or a poem?"

"Maanik, my life, you are about to lose this argument." He smiled.

"Oh?" She stopped on the corner of Seventy-Sixth Street, shifted her weight onto one hip, and raised her eyebrows at him. "How?"

He grinned. "You are young and impatient. I have been where you have been, but you have not been where I have been."

Maanik turned suddenly to the six-foot-two blond man with the crooked nose who stood behind them. "Daniel, do you think that's a good argument?"

"I am neutral in this, ma'am," said the bodyguard with a smile. Behind the reflective sunglasses his eyes were on the pedestrians who moved around them, peripherally watching the cars drive too quickly on the avenue. He looked along the street as they got a walk sign, and they crossed York into a narrow block full of red brick and green leaves just starting to turn.

"Maanik," Ganak admonished, "allow him to do his job." His voice softened quickly. It always did with his daughter. "As for you, your job is to learn patience and to get an education and experience, from which grow wisdom."

"Patience," she said impatiently.

"Do you know that is my primary job? To guide patiently, compassionately. To nudge people along, not to wrench them to my goal, my will. I work toward a Kashmir protectorate, but slowly. Do you see this as less courageous than shaking your fist or raising your voice? I tell you, it is more!"

The young woman suddenly looked like the little girl who was still so green in her father's memory. They walked in silence. He impulsively took her hand in his. She squeezed it tightly.

They reached the stretch of sidewalk before the school doors. It was full of students and a few teachers sending texts or hurrying through conversations before the activities of the first period began at seven forty-five. Today was Human Rights Club, which alternated with Model UN. But Maanik was not rushing to find her friends. Her father saw that she was thinking hard and he almost regretted the conversation.

As he looked around, it appeared as if everyone outside the school was subdued. After he had shown the video of the mother's suicide to the General Assembly, it had gone viral. He regretted that, especially considering that some of these teenagers had probably watched it, and many more of them must have heard about it. But the world needed a push so that the endless tensions in Kashmir could finally be laid to rest. The Security Council had to pressure India and Pakistan or they would only pressure each other until yes, one day, perhaps a mad general would put an end to the tensions in a much worse way.

The ambassador was aware that he had made the situation even more serious. So, after pushing his daughter from a place where she felt she might have some influence, Ganak could not blame her for falling into solemnity.

"Do not dwell on this," he said, kissing her forehead. "Trust your father."

"I do," she said. "It's the others I do not trust."

He smiled. "And that is the problem, is it not? Someone must be the first to lay down his saber and believe that the other wants the same thing."

He waved and turned toward First Avenue. He and Daniel would walk the half hour downtown to the United Nations building, Ganak using the time to mentally rehearse his strategies and make phone calls. Without Maanik by his side he tuned into the city, heard the airplanes and helicopters overhead, the trucks making deliveries, the cars whipping across bumpy streets. He heard the sound of a loud motorcycle but dismissed it without thought.

Daniel did not dismiss the sound at all. The exhaust was so loud that the bike had to have straight pipes, uncommon on the sedate, aging Upper East Side of Manhattan. Daniel stared as the motorcycle turned onto Seventy-Sixth Street—black with red trim, slim rider also in black. It passed a street crew at the corner and roared past a man who was holding a SLOW sign on a pole. That was wrong too: the worker was walking away from the intersection where he should have been managing traffic flow. His strides were long and his gaze leveled on Ambassador Pawar. Shielded by the sign, his free hand disappeared under his yellow-and-red vest—

Outside the high school, no one reacted to the first gunshot. It was just a loud noise under the louder motorcycle. But Ganak turned and froze. That was what the assassins were counting on: paralysis to make him an easy target. That reaction was exactly what Daniel had been trained to overcome.

An instant before the worker had fired, Daniel was already in motion. The bodyguard bear-hugged the ambassador and dropped him hard to the concrete, at the same time turning with his own nine-millimeter drawn. He leaned on his stiff left arm, half-shielding the ambassador, while he aimed toward the street with his right.

With the second and third shots, pedestrians ran shouting for doorways or ducked behind cars. The parked vehicles and trees made it difficult for the gunman to find his target. To the east, the students, the teachers, everyone outside the school started screaming. Half the crowd dropped to the sidewalk, others huddled against the wall; the few still standing were grabbed and pulled to their knees, to their chests, their faces to the sidewalk. Maanik stood still, shaking in fear. The AP English teacher, Ms. Allen, grabbed the girl by the collar and forced her head down.

Maanik struggled against the woman's protective arms and tried to lift her head. She could not scream. She could not even open her mouth. There had not been a fourth gunshot. Did that mean the first three had succeeded? She thought of Daniel, wondered if he was all right, if any of those shots had been his. She felt the cold concrete against her right cheek, a dry leaf crumpled beneath it as she craned to see down the block.

There were sirens in the distance. Ms. Allen hesitated, then pushed herself off her knees. Someone had to check on Maanik's father and it couldn't be Maanik.

"Stay here," she ordered the student.

Mary Allen motioned for another student to stay with Maanik and ran in a crouch toward First Avenue and the bodies on the sidewalk. She did not see any blood, though she glimpsed a figure in a worker's yellow-and-red vest jump onto the back of a motorcycle. She felt her ears blasted by the roar of the bike as it tore east. She picked out the lumped figures of Maanik's father and the bodyguard. One body stirred, sat up, blond hair catching the sunlight. He turned to the body he was half-covering. The man's head lifted. He placed a hand on the sidewalk, struggled to push himself up, collapsed. Ms. Allen ran to his side, added her hands as support, and shouted over her shoulder, "Maanik, he's okay! They're both all right!"

Though that wasn't entirely true: now she noticed the blood on the pavement. She looked all over the ambassador's body before she saw blood gushing from the bodyguard's sleeve and knew that it was he who had been struck. She called for someone to get the school nurse.

• • •

Fifteen minutes later, having just gotten off the phone with his wife, Ganak Pawar gently lifted his daughter's head from his shoulder and helped her sit upright on the couch in the principal's office. He pulled a fleck of dry, broken leaf from her cheek. They were alone, both unharmed. Daniel had been rushed to the hospital, losing blood fast, his right arm useless, but the EMTs had assured them he would be okay.

Maanik had not cried, even as the adrenaline drained out of her. Her deep, ragged breaths calmed into something approaching normal. She was still shaking, but her father could not ignore the knock on the door. The principal looked in.

"Mr. Ambassador, your car is here."

"Yes, thank you," he said. "I will be right there."

Maanik grabbed his hand, held it tight.

"Maanik, I must."

"I don't want you to."

"I know. But I will be all right, I swear to you. Two in one day, it does not happen."

She nodded, unconvinced.

"As soon as you feel up to it, have the principal call Mama and she will pick you up and take you home. You will have a very quiet day."

Maanik looked away from him and was silent. Her grip tightened; she dug her nails into his hand.

"Maanik—"

"It is hopeless. Everything is hopeless. The UN, your speech, everything."

"It is not. *You* must not lose faith."

"I could have lost you. Who can have faith?"

"But you didn't lose me; I am here. And when I appear at the United Nations after an assassination attempt, that makes my voice stronger—"

"I'm not going home." She let go of his hand.

"It's all right—"

"You have to do your job, so I will do mine."

He took a deep breath, gazed at his daughter. This argument was hers. He kissed her forehead, lingering longer than before, and pressed her hands in his as he stood.

"Then I will see you for dinner, and I will call you during the day. I will make sure the principal allows you to keep your phone on. Maanik Pawar, you make me very proud."

"You too, Papa Ambassador." Her smile was weak but it was there.

He gave her one more peck on the top of her head, then left with a strong, purposeful stride. Maanik rose and immediately sat down again, her legs still wobbly. But she attended her second-period class, AP United States History.

The nurse asked the principal to text Maanik's teachers, telling them to keep an eye on her.

Amid the subtle stares from kids she did not know well and thumbs up from those she did, Maanik sat in her seat, opened her notebook, and copied words from the board. Her pen ran dry and she scribbled in circles until the blue ink flowed, then she kept scribbling circles until she caught herself with a jerk. It was as if she had fallen asleep and suddenly there were circles on the page. She forced herself to pay attention.

Maanik listened, moved on with several classmates to Geometry, and midway through the lesson began drawing circles until the paper was full of them. Then she put down her pen and scratched under the sleeve of her dress. She didn't feel itchy. She just needed to scratch.

"Papa . . . ," she whispered, the utterance more breath than word. No one around her heard.

"Papa?" she said, louder this time.

The girl to her right looked over. "Maanik?"

The teacher glanced at her.

Maanik looked at the student beside her and saw a suddenly unfamiliar face. The girl's flesh was pale, almost translucent, like ice on a pavement. Her eyes had a reddish cast, like a ruby in her mother's jewel box. Her lips were a pale blue and very pronounced.

Maanik spoke, her voice wheezing from her chest. "Papa . . . help me!"

The teacher quickly made her way down the aisle. Maanik began breathing rapidly, digging her pen over and over into the desk with one hand and raking the back of her wrist with the other until rivulets of blood rose up.

The teacher gently restrained her hands and sent another student for the nurse.

"Maanik, don't—"

Maanik suddenly threw her arms up, sending the teacher back against a desk, and thrashed in her seat before relaxing for the briefest moment. Then she screamed so loudly that the teacher pulled her close in a desperate, helpless effort to quiet her.

Maanik went limp just as the nurse arrived.

CHAPTER 2

Caitlin O'Hara, MD, PhD, two weeks shy of her forties and three sips into a cup of coffee, toggled keys on her tablet.

"We can't give them the moon, Dr. O'Hara."

"I didn't ask for the moon," she said to the voice coming from her tablet. "I asked for money, Ms. Tanaka, for twenty-five test shelters. You can do that."

On-screen, a 3-D blueprint of a small house revolved and a wall disappeared so that Caitlin could zoom inside and view the interior. The house would accommodate twenty souls who had been sweltering or freezing in decaying tents for months. This new snap-together unit was created by a modular furniture manufacturer under contract to the United Nations High Commissioner for Refugees. It was an update to a previous model that, among other concerns, had lacked a lock inside the front door. It had that now. All it needed was funding.

Tanaka's boss, Director Qanooni, weighed in. "We simply do not have the hundred thousand dollars this project requires."

"Which circles back to where we started this discussion," O'Hara said. "Crowdfunding. I know it won't deliver the windfalls you get from donor nations and it requires valuable person-hours to oversee. But lives are worth the effort."

The conference call with the development officers of the World Health Organization was about to run over its scheduled half hour. But the need for the refugee shelters was absolute. That, and the clock ticking before Caitlin's next client arrived, made her bold.

There was a short silence, after which Tanaka murmured to Qanooni and the director said, "I will take it to the board."

"Please don't," Caitlin urged. "You know what 'board' stands for?" She answered her own question: "Bunch of Argumentative—"

"Thank you, doctor," Qanooni interrupted hastily. "*We* are on the board, need I remind you?"

"You needn't, and I'm sorry if you were offended." Caitlin grinned. "But I cannot abide red tape. It never strangles bad ideas, only good ones. So please, just go to the nearest high school in Geneva, put some students to work for extra credit, and they'll throw a funding website together in a couple of hours."

"If only it were that simple." Tanaka sighed. "There are liability issues."

"I sympathize," Caitlin replied. "I do. I pay more for insurance than I do for rent and office space combined, and that's saying something in Manhattan. But health issues trump insurance. They *must*. Otherwise, why are we in this business?"

"Fair point," Qanooni said as Tanaka made a thoughtful "hmm" sound.

"I'm not wrong about this," Caitlin prodded.

"But of course," Qanooni chided. "When was the last time you were wrong?"

"Cameroon, 2010," she answered. "It was twilight and I mistook a spotted hyena for a dog. I invented the backward broad jump *and* set a record for it, all in one."

Caitlin's phone buzzed, buzzed again. It was a call from Benjamin Moss.

"Director Qanooni, Ms. Tanaka, I do have to go now but I'll follow up by e-mail. Thank you for your time . . ."

The director thanked her—and reprised the issue of liability instead of saying good-bye. Caitlin's phone stopped buzzing, then started again. Ben was calling a second time instead of leaving a voice mail.

Caitlin ended the online meeting, sat back in her chair, and let her eyes rest momentarily on her office walls, full of landscape photos from Thailand, Cuba, the Philippines, her framed degrees and awards—certificates that made her career in adolescent psychiatry easier but didn't matter, not fundamentally.

She called Ben back—he picked up on the first ring.

"Ben, I have a session in one minute, so this has to be—"

"Can you cancel it?"

"What? No—"

"Cai, I'm serious," he said. "I need you at the United Nations as soon as you can get here."

"I'm serious too, Ben, I've got—" There was a knock on her door. "One minute!" she called, knowing it was her assistant, probably announcing her client. "Ben, my eleven o'clock is here."

"Please cancel the appointment," Ben implored. "You know I wouldn't ask if it weren't important."

Caitlin frowned. "This is important too. At least tell me what it's about."

"I can't tell you over the phone. This area gets electronically swept by every government on the planet. Please, Cai."

"It's that serious?"

"That serious."

Caitlin rose and started toward the door. "Give me five minutes here and I'll come over."

"Thanks. I'll text you where to meet."

Caitlin ended the call, opened the door, and explained the situation. After rescheduling with her client, she caught a cab and headed for the United Nations.

Ben's text read *48th and 2nd*. As Caitlin's cab pulled along the curb, she spotted him pacing in front of an apartment tower. He was wearing a tailored suit and a grim expression. She watched her old friend as the cabbie processed her card. A long, dim portico with square arches stretching behind him made his taut stride seem even more restless, as if the arches were boxing him in. He was carefully eyeing every cab that passed. When he eventually registered hers he brightened slightly and hurried over.

She had only noticed fear in Benjamin Moss twice since she met him as an undergrad at New York University: on September 11, 2001, watching the Twin Towers burn from the foot of Washington Square Park, and in Thailand after the tsunami of 2004 as bodies began to wash up onto the shore. But he seemed fearful now.

They hugged. The air felt unusually chilly, even though the sun was shining directly on them.

"I owe you big-time," he said.

"Time and a half," she said. "Why am I here?"

With a gentle hand Ben steered Caitlin back to the portico. He stopped there and glanced surreptitiously at the doorman. Caitlin suddenly felt trapped with Ben in his imaginary cage.

"Ben, what's going on?"

"How's Jacob?" he asked quietly. "Still ten?"

"He's fine. Taking cooking classes. He wants to take Tai Chi now like the people in the park."

"I know a good teacher," he said. "From China."

"Ben? Where's the graveyard and why are you whistling?"

He took a breath. Ben was a translator at the United Nations. She had seen him at work: there was always the briefest delay between what he heard and what he said as he processed exactly how to say it. He was doing that now.

"Early this morning the Indian ambassador to the UN was walking his daughter to school," he said in a voice barely above a whisper. "You may have heard about it—"

"Attempted assassination," she said.

"Right. The police commissioner put the Counterterrorism Bureau on it and all they've turned up is a nameless guy and a fuzzy surveillance video showing two men on their motorcycle racing down York Avenue."

"No one's claimed responsibility?"

Ben shook his head. "The NYPD thinks the men were lone wolves but both India and Pakistan are pointing fingers."

"So no one even knows why this happened?"

Ben shook his head. "Lots of people have reasons for wanting him dead, or at least sidelined. He's a pacifist who's too high-profile to simply recall. More importantly, peace talks started a week ago and most of the United Nations delegates and the Security Council requested that he attend them, over the misgivings of India and Pakistan."

"And you're his interpreter," Caitlin said.

"With Hindi, Urdu, Uighur, Shina, and occasionally a tribal language." He grinned for the first time. "My brain's kind of spinning."

"How's *his* brain?" Caitlin asked.

"Pretty good," he replied. "It takes a lot to rattle that man."

Clearly if he was fine, the ambassador wasn't the reason she was here. Caitlin waited for Ben to resume.

Ben's voice got even softer and he leaned forward conspiratorially. "Everything has been proceeding slowly and cautiously—until today. Ambassador Pawar got a phone call about his daughter and left, canceling the rest of the session. It took about a second for the Pakistani delegates to get annoyed, and we don't know how long they're going to stay accommodating. A half hour later the deputy ambassador of India—who was also pretty concerned—pulled me aside and asked me to come to the ambassador's condo and get him. Which is right here." He nodded up at the skyscraper above their heads.

"The man was shot at," Caitlin said. "Can't they give him a couple hours off?"

"It's not *about* him, Cai. It's about using events as platforms. The ambassador was already late and his absence gives everyone time, and an excuse, to get back on a partisan soapbox."

"I understand," Caitlin said. "But the ambassador isn't why I'm here."

"No," Ben said solemnly.

What would pull a diplomat out of a crisis session but a crisis at home? Caitlin felt a twinge as she remembered her own father's careful, loving attention. "The daughter?" She had heard about the shooting on the news.

Ben nodded, stared down the street, then back at the doorman.

"What's happening with her?" Caitlin asked.

"It's . . ." Ben's mouth tightened, then he exhaled. "It's disturbing. Cai, you'll have to see for yourself."

Taking her by the elbow, he walked her into the building. The concierge at the desk did not bother calling up, obviously familiar with Ben.

"They brought her in through the service elevator," Ben said.

There were security cameras in the lobby and one in the corner of the elevator. *Loose lips sink ships*, Caitlin thought as they rode up to the penthouse. Ben had not spoken another word. She could not imagine what was so dire that it could not be spoken about . . . and had unsettled him so much that he still had not released her elbow.

The elevator door opened on a corridor that was eerily silent. There was a vacuum cleaner running in an apartment but the hallway's thick carpet muted the sound.

But it's more than the silence, she realized as they headed toward an apartment at the far end. There was the kind of stillness one felt at sunset in the wild, when all decent things went into their huts, tents, or burrows, and predators woke to feed. It was a strange and surprising sensation here.

On their first knock an anxious-looking woman in a red-orange sari opened the door.

"Thank you, Benjamin," she said, but was looking at Caitlin, studying her with experienced eyes.

"Dr. O'Hara, this is Hansa Pawar, wife of the ambassador."

"Hello," Caitlin said as a young beagle tried to slip through the door into the hall.

"Jack London!" Mrs. Pawar snapped, and the beagle slunk back inside. The dog was low to the ground and subdued as he turned to sniffing Caitlin's ankles. His attentions were brief, perfunctory.

Caitlin ran her hand down the dog's back as she reached down to take her shoes off; she had spent enough time in Mumbai to know that removing shoes was the cultural norm.

Mrs. Pawar stopped her. "Don't worry about that. Please just come with me."

Caitlin felt another chill as the woman hurried them through a spacious room. It was filled with light from a wall of windows facing the UN building and the East River. There was a pleasant hint of jasmine tea in the air. The apartment was overflowing with artifacts—Caitlin recognized not just Hindi sculptures and Muslim painted texts, but a Sikh helmet, a Christian cross, a Georgia O'Keeffe landscape.

Ben noticed Caitlin's wandering eyes. "Ganak calls interculturalism 'the peace of many choices,'" he murmured to her. "He's trying to embody it and teach it."

Caitlin didn't have much more time to look around before they were ushered into a bedroom, the second off a long corridor.

Though the drapes were drawn, enough sunlight filtered through for Caitlin to see that each wall was painted a different jewel color, amethyst, sapphire, emerald, and cherry opal. On a desk in the corner, an electronic photo frame flashed groups of friends laughing, smiling, hugging—in sad contrast to the girl who was unconscious in her father's arms across the room. Urged by Mrs. Pawar's outstretched hand, Caitlin moved slowly past her to the girl's four-poster bed. The beagle followed and sat on the floor beside her. Ben stayed by the door.

The man looked up. "I am Ganak Pawar."

"I'm Caitlin O'Hara," she said gently.

"Thank you for coming," he said, his voice cracking. "This—this is our daughter, Maanik."

Caitlin smiled reassuringly but her attention was on the girl's forearms, which were wrapped in gauze that was heavily spotted with blood. She sat on the bed and gently moved the girl's arms to look under the bandages. The teenager showed no response, the limbs dead weight. The bloodstains were smeared and unusual. Cut marks were typically linear; these were S-shaped and they were fresh. Even in the subdued light, Caitlin could see blood on the girl's fingernails.

"Maanik insisted on going to class," the ambassador said. "She was only there an hour when she began shrieking, doing this to herself."

"Nothing before that? No hyperventilating, faintness?"

"Her second-period teacher said she was staring, but otherwise normal," Ganak said. "This happened in her third class. When she came home she fell asleep but awoke screaming. For a while now she has been falling asleep, waking up screaming, speaking in gibberish, then sleeping again. Our doctor said it is post-traumatic stress from the shooting."

"Symptoms in cycles don't fit with PTSD," Caitlin mused, more to herself. "Did your doctor leave a prescription?"

"Yes. Kamala, our housekeeper, just picked these up." He nodded toward pills on the night table.

There was a paper pharmacy bag, still stapled at the top. Caitlin noted the physician's name, Deshpande, and the recipient's name, fabricated most likely, which did not include "Maanik" or "Pawar."

Caitlin opened the bag and retrieved a pair of amber containers. "Vasoflex. This is for insomnia and recurrent nightmares." She looked at the other, surprised. "Risperdal. This is a potent antipsychotic."

"That is a correct medication, yes?" Hansa asked.

"If you're bipolar and haven't slept for a few days," Caitlin replied.

"We don't use it as a prophylactic, 'just in case' medicine. Mrs. Pawar, your doctor *did* come by and see her, yes?"

There was silence. He hadn't. That was illegal in New York State. Caitlin glanced over at Ben, who gave her a cautioning look. Rules were obviously being bent here.

"That's a potent mix to put in her body without an examination and after just a few hours," Caitlin said.

"I am sorry," Mrs. Pawar said, more to her daughter than to Caitlin. "We did not know what else to do."

"It's not your fault," Caitlin lied, not wanting to make a bad situation worse. "But until we know the trigger, we're not going to give her these."

"Dr. O'Hara, we are watched," the ambassador said unapologetically. "Our doctor is also with the United Nations. He keeps a log. Confidentiality means nothing in diplomacy; word would spread. I'm afraid the delegations will see my distraction as a potential weakness and press for advantage, or worse. There is still a stigma against mental illness in both India and Pakistan. If anyone were to find out she was receiving psychiatric treatments—"

"Sir, there is no illness if a situation is treated."

"That is a technical distinction," the ambassador said. "I know it is difficult for Americans to understand the concept of family shame, and though Hansa and I do not subscribe to the idea, many still do."

"I do understand and there is no need to explain or apologize—"

"But there is," he interrupted. "I am in a delicate position. Accusations of evil spirits are still a quite common response to mental illness in both countries. If her condition is known—in fact, *when* her condition is known, as I am sure we have only a week, two at most, before discovery—I could be removed from the negotiations, Dr. O'Hara, or either side could use it as an excuse to leave the negotiating table and turn this matter over to their military forces. A doctor's visit to my home could be used to prove not just that I am incapable of mediating, but that the entire negotiation process is forfeit."

"We needed a caregiver no one knows," Ben said. "That's why I called you."

Caitlin didn't like it but she understood. The good of the many outweighed the needs of a few.

Ganak went on. "I know this is a terrible imposition, but Ben gives you a glowing report. Will you help?"

"Of course."

Ganak and his wife shared a relieved look, then smiled gratefully at Caitlin.

"If you will excuse me, doctor, I must get back," the ambassador said. He gently moved the girl out of his arms so that she was lying against her pillows. She still did not stir.

Caitlin moved closer to the young woman. "Ben, will you call my office and tell them I'm tied up in an emergency? This is going to take longer than I thought."

"Naturally."

"Mrs. Pawar, we're going to have to impose on your housekeeper again," Caitlin said. "Please ask her to pick up several boxes of cotton pads, six-ply bandage rolls as wide as they make them, and oregano oil. That won't sting your daughter awake; we want her to sleep."

Mrs. Pawar nodded. The ambassador rose and cupped his wife's face briefly as he passed her. She followed him out of the room. Ben nodded to Caitlin and smiled briefly in gratitude, then left the room, closing the door behind him.

Alone with the girl, Caitlin experienced another chill. The isolation and dread she had felt in the hallway seemed magnified here. There were no street sounds, no hovering air traffic anywhere near the United Nations, no sense of the time of day, no fresh air. She realized, though, that she might be responding to more than the environment and the girl's condition. Politically, what happened here would radiate in all directions, affect countless lives. There was no room for mistakes.

Good thing you never make any, she needled herself, thinking back to her conversation with Director Qanooni.

Maanik continued to sleep, her breathing shallow, her pulse at the low end of normal but not a cause for alarm. Her skin was cool but not cold. Caitlin asked for a thermometer; her temperature was normal. She checked for bruises on her neck, felt her scalp for abrasions or any sign of concussion.

When the housekeeper returned, Caitlin removed Maanik's bandages, then soaked several cotton pads with the oregano oil and gave them to Mrs. Pawar to hold ready. She picked up the girl's right arm with a gentle hand, held a soaked pad over one of the wounds, then wiped down gently but firmly to the wrist.

There was no reaction from Maanik. Her forearm twitched, but the girl's eyes did not even move behind her eyelids.

"My poor girl," Mrs. Pawar said.

Caitlin was concerned, not by the cuts, which were fairly superficial, but by the near-complete lack of response. This was not a normal slumber or the common numbness and disconnection that arose from an unexpected emotional event. She dropped the cotton pad and, taking Maanik's hand, applied sharp pressure to the nail bed of Maanik's pinky, trying to gauge her level of consciousness. The girl did not react. Caitlin pulled up the girl's left eyelid and the pupil immediately began to dilate.

That's strange, Caitlin thought. *There's no light here—*

"Help!" The girl screamed and bolted upright.

CHAPTER 3

Cries of terror seemed to explode from deep in Maanik's chest. Caitlin jolted back, giving the girl room to move but holding firmly to her wrists. Maanik was trying to scrape at her forearms while flinging her body back and forth on the bed.

"Maanik!" Caitlin called.

"Maanik!" Mrs. Pawar repeated from a corner of the room. "*Ise banda!*"

But the girl did not stop. She shook her head back and forth, not in resistance but in what seemed like rage. Caitlin wasn't sure she was even hearing them.

Releasing Maanik's wrists, she pressed her palms on the girl's shoulders and shifted them, not holding her down or shaking her but simply moving one shoulder up and the other down with strong purpose. It was an adaptation of a Chinese Qigong method Caitlin had used before to calm panic attacks.

Within moments, Maanik's screams became slightly more subdued—but only slightly.

"Mrs. Pawar, turn on the light," Caitlin said.

The woman hurried to the switch. An overhead fixture glowed. Caitlin angled Maanik's body slightly so she was looking up.

"Maanik, listen to me," Caitlin said. "You are looking at a large TV screen. Whatever you are seeing is on the screen. Do you understand? Look at the screen. Everything is on the screen."

Caitlin watched the girl's pupils focus on a point over her shoulder. The pauses lengthened between the screams, and they sounded like urgent announcements now instead of bursts of pure terror.

"Maanik, move your right foot."

The girl did not move.

"Maanik, keep looking at the screen and move your right foot."

The girl slid her right foot down the bed. Her breath had turned ragged and panting but she was not summoning breath for another scream. She was starting to recover.

"Maanik, I am going to count now. When you hear me say a number, you will see that number on the screen. When you hear 'eight,' you will want to go to sleep. When you hear 'five,' you will let yourself go to sleep. Okay?"

Her breathing was growing calmer. But there was no indication that she'd heard or understood.

Caitlin glanced around the room, the movement of her head easing the tension in her shoulders. She noticed that Jack London, instead of staying near his human like most worried dogs would have, was behind the curtains. He was sniffing hard and appeared to be moving along the edges of the windows.

Caitlin took one more deep breath, then said, "Okay, I'm going to begin counting." She maintained a light pressure on Maanik's shoulders. "Ten. Look at the ten on your screen. Keep looking. Nine. Eight."

Nothing changed.

"Maanik, when I say the word 'eight' you will feel how tired you are, how nice it would be to go to sleep. Look at the screen. Eight."

The girl's shoulders sagged under her hands.

Caitlin felt Jack London sitting down on her foot. Now he was watching Maanik.

"Very good. Seven. Six. You can feel your eyelids closing. Five."

Maanik's eyes closed as the countdown finished.

Jack London shook his head, sensing the crisis had passed, then yawned and trotted from the room.

Caitlin relaxed as well. She stood, pulled a light cover over Maanik's resting form, and backed toward the corner of the room where Mrs. Pawar had found safety. She could see that amid the mother's concern for her daughter, this protective and dignified woman was also scared of Caitlin.

"Hypnosis is a very common tool for psychiatrists, please don't worry."

"But how did you . . . she was unreachable!"

"Only to normal forms of communication. Maanik was actually very responsive to hypnosis, almost as if she has experienced it before. Has she ever been hypnotized?"

"No, never."

Caitlin was used to skepticism, but under Mrs. Pawar's gaze she felt like a wizard.

"This is just a temporary fix," Caitlin said. "At this point I would strongly suggest that you admit Maanik to a psychiatric hospital—"

"Absolutely not," Mrs. Pawar interrupted.

"But she's already a danger to herself, and at any minute—"

Mrs. Pawar was shaking her head. "It would be noticed and it would be publicized, doctor. It is not possible at this time."

She folded her arms and rested the back of a hand against her lips, and Caitlin saw how hard she was working to keep it together in the face of the day's events. Pushing the matter would worsen the situation for the mother and do nothing for the daughter.

"All right," Caitlin said, pulling her prescription pad and a pen from her purse. "I'm going to give you a different prescription—clonazepam. It's a sedative and a muscle relaxant, less radical than the others, and Maanik can be named the recipient without raising suspicions, in case anyone finds out. Give her the pill on a full stomach and when it takes effect, clean her forearms with the oil, all right?"

Mrs. Pawar nodded.

Caitlin indicated that they should leave the room. Mrs. Pawar followed her into the hall. As Caitlin left the door ajar she asked, "If you'll excuse me, Mrs. Pawar, I must ask: has Maanik ever suffered any kind of trauma? An attack, abuse at any age? Sexual abuse? Physical or emotional?"

Caitlin watched the woman grow weary under these most difficult of questions. She shook her head no. Caitlin pushed a little further.

"I know that you lived in New Delhi not long ago, and I know that New Delhi is experiencing an epidemic of sexual assault. Is there *any* chance at all that Maanik could have been assaulted and not told you?"

Mrs. Pawar did not look Caitlin in the eye but Caitlin knew that was cultural, not deceptive. "There is no chance," Mrs. Pawar said. "We raised a miracle. We raised a safe child. She was unscarred until she saw the attack on my husband."

Caitlin reached out and held Mrs. Pawar's hands for a moment. "I believe you," she said.

"Thank you."

"Thank *you*," Caitlin replied. "I know this isn't easy but it's necessary. We will find the cause of this. We will make her world safe again."

"How long will that take? Do you have any idea?"

"I don't," Caitlin admitted.

"What if—if it happens again?"

"It may very well. I'll leave you my number. If there is another episode, even a very mild one, call me. I'll come right over."

The relief in Mrs. Pawar's eyes was profound.

The housekeeper stepped forward—a small woman with the first touches of gray in her hair—and showed Caitlin to the door. But Caitlin turned suddenly. She felt goose bumps along her arms, as though cold air was blowing up her sleeves.

"Doctor?" Mrs. Pawar asked. "What is it?"

Caitlin looked down at her arms. Her sleeves weren't moving. There was no vent on the floor or the wall.

"Sorry," Caitlin said. "I thought I left something back there."

Smiling and wishing the women a good day, Caitlin walked into the hallway. The odd feeling passed as the elevator descended and the course of her day resumed and the lives of the patients she had to see crowded Caitlin's mind.

• • •

The rest of the day passed swiftly and without incident. Caitlin attributed her earlier restlessness to Ben's anxiety, the Pawars' fear, and the uneasy zeitgeist of a city that seemed to be waiting for bad news. Something about the Kashmir crisis was gripping people who usually forgot about major news events within a day or two. She overheard several conversations about the assassination attempt and whether nuclear war was likely. It was the top trending topic on Twitter, and her colleagues were sharing news articles over e-mail. An Associated Press update mentioned the ambassador's return to the negotiations and his cold reception. The talks had not recovered from the damage of Ganak's sudden departure—his "unexplained abandonment," one Indian delegate had called it.

Ben was right, she thought. *They're just looking for reasons to be petulant. Little girls and boys with very dangerous toys.*

Late in the afternoon, Caitlin headed to a café on Twenty-Seventh Street. Jacob's cooking class, held in a test kitchen one floor up, would be finishing in twenty minutes. She sat in a private corner with a cup of jasmine tea, hunched over her phone for an overdue conversation.

The man on the other end was unhappy and more than a little condescending.

"Dr. Deshpande, I assure you, it is *not* post-traumatic stress disorder," she said to Maanik's physician. "I have never heard of a rapid, cyclical repetition of PTSD symptoms."

"Perhaps a review of the current medical literature might convince you to revisit that opinion?" the doctor suggested.

Caitlin bristled but decided that methodology was not the battle she should be fighting.

"Yes, of course, I will be doing that," she said. "But in my experience with crisis survivors locally and globally, this is wholly atypical. Now," she continued before he could interject another cover-his-ass approach, "are you sure there is nothing in Maanik's history that could be a precursor to this?"

"Nothing. I am certain you checked for head trauma while you were there, Dr. O'Hara? She was thrown to the sidewalk when the shooting occurred—"

"There were no bruises, no reason to infer nausea, no reaction that would suggest headaches—"

"'Infer,' 'suggest,'" he said. "That is why I prescribed what I did. Because you frankly do not know."

"And *you* didn't request an MRI," Caitlin shot back. "I understand why, I do. But that doesn't justify nuking her body with that cocktail you prescribed."

"The ambassador was needed. Another incident had to be averted. And your method did not work, I understand? Not quite?"

This discussion was pointless. Caitlin got back on topic. "What about when she was a child?" she pressed. "I know the Pawars have only been here two years, but you have her records from India?"

"I came to New York with the Pawars," he said. "The ambassador arranged for my post at the United Nations. As for Maanik, the most serious ailment I have ever treated was a sprained ankle last winter from ice-skating. And before you interrupt me again, no, her head did not touch the ice. She is supremely healthy in every way. Which is why I felt—and still feel—she could handle that 'cocktail.'"

"What about psychologically?" Caitlin asked. "Has she ever exhibited an extended period of despondency, withdrawal?"

Dr. Deshpande laughed. "Those are words that could never apply to Maanik. She is a precocious, vital, outgoing girl, Dr. O'Hara, and has always been so."

"The drugs you prescribed. Had Maanik ever taken those or anything like them?"

"No, and I will spare you the discomfort of asking: Mrs. Pawar is concealing nothing about domestic abuse or assault. Her family is strong and loving and Maanik is one of the happiest teenagers I have encountered. I have no doubt that the mental trauma of witnessing her father's attack altered her body's chemistry and it is manifesting mentally. We can *safely* use medications temporarily to remind the body of what normal is, and she will adjust and return to herself."

"*Or* we can look for an approach that addresses the cause and not just the symptoms," Caitlin replied. She saw no reason to press this further. She thanked the doctor and ended the call. At least he had agreed to stick with just the clonazepam for now, since the immediate crisis had passed.

But Dr. Deshpande was right about one thing: had it passed for good? She flashed to the bloody S-curves on Maanik's forearms. Every day Caitlin provided therapy to high school students for Roosevelt Hospital. She counseled college students from the John Jay College of Criminal Justice, consulted for international agencies, oversaw the development of a mental health program for refugees, and closely monitored world news for potential hot spots of trauma where she might be needed. This work was her life and her passion. And yet, with all her specialized experience behind her, she was stumped by Maanik. Something about the terror, the scratching, the look in her eyes. To say it unsettled her would be an understatement.

Caitlin lifted her shoulders high and dropped them—a literal effort to shrug off the residue of the afternoon. Ten more minutes before Jacob would be down. She discreetly massaged just above her eyebrows, the tips of her ears, behind her ears, down her skull to her neck. It helped.

Her phone vibrated once—a text from her younger sister, Abby, a surgeon in Santa Monica, California: *How was it??*

Caitlin sighed. She knew what this was about: last night's date, which now seemed a hundred years ago. She'd text back later. She signaled the server for the bill, closed her eyes, and listened to the low murmur of conversation around her, cars outside, the flutter of a paper pinned to the wall near a heating vent.

Maanik came back to her thoughts—would she remember what happened when she woke? Caitlin thought of Ben, how scared he had seemed. Did he know something he wasn't sharing? She thought of all her clients whose appointments she'd had to cancel that afternoon, and the UN negotiations.

"Will that be cash or charge?"

Startled back to the room, Caitlin gave the server seven dollars and gathered her things. She exited the café into the lobby, peered through its windows onto Twenty-Seventh Street, saw nothing unusual. She checked her messages. Nothing new. She walked around the lobby twice, sat down on a bench made of recycled plastic, thought of Jack London back at the Pawars' apartment. She smiled, then called her own therapist and left a message, asking for a call back. "Nothing urgent," she said. Caitlin just needed to talk.

Then Jacob was hurrying across the lobby, still young enough to be excited to see her, saying and signing, "Hi, Mom!" at the same time. At school he leaned toward sign language as a means of communicating; after school he usually used his hearing aids. Caitlin marveled at how he straddled both worlds, even when faced with occasional pressure from other kids to "pick one."

He shoved a food container into her hands and made her try some of the salad he'd just prepared. She smiled as she accepted a plastic fork from her son and jabbed it into the julienned carrots and jicama doused in what appeared to be a light vinaigrette. It was delicious and she said so.

As they left the lobby for the cab ride home, Jacob enthused over the chemistry of cooking with eggs. Fire engines loudly raced by and she winced but quickly forgot them, completely and gratefully absorbed in the moment, in their shared signing, laughing, and camaraderie.

CHAPTER 4

Caitlin and Jacob were wrapped in a blanket on the couch in their Upper West Side brownstone apartment. The curtains were closed, the dishwasher was humming quietly, and Jacob was rapidly flipping through channels on TV. At this speed she wondered what could possibly be registering in his brain.

Caitlin wondered whether this was a sign of his transition into a preteen: where once he had shown tiredness by curling into a corner of the couch with his head on the armrest, now he channel-surfed like a zombie. She would wait to see if the behavior repeated on other nights.

But besides his restlessness, their time together was blessedly normal, and Caitlin cherished that. Each day was a challenge, today more than others, and she embraced these moments as if each were a little bit of Christmas morning.

"Okay, you," Caitlin said and signed, though his hearing aids were on. "My eyeballs are getting whiplash. Time for bed."

She was expecting an argument but didn't get one. He just headed for the bathroom, tapping the glass of the aquarium on his way out but not waiting to see if his bandit cory would peek out of her plastic castle.

"Teeth and face," she called. She heard the faucet start.

She turned off the TV, booted her tablet, and picked up their high-strung cat, who was prowling on the couch. Five minutes later, Jacob and their tabby Arfa were both asleep.

Even Jacob's slightly off mood had felt like a relief from Caitlin's day. He anchored her hectic life, tuned the world for both of them to a mellow pitch. But the mood never seemed to stick when she was on her own again. Even now she was losing the magic as she focused on e-mails, got back into her work head. As if on cue her phone buzzed. It was her therapist, who had become a dear friend long ago.

"I hope I'm not interrupting anything," Barbara said.

"Just finished TV time with Jake."

"Excellent. I'm glad you weren't working after six o'clock for a change."

"Says the shrink who's doing just that," Caitlin replied.

"Touché," Barbara said. "I blame the inventor of cell phones."

"Remember when the world turned without us for hours at a time?"

Barbara laughed. "And then there were vacations. Remember those?"

"I'll keep it short," Caitlin promised. "I've been restless today in a way that's different for me."

"Who or what was different in your routine?"

"There's a case that's much more personal and emotional, but I treated the condition, not the patient." Caitlin's answer had anticipated Barbara's next question. "What I'm actually wondering is, could my unease be perimenopause?"

"When did you get back from the relief camp?"

"Two weeks ago."

"Well good lord, Caitlin—"

"Okay, point taken. I'm still readjusting. But maybe I should be tested?"

"I think the result would be turningfortyosis," Barbara said. "You forget that it's the new thirty. Don't let the social programming kick in."

"I know, I'm not a hypochondriac. It's just, something is off."

"Sure, but I'd vote for exhaustion. And the peri tests are inconclusive anyway. I'd prescribe a couple weeks of dedicated health—real exercise, not just running for a cab. Take your vitamins, especially B and D, eat more vegetables—"

"I've been good about that. Well, Jacob's been good about it and I've benefited."

Barbara laughed. "And sleep. Actual sleep, not the occasional Ambien. Also, take some time off."

"You don't want much, just miracles," Caitlin said as her phone beeped with another call. It was from a private caller. Her gut burned a little; she had a feeling who it might be.

"You asked, I answered," Barbara replied.

"All right, will do. Hey, I need to take this other call—"

"Okay, but keep it short. Maintain your boundaries."

"You're a mind reader. Talk soon." Caitlin switched to the other call. "Hello?"

"Dr. O'Hara?" said a man's voice.

"Mr. Pawar."

"Please, it's Ganak. I am sorry not to be visiting you in person, to thank you. But eyes are upon me."

"Not a problem. How is Maanik?"

"She is a little better."

Caitlin heard strain in his raw, raspy voice. "Did she have another episode?"

"Yes, but not like before."

"Tell me about it."

"We're not sure. It was—forgive me, I am not used to describing these things. It was as if she was there with us at dinner, eating her soup, but she was listening for something else."

"Did she talk at all? Respond to you?"

"No. It was as though she was on the alert for something. But not in an urgent way. It's very difficult to explain."

"How long did that go on?"

"Perhaps five or six minutes. She said nothing the entire time and we did not want to question her until we spoke with you."

"I understand." Caitlin paused to consider the situation. "Mr. Pawar—Ganak. Maanik may have been suffering from a mild, self-induced trance."

"I'm sorry. Do you mean she hypnotized herself?"

"Not exactly," Caitlin said. "Did Mrs. Pawar tell you I used hypnosis to stabilize her?"

"Yes. And I must be candid, Dr. Deshpande expressed some concern—"

"Dr. Deshpande may be a fine doctor but he was prepared to over-medicate your daughter," Caitlin interrupted. "That's like washing your eyeglasses with a hose. It's not my way."

"Please, I did not mean to question your judgment. This is all so unfamiliar to us."

"Completely understandable," Caitlin said. "My point is, occasionally, individuals who have been given hypnotherapy will return to that state if they feel threatened in the same way as before."

"You mean her mind self-hypnotized to fend off a relapse?"

"In a manner of speaking," Caitlin said.

"I see." The ambassador was silent.

"Sir, may I make a suggestion?"

"Please."

"There is an obstruction in her mind, something that is redirecting her natural response to ordinary thoughts and stimuli. My guess is it has something to do with a traumatic event—in this case, the shooting. Maanik was very responsive to the superficial hypnosis I used earlier. I'd like to put her into a deeper trance."

"Deeper? What does that mean?"

"I only helped her to sleep before; I didn't fully engage with her.

It's clear that something is blocking her normal self and we must un-
cover what that is. This process is a proven tool for enhancing memories." She added, "Leaving her untreated could make the situation
worse."

There was another silence. Caitlin had the impression the ambassador was not considering her suggestion but thinking about how to
refuse it respectfully. She was right.

"Hypnotism is a practice honored across time and across many
cultures," Ganak said. "The Hindu Vedas call it a 'healing pass.' Yet I
believe a mind moves between different strata of consciousness for its
own good reasons. Interfering with that self-organization may be premature, if not dangerous."

"I respect what you are saying but you're forgetting an important
point—the self-mutilation," she said carefully. "The sounds she was
making while scratching at her arms alerted those around her. But it's
possible that she could harm herself in silence in the future, without
anyone knowing in time to prevent it."

"Then someone will stay with her constantly," Ganak said.

"Which could bear a psychological cost, drive her farther into hiding," Caitlin pointed out. She let that sink in for a moment, then said,
"One thing I can do for Maanik under hypnosis is guide her into symp-
tom transformation."

It took the ambassador a moment to rediscover his voice. "I am
not familiar with the term."

"We would choose a physical movement such as twitching her finger and associate it with her scratching at her arms. When fully conscious, any self-attack would be preceded by her finger twitching. As
she exercised control over her finger she would also shut down the
scratching."

"An off switch," he said.

"Exactly. It's one of many useful tools. And please understand,
while she is in a trance she retains her power of choice. In hypnosis I
am not operating her. We work together."

"I will certainly keep that in my mind."

"I appreciate your willingness to hear me out," Caitlin said. "You may call at any time if the situation changes."

"Dr. O'Hara, I may not have been sufficiently clear earlier about my reasons for caution."

"Not at all. I can see that you're in a difficult situation."

"Many political experts already feel that I am not the best chance for a peaceful and long-term resolution in these negotiations—I am the only chance. That is why radicals on both sides want me out of the way, by any means possible."

"Does your daughter know this?"

"She has made a point of studying the situation," Ganak said with a hint of pride. "You see, I am descended from the Pawar Rajputs, princes of Kashmir, so we are respected in India. But my family owns land in Gurdaspur near Jammu and Kashmir. It remains highly contested territory for the strategic importance of its road and railway. Because my family has never denied anyone access, the Pakistanis do not entirely mistrust me. So I have become the agent of all voices. There must be no blemishes on my perceived ability to engage fully. Please do not think I would risk my daughter's well-being—"

"I don't," Caitlin replied. "Maanik's symptoms may not recur and this could just be a posthypnotic echo, but we have to be prepared either way."

Ganak sighed. It was not relief exactly but cautious optimism. Tendering further apologies for interrupting her evening, the ambassador said good night.

Caitlin hung up and tapped a pen on the desk as she stared at her tablet. The fate of the region was on the shoulders of a sixteen-year-old. Perhaps Maanik knew that too.

After answering work-related e-mails—over two dozen in all—Caitlin was surprised to see that it was nearly midnight. It was past her bedtime but she was halfway through a weekly newsletter summarizing reports of adolescent schizophrenia episodes from around the world and she wanted to finish. There seemed to be an uptick in the number of references to an "apocalypse" by teenage patients, but Caitlin was wary of seeing trends where there were none. She decided she was just tired and overwrought.

"Enough!" she said, and closed her tablet. She brushed her teeth, washed her face, and got into bed.

As she lingered between wakefulness and sleep, she had dreamlike visions of smoky waves of red and blue rolling in from the distance, a nightmarish surf, creeping toward her on shapeless fingers, finally oozing and sputtering, throwing off ugly clouds of suffocating dust.

"Dad . . ."

She was looking for him—for someone—but the waves were everywhere, undulating and crashing, rising and engulfing her—

Caitlin gasped herself awake, surprised to find that two hours had passed. She blinked away the nightmare, looked around at the dark familiarity of her bedroom. She let her head sink back, breathing regularly, easily.

"Night terrors," she told herself. Everything was normal and right again, the room inside and the sounds outside. Everything—except one thing.

She was still afraid.

CHAPTER 5

The University of Tehran
Central Library and Documentation Center

Atash Gulshan sat alone at a long wooden table looking over the first draft of his paper on the tariff protests that shook Tehran in 1905. He had been staring at the printout for some time without reading the words.

He blinked twice, three times, and refocused. Eyes were upon him, furtively, accusingly—he had an acute sense of them, forced himself to ignore them. *The population did not want to repay the Russian czar for lending money to the Persian king for his personal use.*

A wave of nausea engulfed him, pushing from his mouth to his belly. Looking up, his gaze was misty.

Rashid, he thought miserably. *Brother . . .*

The nausea came a second time and he leaned forward on his forearms, shut his eyes. Atash saw the crane from which they hanged him, his brother's frightened but unrepentant expression as the stool was knocked away and the rope tugged his mouth and face horribly, unnaturally to one side.

Unnatural. That was what they had called Rashid for being a homosexual. Atash had been questioned mercilessly after his brother was found with another man. Queried, pushed, slapped. He wanted to tell them he must be a homosexual too, for after all, he loved his brother . . .

When he opened his eyes, a featureless wave rolled at him from a pinpoint in the distance. It was not an object so much as a billowing movement. It reminded him of his mother shaking out one of the quilts she made—a bulky mass moving thickly and in slow motion. The wave was a low, glowing red growing brighter with each moment. As it moved it shook off charcoal-colored clouds that seemed almost like black cats leaping as a rug was pulled from under them. Atash stared, transfixed, as the wave writhed toward him, filling more and more of his view. His head suddenly began to throb above both eyes. He winced but remained very still. A part of the young man's mind remembered that there were strict rules in the library. Quiet. Respect. No electronics. If he moved now he was afraid he might stumble . . .

"*Ulzii,*" he whispered.

The library rules became a haze of meaningless sounds in his head.

"*Ulzii?*" he repeated.

He pushed the chair back, scraping it along the floor. There was someplace he had to be, but *ulzii* was not a place. It was . . .

He reached into his backpack under the table. Feeling his way through the lentils and onions, he found the sunflower oil. He grasped the small plastic bottle and held it tight to his chest with his left hand.

Ulzii. He somehow knew he needed *oil*. Now he had to go as fast as he could.

The young man rose unsteadily, the legs of the wooden chair dragging again on the floor. He drew annoyed glances from half a dozen students at different tables. Atash was oblivious to their presence. He was walking now, bumping into the edge of the next table, pressing past it, bumping into another, slipping through a door.

"You cannot go there!" a student hissed as the door eased shut behind him.

Atash heard his words but they did not make sense. He saw glimpses of dark stone through a haze of red and black. He saw sheer fabric, white and yellow, spinning hypnotically as if caught up in a cyclone. This was where he had to be.

Ignoring pinpricks of pain on his cheeks and hands, the young man reached into his shirt pocket and pulled out cigarettes. He dropped the package to the floor and fished again blindly, pulling out a lighter. He flicked it open, uncapped the bottle of oil, released it spewing at his feet. He ignited the lighter and let it fall from his fingers. The flames crawled and then leaped up his pant legs.

He bellowed from deep in his throat.

Niusha Behnam, the librarian, jerked open the door and ran toward an orange shadow that could be seen among the stacks. Several students ran in after her as the smell of smoke reached the main room. They crowded the narrow alleys of books, pushing and shouting but also just staring. The students in the rear were forced back as Niusha called for the fire extinguisher. Someone yanked it from the wall and the crowd passed it toward her like an old-fashioned bucket brigade, and she turned the spray toward the fiery column. The flames had reached the paper-filled shelves and it took some strength and great sweeping movements to soak the rapidly expanding inferno. But at the heart of it, at the center of its blazing anonymity, was Atash, a boy, on fire and screaming.

CHAPTER 6

Caitlin woke to the sound of Jacob drumming on the wall that separated their bedrooms.

It had started a year earlier and it happened on average once a week. She'd naturally considered a number of psychological explanations, from recurring dreams to unexpressed emotions, but he was usually asleep when she went to him, tapping hard with his fingertips, like he was hitting a bongo. It ceased when she woke him, and he had no memory of having done it. After several weeks Caitlin tried a different tack: she rapped back, hard enough for him to feel the vibrations. He immediately stopped and fell back to sleep. She realized then that this was his way of connecting with her when he felt alone. It was a common feeling among children, who, after all, were vulnerable on every conceivable level, hence the very crux of her practice. The world had little patience or concern for innocence.

Though Jacob slumbered on, Caitlin did not. Her restlessness poisoned her sleep. She couldn't recall the nightmares but was left with the familiar feeling of hot, ashy, gritty mud. She reached for her cell phone and saw a text: *So either the date was so amazing u disappeared with him for 2 days or it was a dud and ur avoiding talking about it.*

Caitlin had forgotten to text Abby back. She quickly typed: *Dud. And life is crazy right now, promise I'll call soon.*

OK love u

Love u 2

Gradually Caitlin calmed and drifted off.

The alarm on her cell phone snapped her awake.

"Crap."

That was the Beep of Death, the last warning. She had slept through sunrise, through Jacob using the bathroom, and through the first "ocean wave" alarm on her clock.

Dressing while hurrying into the living room, Caitlin caught Jacob waggling his arms at his fish like a giant squid instead of putting on his shoes. He didn't acknowledge her arrival.

Well, a squid wouldn't, she thought. Jacob's imagination was nothing if not immersive and absolute.

When they eventually left their building he ran ahead of her to the subway and forgot to hug her good-bye when they reached his school on East Twenty-Third. *Maybe that's impending tweenitude too,* Caitlin thought. Left alone, she realized that she had felt sad all morning. But it would pass, she told herself in the same tone she might a patient.

And as a matter of immediate fact she had a breakfast appointment with Ben. She speed-walked the eleven blocks to the rendezvous. Since this was taking up her gym time, that would have to pass as her exercise for the day.

She was first to arrive at the French bistro in Murray Hill, a ten-minute walk from the United Nations. The warmth of the restaurant steamed the corners of the street-side windows and made Caitlin feel like she was walking into a protective bubble. She hung her coat on the booth-side rack, sat with a thump on the well-worn seat, and ordered coffee for two.

Then she could not resist checking her e-mail again. She found that an addendum to the adolescent schizophrenia newsletter had been e-mailed to the list—an item odd enough, and tragic enough, not to wait for the next scheduled newsletter. A college student in Iran, Atash Gulshan, had set himself on fire in a library and was now hospitalized. The act did not appear to be politically or religiously motivated, although two days before, his older brother had been hanged by the government for an unspecified crime. Little other information was available, but one sentence jumped out at her: "Witnesses reported that Gulshan exhibited logorrhea shortly before attempting suicide."

"Logorrhea"—saying nonsense words. Maanik's father mentioned that Maanik had spoken gibberish at one point. Caitlin made a mental note of it.

Then Ben arrived, with a huge smile, and Caitlin's tense concentration happily dissolved.

"Thanks for that smile," she said.

"You're welcome," he replied, lifting her small coffeepot. "Coffee in your lap?"

"Please." She laughed at their old joke. Though they had become firm friends nine years ago when Ben taught Caitlin how to sign, their first meeting had occurred years before, when they were both English majors at NYU. Ben had accidentally spilled a cup of coffee on her in a crowded diner and, after purchasing a replacement, spilled that on her too.

"How was your night?" he asked as he poured himself a cup.

"I live with a ten-year-old," she said. "When I'm with him, I'm fine. We live in a wonderful little biosphere."

Ben turned suddenly somber. "How do you do it, Caitlin?"

"What?"

"Maanik," he whispered to protect her anonymity. "She isn't my kid and yet I've been so worried about her I couldn't sleep. How do you have a child without being terrified all the time?"

"Well, that's the big secret to parenting, Ben." Caitlin whispered. "You *are* terrified all the time. You get used to it. It becomes part of the background. Except for the times when it stabs you through the heart."

He gazed at her a moment, then looked down at his menu.

"That was probably the worst sales pitch ever for having kids," he said.

Caitlin laughed. "You were never really tempted anyway."

"I'm tempted all the time," Ben said to his menu.

"Oh?"

Ben allowed the silence to stretch until the server appeared. Caitlin let it rest. Ben would talk if and when he was ready. Thinking of Barbara's culinary suggestions, she ordered roasted vegetables and an omelet. Ben stuck with coffee.

He sat back. "I'm tempted by the same desire for stability that I guess everyone wants. Home, family. But I'm chin-deep in the world's worst crises, every day, so there's not much point in letting my mind go there."

"Your current boss does it."

"The ambassador has a staff, he has a bunch of years on me, he has experience, and he's *still* stressed."

"Maybe if you looked at it as adding to the world at large, rather than taking away from yours . . ."

"Adding what? Besides worry," Ben said.

"I didn't say it was free," Caitlin told him. "You can't understand until you actually experience the parts that are transcendent."

"Is it worth what our friend is going through with his child?"

"You tell me. You've seen them when she was her normal, happy self."

Ben was silent. Eventually he nodded.

"All parents have challenges," Caitlin said quietly.

The server arrived with Caitlin's meal. Ben leaned in after the woman walked away. "What kind of a challenge is he looking at? Is she schizophrenic or something similar?"

"I can't make that diagnosis yet, and I shouldn't tell you anyway."

"But you will, right?"

"I *will* say she's missing some key symptoms," Caitlin confided.

"There are usually warning signs for a psychotic break. But in this case, by all accounts she hasn't shown a progressive disconnect from her life. This girl was very suddenly ripped from her reality."

"Meaning what?"

"Meaning I'm not sure what to make of that yet."

"There is such a thing as sudden onset, though."

"I won't say there's no such thing, but not this sudden, not usually. And there's something else." Caitlin took a bite of omelet as she collected her thoughts. "This is harder to describe. Typically, schizophrenics attempt to apply order to the disorganized information they're receiving. That's when you get diagrams, notebooks full of things that don't make sense. In this case, there seems to be something very organized about what she's experiencing."

"Organized," he said. "You mean this is making sense to her?"

"Perhaps on some level. The cycles of stimuli she's reacting to are producing clear, repetitive effects."

"The effects being fear."

"I'm not convinced that's what we're seeing. It may be part of the mix, but it's not the external part."

"You lost me."

"We don't know what's going on with her, other than her expression seems disorganized. We're reading that confusion as panic, fear."

Ben brightened. "I think I get what you mean. I've seen it in linguistics. She's like a small child who doesn't have enough language to communicate what she needs to say so there's a huge amount of frustration, almost anger. But inside, things make sense."

"Mm-hmm." Caitlin had a mouthful of egg. She swallowed and nodded.

"What can you do to treat that?" Ben asked.

"Ideally, as I tried to explain to her father last night, we do another round of hypnosis and try to find and quarantine the problem, keep it from expressing itself as we saw yesterday."

"'Tried to,'" Ben said. "I take it he was not enthusiastic about that?"

"He was diplomatic, but no."

"I'll see if I can help the idea take root."

"He's sensitive to the pressure put on him," Caitlin said as she bit into her toast.

"Yes," said Ben, concerned for his friend.

"So, how's Marina?" Caitlin grabbed a different subject. "Has she changed your man cave unrecognizably?"

"She started to," Ben replied as he sipped his coffee. "I've changed it back."

Caitlin paused her chewing. "Oh."

"Yeah."

"I'm sorry."

He shrugged. "It was a good seven months. She went home to Ukraine. I was specifically disinvited to come along."

Caitlin continued eating. "You shouldn't have kept pouring coffee on her."

There was a glimmer of laughter in Ben's eyes. "With her, it was tea. She had a tea press."

"Oooh, heavy-duty."

Ben smiled, gazing at her. "I've never actually asked you out, have I?"

Caitlin fired him a look and immediately waved a *Stop! Cease! Desist!* hand at her old friend.

"Ben, you"—she motioned *you over there*—"and me"—she motioned *me over here*—"are perfect as we are. Let's keep it perfect."

"Okay," he agreed readily. "It was just a question, it wasn't a proposal."

She laughed. "Oh, it wasn't, huh?"

"No! I couldn't remember. I was asking."

"Uh-huh. Do you really want me to analyze that 'question'?"

"No. Okay, fine. Maybe I was talking about possibly asking you out. Dinner, movies, a concert? I get a lot of invites from consulates and now I have no one to go with."

"Events, yes. Dates, no. 'Friends' "—she tapped the table for emphasis—"means we don't let things get deep and messy."

"Messy?" He grinned. "Who says the past has to inform the future?" He picked up a fork and dug into her cold omelet. "Anyway, the Friend Zone doesn't exist after forty."

"Put a sock in it, Moss." She smiled.

Before he could answer, her phone rang in her bag. Someone was calling from the Pawars' number. Her expression changed and she held up a finger to Ben as she answered.

"Hello?"

"Dr. O'Hara"—Mrs. Pawar's voice was taut—"can you please come to us immediately?"

"What's happened?"

"Please," the woman said.

"I'm on the way," Caitlin said.

CHAPTER 7

They shared a cab to Forty-Eighth Street, then Ben went on to join the ambassador at the UN. Today marked the beginning of the second week of talks; Ben said they were expecting the Indian and Pakistani delegates to shed what little politeness they had managed to maintain thus far. It was not likely to be a pleasant week at the negotiating table.

When the housekeeper ushered Caitlin into Maanik's bedroom, Caitlin resisted the urge to recoil. Maanik was standing upright in her pajamas, fighting against her mother's restraining arms. The young woman was absolutely silent, even though the muscles in her neck were straining and her mouth was stretched so wide that her lower lip had split. Her abdomen was pushing in a controlled rhythm, timed with the straining of her neck. Maanik was clearly screaming as hard as she could—but without a sound. Kamala backed from the room, fighting sobs.

Caitlin started into the room just as Maanik wrenched herself forward so hard that Hansa lost her grip and fell to her knees. The girl remained where she stood, trembling from head to toe, leaning forward—not toward Caitlin but toward the windows. Caitlin could just make out the small shape of Jack London behind the curtains. Then she looked back at the girl.

For one second Maanik's eyes rolled to meet hers and Caitlin felt raw horror wash down her spine. She had seen young people trapped in terrible circumstances—held hostage by a parent, pinned by a landslide—but here she felt as if she were looking at someone who had wakened in a coffin and found herself buried alive. The girl took an uncertain step and her eyes rolled to the ceiling. She was still trying to scream.

Caitlin grasped the girl's shoulders. "Maanik, I'm here. You hear my voice, feel the weight of my hands . . ."

The girl stopped moving and stood shaking. Suddenly her hands whipped into the air, throwing Caitlin off balance, forcing her to break her fall against the four-poster bed. Maanik's hands remained in front of her, her left hand clutching at the air and her right hand curled, the forefinger and thumb pinched tightly together. Her arms were jerking and spasming but the hands stayed front and center. Caitlin grasped Maanik's shoulders and gently moved her from side to side to break her rigid stance. The spasms decreased slightly but she was still screaming in silence.

"That's good, Maanik," Caitlin said. "Mrs. Pawar, what is your daughter's dominant hand?"

"Her left," she said, tears streaming from her eyes.

"She writes with her left hand?" Caitlin said, not sure the woman had understood.

"Yes, yes!"

That's not what I would have guessed, Caitlin thought. So why was Maanik pinching her right hand? Was she trying to pull at something?

No . . . that isn't it.

Caitlin decided to try something. If a split personality were forming here, new or once-latent personalities sometimes switched the hand they wrote with.

"Mrs. Pawar, can you please get me paper and a pen?"

The woman was frozen as though she were in a trance of her own, staring at Caitlin but seemingly uncomprehending.

"Hansa!" Caitlin overenunciated for effect without volume. "Pen and paper please!"

Mrs. Pawar stood clumsily, wiping her face, and moved to Maanik's desk to search through the mess there. Soon she held out a pad of turquoise paper and a black marker. Caitlin took the marker and instructed the woman to stand in front of her daughter with the paper. Caitlin then moved behind Maanik so that she could support the girl's torso with her side. She reached around her and inserted the marker into Maanik's right hand, uncurling the forefinger and thumb and pinching them together on the marker. She beckoned for Mrs. Pawar to hold the pad of paper under the nib. Jack London began to whine from behind the curtains.

Maanik touched the marker to the paper, had a moment of physical recognition, then scrawled across its surface, long swooping lines, then short jerks, more long lines. She then released the marker and her full weight dropped in Caitlin's arms. Caitlin struggled to brace herself as she helped the girl's body gently to the floor.

With one arm under Maanik's shoulders, she reached up for the pad of paper and inspected it. The drawing looked like a steep cliff with wavy lines around its base like water. Caitlin turned the pad around and now the lines meant nothing, just chaos. She kept turning it but nothing stood out. When she returned it to its original position, Caitlin was no longer sure there was a cliff and water.

She handed the pad back to Mrs. Pawar and after helping Maanik to the rug, she stood. Maanik was finally, thankfully still but Caitlin realized she herself was trembling. She placed her hands on her knees and took a long, deep breath before straightening.

"Is it over?" Mrs. Pawar asked in a ragged voice.

"I don't know," Caitlin said quietly, her head still spinning. "May I have a glass of water?"

Jack London slunk out from behind the curtains. Dragging his belly on the ground, he slithered toward his young mistress. Suddenly the beagle lurched forward, seizing Maanik's right sleeve and pulling with all of his strength. Maanik's body jerked, her jaw opened, and with her eyes closed, she began to scream. This time there was sound.

Caitlin grabbed Jack London, tried to wedge a finger in his jaw to get him to release Maanik's sleeve.

"What is happening now?" Mrs. Pawar cried. "Maanik!"

"Mrs. Pawar, I need your permission to put Maanik under deep hypnosis."

The girl's mother seemed entranced. Caitlin didn't know if she'd even heard her.

"Mrs. Pawar!"

The woman blinked, looked at Caitlin. "Yes?"

"Your daughter is in crisis. She must be stabilized."

"I understand. What . . . what about Dr. Deshpande's medications?"

"I said *stabilize* her, not *bludgeon* her. I want to employ depth hypnosis, Mrs. Pawar."

"I see. I—I will ask my husband."

"No time!" Caitlin insisted.

The woman nodded. "I will just send him a text now." With unsteady hands she pulled her cell phone from a pocket in her sari and typed.

Caitlin finally managed to separate the beagle's jaws from Maanik's sleeve. He didn't bite her but he did bark. "Is there somewhere you can put him?"

"His crate," Mrs. Pawar said as she stopped texting and took the dog. He struggled to get out of her hands as they left the room.

Caitlin crouched on the floor next to Maanik. The girl's screams were relentless, each one weighted with deep sobs. Her hands were motioning in a peculiar way—not scratching, not writing, more as if she were pulling things off shelves frantically. Somehow in the breaths between cries, she was murmuring something, and Caitlin leaned close to catch it. It sounded like "null zee."

Mrs. Pawar shuffled back into the room with the requested glass of water.

"Thank you," Caitlin said, then drained the glass. She was perspiring and didn't want to dehydrate.

"I have not heard back from my husband," Mrs. Pawar said.

"We can't wait for the ambassador. I have to do something before she hurts herself. Do you understand?"

"Yes, yes."

Caitlin leaped up and dug in her purse for her phone. She set it to video and placed it on a pile of books, framing Maanik's head and torso. She double-checked the positioning, then tapped record.

"What—what are you doing?" Mrs. Pawar asked.

Caitlin gently hushed the woman and motioned for her to sit back as she knelt beside the girl. "Maanik, remember the large television screen I told you about? It's there right in front of you."

Caitlin guided the girl through the same steps of hypnosis as before and she was just as responsive. At eight she became heavy and tired and her eyes shut, but at five Caitlin did not tell her to sleep. Instead she asked Maanik to raise her right arm in the air and wiggle the smallest finger. The girl calmly complied.

"That's very good, Maanik. You're doing great. You're taking care of yourself by letting me help you. Now I'm going to make some suggestions and ask some questions and you do what feels right for you, okay? If anything I'm saying doesn't feel right, you just let it go, don't bother with it." Caitlin waited for her to process the instructions, then said, "Tell me how you're feeling."

Immediately Maanik said, "I'm fine, I guess."

Mrs. Pawar gasped from across the room.

Caitlin was equally startled. She had not yet heard Maanik talk as a normal teenager. It was disconcerting but profoundly hopeful.

"I'm glad you're feeling fine. I'm going to ask you to picture a place that makes you happy. Imagine that you're there—"

"I don't have to imagine it," Maanik interrupted. "I'm there."

She had the classic teenager tone of, *Why are adults such idiots?* In this case, she might have been right. Caitlin was surprised by the response, but she went with it.

"That's great, Maanik. Where are you?"

"I'm home," she said, as if it were obvious. Then she said, "Oh, hi." By the change in her tone it was clear she wasn't speaking to Caitlin. "Hi, baby," she cooed.

"Are you saying hello to Jack London now?" Caitlin asked.

"Who's Jack London?"

Mrs. Pawar sat heavily in a chair, as if her legs had given out.

"Maanik, you can stay at home, you don't have to imagine anything else or go anywhere. Do you understand?"

"I understand."

"All right. I'm just going to ask you for a favor, okay?"

"Sure."

"Maanik, do you know that you've been having trouble lately? You've been very disturbed sometimes?"

"Yes, I know I've been screaming. I can feel it in my throat and my sides hurt. My arms hurt, too. Not hurt, actually—ache."

"Well, I'm going to ask you to respond to a cue in the future, a signal. The cue will be when someone says the word 'blackberries' and touches your ear."

"Which ear?" Maanik asked.

At least her cognitive functions were clear and focused—sharper than Caitlin's. "Either ear. Does that cue sound all right to you?"

"Yes."

"So when anyone says 'blackberries' and touches your ear, you will respond by calming down, just like when I'm talking to you about the television screen and counting backward. Any other time you hear the word 'blackberries' it just means 'blackberries.' Is that clear?"

"Okay, fine," Maanik agreed. Then she cooed to whatever was not Jack London.

Caitlin knew that a posthypnotic suggestion of this caliber was a much bigger step than the one she had discussed with the ambassador, but she felt sure she could convince him of the necessity. They needed a kill switch for all of the behavior, not just the scratching.

"Thank you, Maanik. Now tell me a little about your home."

"What do you want to know?"

"What are you seeing? Who is your baby?"

"That's my little guy," she cooed, smiling. "He's licking my hands. And"—her eyes moved under her closed eyelids—"there are the trees next to the door, I'm coming back from the hot pool, it's nighttime, there's some *thokang* down by us but high up the stars are out—"

"There's some what down by you?"

"Wow, the stars are so beautiful tonight. There are so many of them!" The smile became almost blissful. "*Khasaa.*"

Caitlin decided that keeping the flow going was more important than backtracking for every detail. "Your little guy, he met you outside of your house?"

"Yes, he slithered up from the water as he always does."

"What does your little guy look like?"

"Like *thyodularasi*," Maanik burbled in a *duh* tone. She was speaking so quickly now that Caitlin couldn't follow. It took a moment for her to realize that speed wasn't the problem.

"Maanik, can you use English words for me?"

But the girl kept pattering in gibberish. She had begun to move her arms again, not frantically this time but in wide motions that didn't seem to resemble anything. Caitlin thought of Jacob waggling his arms like a squid. Was Maanik just being playful?

Suddenly the girl sat up and her eyes snapped open as she craned to look up at the ceiling. Her speech sped up, as did her arm movements, except that her right hand was drifting toward the left, as if she wanted to scratch.

Caitlin put her hands on her shoulders. "Maanik, tell me what you see in the sky."

The patter came faster now. Caitlin glanced questioningly at Mrs.

Pawar, who looked like the sins of the world were written on her daughter's face. Mrs. Pawar understood Caitlin's glance but shook her head—the words weren't Hindi. *But there's something Asiatic about them*, Caitlin thought, *yet not. If only Ben were here* . . . And then Maanik was shouting at the sky, pushing up at it, and slapping her arms, trying to scratch through the gauze.

"Maanik, English, please! Tell me what's happening!" she yelled as she tried unsuccessfully to prevent the girl's hands from making contact.

Maanik started to scream again. Her whole body slammed down onto the floor as she bucked and thrashed, and suddenly from nowhere Caitlin felt like she was grabbed and thrown across the room.

CHAPTER 8

Caitlin was thrown back into a wall, and the breath was knocked from her. Her arms felt weak as water as she tried to prop herself up.

If this is a personality split, she thought, *please let increased strength not be part of it!*

Caitlin jerked herself onto her knees and reached out through Maanik's flailing arms to touch her left ear. "Blackberries," she said.

The girl's hands dropped. She took a violent, deep breath, as if she might scream to the heavens, and then exhaled slowly, until the in-breath came and a natural quiet rhythm took hold. Within seconds, Caitlin heard the soft deep breaths of sleep.

After lifting Maanik onto her bed, Caitlin and Mrs. Pawar left the girl to rest and retired to the living room, where Kamala had made tea.

"If you don't mind, I'd like to wait a few more minutes, make sure everything is all right," Caitlin said.

"Of course," said Mrs. Pawar as she sat in an armchair. "I am sorry to take you from your work."

"This *is* my work," Caitlin said.

Mrs. Pawar smiled, but only briefly. "What's wrong with my daughter?" she asked.

"I don't know," Caitlin admitted. "But we're going to find out."

"We did the right thing? Just now?"

"Absolutely."

The older woman sipped her tea. "Nothing like this has ever happened in our family."

"I was about to ask, Mrs. Pawar—were there ever rumors or whispers, about an aunt, a grandparent, a cousin?"

"Whispers?"

"Their mind, their behavior, habits—anything. I understand there would have been a reticence to discuss it."

The woman shook her head and looked down. "We do not speak of such things, but one knows. There was nothing."

Caitlin believed her.

"Mrs. Pawar, I understand that you must keep this matter quiet. But if your daughter continues to have episodes you're going to have to get her to a clinic for tests. She might have hit her head during the assassination attempt—"

"The school nurse checked her, said there was nothing."

"There are conditions an MRI or CT scan can explore that a doctor cannot. I already mentioned this to Dr. Deshpande, and you may need to be a little more aggressive . . ."

"I see," the woman said helplessly.

"Surely your husband won't object if it's necessary."

Mrs. Pawar regarded her. It was a look that told Caitlin: *Yes. At this moment, given the Kashmir situation, he might resist.*

Jack London, released from his crate by the housekeeper, made the rounds, sniffing at their feet.

"She seems so vulnerable, so fragile," said Mrs. Pawar, "so unlike herself."

"She's stronger than you think, and she's not alone in this," Caitlin said. "Whatever's going on, if she shows any unusual signs of unrest, remember what to do: you touch her ear . . ."

The woman nodded, more to reassure herself than anything, but Caitlin left the Pawars' apartment with a knot in her stomach.

During the cab ride back, she called her office to tell her receptionist that she would keep her eleven thirty. Then she texted Ben: *Some progress today, I'll call u tonight. Send me ur most secure email address.*

There was no immediate response, but she wasn't expecting one. He would be at the talks. She watched the news crawl on the TV monitor in the backseat of the cab. The tensions between India and Pakistan were being described as "volatile," with more troops being moved to the borders. The United States ambassador's proposal for a demilitarized zone between the nations had been met with derision in India, whose pundits pointed out that Pakistan could not even establish a de-terrorized zone within its own borders. Meanwhile the local news reported that in Queens, fistfights were erupting among Indian and Pakistani neighbors. Police presence in the subways had tripled, and the emergency management department had been quietly checking on the state of the city's old fallout shelters as potential neighborhood command centers. Nor was New York alone in its anxiety; across the nation survivalist and prepper groups had replenished their stocks of ammunition, causing a shortage, and disappeared off the grid. An Internet questionnaire called "If This Is the End, I Will . . ." had gone viral.

Caitlin turned the screen off and spent the rest of the cab ride in uncomfortable silence. It seemed that war fears rode the air with their own wireless source: people. Maanik and her mother had given them a personal face for Caitlin.

It was with a great sense of relief that Caitlin walked into her top-floor office on West Fifty-Eighth Street. She experienced such a sudden feeling of comfort that there was almost an audible click. After going through her routine—coffee on the thumbprint coaster Jacob made when he was five, purse in the lowest desk drawer, phone in the top drawer and muted, coat on the hanger behind the door—Caitlin reviewed her schedule, but her mind kept shifting back to Maanik.

A diagnosis of schizophrenia was premature and sketchy, since schizophrenics understood that there was a "them" and a "me." Maanik had no "me" during her episodes, at least not the "me" she'd been for sixteen years. But a diagnosis of dissociative identity disorder—a split personality—wasn't accurate either because multiple personalities rarely had delusions. They lived in the real world. Maanik was obviously reacting to something that wasn't there. A form of petit mal or grand mal was a possibility, yet sufferers would not respond to hypnosis the way Maanik had.

One size did not fit all here. What was Caitlin missing?

She wanted to see the girl when she wasn't experiencing the cycle of behaviors. Even watching her quietly eat dinner would help Caitlin establish a baseline and get a firsthand sense of who she was.

Give it a rest, Caitlin told herself. She had never healed anybody on day one, and besides, lingering over one case was a poor way to greet another. Her eleven thirty appointment would be arriving in about ten minutes and she felt the relief of . . . not normality, there was no such thing, but of having an established therapeutic history and many more months to devote to the work. Neither of these essentials was available with Maanik.

Why was she so different from any kid Caitlin had ever seen?

She had a sudden inspiration to search for her online, to see if there were any videos of her before the assassination. She kicked herself for not thinking of it before. She expected the Pawars to keep something of a lock on her public persona; the daughter of a diplomat had to have a strong concept of privacy. But there were several videos on her school website of Maanik engaging in debates as part of their Model UN. Caitlin clicked on one and noticed immediately how sure the girl was of herself. She certainly was not faking extroversion, which made these repeated inward collapses even stranger. In another video, Maanik was starring as the fiancée of an eccentric British aristocrat in a school play; at one point she gestured excessively and intoned, "I'm not diseased. I'm mismanaged." Maanik rolled her eyes and the line got a huge laugh from the audience.

She seemed utterly normal, entirely comfortable in her own skin, impressively so. There were none of the tics or hints of darkness that shrouded most of the kids Caitlin saw. Could the assassination attempt have done so much damage? If her father had died or been wounded, yes. If her mother had suffered some kind of collapse, perhaps. But those severe triggers did not exist here. The reaction simply was not proportionate. Caitlin needed to think this through further but her eleven thirty was knocking on the door.

Hours later, after five more appointments and two conference calls, it was time to pick up Jacob. She could tell as she approached the front door of her building that the temperature outside had dropped considerably. She snuggled into her coat collar and caught herself humming "Let It Snow." As she stepped outside her humming stopped and she suddenly felt a chill that had nothing to do with the weather. It ran up her backbone and tickled out along her shoulder blades like a small animal. Instinctively, she moved closer to the wall, stood still, and looked around.

What the hell?

Her heart was thumping harder; her breaths grew shorter. There seemed to be a cold wind against her arms but there was no motion in her sleeves. She had goose bumps.

Get a grip, she told herself.

She saw people picking up their cars from the garage across the street, a smoker by a tree in the tiny park on top of the garage, a group of college students hurrying by her, but nothing to explain the chill that remained. She felt exposed, pinned there as though these other people existed on another plane and she was alone. Or nearly so.

There was also an unsettling sense of being watched. It was not a flash of exposure, like walking in front of a tourist taking videos.

Barbara was right, she thought. She was so deep in other peoples' issues she had lost her own protective skin.

A burst of greetings startled her as students from the Roosevelt Hospital day program hustled out of the building and enfolded her in their group. Caitlin walked to the subway with them, pushing the noise and shapes of the city away, but not the creeping chill that danced along her spine.

CHAPTER 9

Dodging and maneuvering with Jacob through the crowded subway, Caitlin tried hard to shake the odd paranoia that had seized her outside her office, but it was like swallowing an oversized bite of a sandwich. She usually tried to make a game of their dash through rush hour—Crazy Football or Running with the Gazelles—but not today. Jacob was deep in his own thoughts and she just wanted to get home.

The third-floor hallway seemed unusually quiet, the clang of the keys uncommonly hollow. It reminded her, unpleasantly, of the feeling she'd had at the Pawars' apartment. A sense that she was somehow in danger. Not Jacob, just her.

Unlocking the door, she made a mental note to talk to Barbara about this, then happily turned her attention to roasting broccoli and defrosting and heating a container of congee for dinner. Jacob went straight to his room. They had arrived home just in time for his weekly online chat with his father. Caitlin was surprisingly glad for Andy's call right now; even abnormal normalcy was welcome.

Andrew Thwaite, divorced with three kids, was a sociologist from Sydney whom Caitlin had met in Thailand three weeks after the 2004 tsunami. He had joined one of her relief efforts, which Ben helped to coordinate through the under-secretary-general of the UN Office for the Coordination of Humanitarian Affairs. When they met, Caitlin felt that he was "right for right now," as she'd expressed it to Ben.

"The people I've talked to say he's kind of a d-bag, Cai," Ben had said.

"Oh, you checked?"

"Captain of your team," he said evasively.

"Well, he's smart, he's entertaining, he isn't making any promises to be something he's not, and he's six-three and ripped."

"Uh-huh. I know the type, a swaggering narcissist."

"Strong words, Ben."

"I've been living in the shadow of miserable hotshots like him my whole life. He'll use you and leave you in the dust."

"Only after I leave him in mine. Hey, is this about me or you, Ben?"

"Fair enough," he conceded, "but I think you've entirely misunderstood the meaning of 'relief efforts.'"

The disagreement ended in laughter. But after passion trumped caution and she found out she was pregnant, she decided to keep the child. Andy was notified and had stayed far away, making everything blessedly simple.

Until recently.

Around the time Andy's youngest kid went to college, in 2011, he'd suddenly asked for weekly video calls with Jacob. She had no objection to that. She and Jacob had discussed it repeatedly and Jacob seemed happy to accept him on the same level as an upstairs neighbor. But six months ago Andy had asked Caitlin why she hadn't chosen a cochlear implant operation for Jacob when he was younger.

"Because it's Jacob's choice," she said.

"Jacob is ten," Andy pointed out. "The earlier the operation is performed, the easier the learning curve—"

"Having to work a little harder is a fair price for his freedom of choice."

"I don't think that's a choice a fifth grader should be allowed to make."

At that point Caitlin had descended with Thor's hammer. Under no circumstances was Andy to have that conversation with her child. She delivered the message in a mode that had cowed recalcitrant bureaucrats around the world, and it seemed to work on Andy.

Still, Caitlin always checked Jacob when he came back from their video chats for signs that he'd had an uncomfortable conversation with his father. There were none today; he moved right along from a question about whether kids rode kangaroos in the outback to the topic of his homework, an opinion essay on the ethics of zoos.

As they discussed the different sides of the zoo issue, the back of Caitlin's mind was chewing over her own ethical dilemma: sending the video of Maanik's hypnosis session to Ben. She had already received his secure e-mail address, and she already knew she was going to send the file to him, despite it being against the rules of doctor-patient confidentiality. She concluded that because Ben was a friend of the family there was a chance the Pawars would agree if she asked—but she needed more certainty than just a chance. Sharing it with anyone other than Ben would be indefensible, yet she needed an outsider's perspective, confirmation of something she had begun wondering about, something she couldn't be sure was true. A full understanding of Maanik's very elusive inner world depended on this.

· · ·

After dinner, when she and Jacob had finished washing the dishes, Caitlin sent Ben the file, then called him online. When his image appeared he was looking at something else on the screen and typing, and she could tell he was beat.

"Hey," he said.

"For horses," she replied.

He smirked. It wasn't funny, but Caitlin was. They were. That had always been their way: when one was down the other always took the high, droll road to help out.

"It's taking this long to download?" she asked.

"It's getting here 'bit by bit,' " he joked back.

"Yikes. Is the UN giving employees hand-me-down computers from 1995?"

"Clay and styluses." He smiled. "I'm using the landline to download the file, plus I'm jumping it through a few other hoops. Extra protections." He finally glanced at her. "I'm surprised you sent it, Cai."

"It wasn't an easy decision but desperate minds call for desperate measures."

"Are you feeling desperate?"

"I meant Maanik's mind." She thought for a moment. "No, I'm not desperate. Yet."

Ben glanced away, somber. Then he fixed on her again. "How *are* you feeling?"

"About what?" she said, hedging.

"Managing this in the epicenter of a world crisis."

"I think we're all in that epicenter," she said. "Any progress there?"

He shook his head. "You avoided the question."

Now it was Caitlin who looked away. What she wanted to say was, *Honestly, I'm not myself and I don't know why*. But this call was not about her.

"I'm very, very concentrated," she said. "Sharp as a knife."

"Don't lose yourself in this, Cai."

"I won't. I know how to work my switchboard pretty well." She smiled.

" 'Switchboard,' " he muttered. "You realize we may be the last generation who knows what that means? I had to translate 'VCR' for a young observer from Bhutan today. They had no idea what I was talking about."

"I have no idea what you're talking about," she teased.

"Nice." He grinned. "You got any new 'someone walks into a bar' jokes?"

Caitlin laughed and shook her head. "Those were the worst jokes ever," she said apologetically.

"That's what made them so good. My all-time favorite? Ahem—'A skeleton walks into a bar and orders a gin and tonic. And a mop.'"

"I worry about you, Ben." She rolled her eyes. "And no. I kind of outsourced the bulk of my sense of humor to Jacob a long time ago. He's got natural silliness and it's more than enough for one household."

Ben shook his head. There was an imperceptibly longer, perceptibly more awkward silence. "What about the other parts of your life? Are you seeing anybody?"

"No. And why do we always have to have this conversation?"

"Not always—"

"You're like my mother," she went on. "Or more accurately, my sister, who's due to gently kick me in the ass about that any day now, so I don't need it from you too."

"Okay, okay," he said. "I wasn't gonna kick you."

They looked at each other. "Sorry," she said. "I didn't mean to go off on you. Just a little stressed. Won't happen again."

"Great. Anyhow, the video's downloaded. Let's see what we've got."

Caitlin didn't miss the quick change of topic but filed the observation away for later.

Ben opened the video and tucked it in the corner of the chat window so they could both watch.

"Jeez," he said when Maanik started speaking in gibberish.

"I know."

"Wow," he said again at the moment in the hypnosis when Caitlin felt she had been thrown into a wall. "What happened there?"

Caitlin didn't answer so that he could focus on the use of the "blackberries" cue. She wanted him to know the cue in case the ambassador asked about it, but that wasn't the only reason she'd shared the video.

At the end of the video Ben ran it back again to the segment with Maanik's gibberish. Then they watched it a third time.

"You think that could be a language?" she asked.

Ben made a noncommittal sound and paused the video. He sat back, thinking. "There's a clipped similarity to Japanese in it," he mused.

"I thought that too."

"Right there," he said, and rewound the segment again. "You hear that?"

Maanik was saying, *"Thyodularasi."*

"Yes . . . ?" Caitlin said.

"That's a distinctly Asiatic 'r,'" Ben told her.

"It's prevalent throughout," Caitlin said. "That's what makes the whole thing sound like Japanese, right?"

"That's part of it, along with the alveolar stops on the 'd's and 't's. But at the beginning of that word, that's a very hard 'th.' Those sounds don't coexist in any language."

"Not anywhere?"

"Well, we don't have every tribal language on the planet down, but as a rule that 'r' and that 'th' don't evolve in the same tongue."

The video flicked off and the screen reverted to just Ben, who was rubbing his eyes.

"Pretty amazing, right?" she said.

"What the hell is going on with that girl?"

"That's what I'm trying to find out, if the Pawars will let me."

"Hold on, Caitlin. All you have to worry about is getting them through this period of the negotiations."

"What?" She felt as though she'd been head-butted.

"That's why I brought you in," he reminded her. "There are teams of people who can help once the ambassador doesn't have to worry about the media."

"I understand that, but I'm not—I mean, I don't just want to be some stopgap."

"Cai, I didn't mean that—I meant that this isn't in my control. I suspect they'll take her back to India as soon as we're clear of all the political barbed wire."

"And what about Maanik? Ben, something is happening to that girl. I'm not just going to spackle her."

"I wasn't implying that," he said defensively. "Look, we're both tired and I shouldn't have said what I said. I'll back your play, whatever it is. I just know how you get when you're invested in a case, so keep a distance, okay?"

"I don't know if I can."

He smiled. "A small distance. For your own mental well-being."

"A small distance," she agreed, and forced herself to smile back.

"And now I'm going to put myself to bed," he said. "We'll see what my subconscious has to say about all this."

"Is that all you've got?" she teased.

"I'm not a university go-getter anymore," he said. "Those days ain't comin' back."

Caitlin hid her disappointment. She'd shared the video with him so they could discuss that last part of the hypnosis, the wall moment. But the man needed rest before going back to the peace table.

"Good night," she said.

"Good night, Cai," he said, and raised a hand with effort as he signed off.

She raised a hand at the dark screen.

After answering a few e-mails and reading a few headlines in the professional newsletters, she went to say good night to Jacob. He was buzzing with energy and Caitlin had to sign "good night" to him so many times, curving her right hand over her left hand to say, "Night, night, night!" that she felt like a robot—so she walked stiff-legged, arms outstretched like the Frankenstein monster, toward the door. Many giggles later, Jacob finally drifted into silence.

Amazingly, Caitlin too managed to fall asleep at a decent time. But just a few hours later, she woke in a panic, feeling like she was clawing upward through blankets. The sign for "night" was stuck on a loop in her head like a song refrain, along with an old memory of Jacob trying to coach her signing.

"Mommy, it's in your elbows, fix your elbows!"

Damn it, Caitlin thought as three o'clock became four o'clock. Why were elbows stuck in her brain? It had to be Maanik.

She got out of bed and turned on her tablet, booted the video of Maanik. She watched it from the moment the girl began speaking gibberish. Caitlin's spine straightened and her brain woke up. There was a definite change to how the girl's elbows were moving. After several viewings she was certain that they were inscribing specific arcs at specific times. Maanik was repeating some of the gestures, which suggested they had meaning—and might indicate that the gibberish had meaning too.

Caitlin took a deep breath, trying not to get overly excited. But she felt that she had just made a major breakthrough in this case. And if that were true, it might be possible to guide Maanik out of the morass sooner than she'd thought.

CHAPTER 10

Montevideo, Uruguay

Heading from Port Stanley toward its first refueling stop in Montevideo, Uruguay, the Learjet Bombardier cut gracefully through the dawn sky like a white arrow.

Mikel Jasso—born in Pamplona, educated at Harvard, elite member of the Group—was the aircraft's sole passenger. He had begun the two-thousand-mile journey alone with his thoughts, his camera case, and a celebratory glass of Royal Salute scotch—a tradition after every successful mission. The Group routinely monitored that large southern swath of the hemisphere, and in ten years Mikel had successfully retrieved all eight of the relics they had instructed him to acquire. The relics came from museums, scientific research ships, military vessels, and tourists. This time the quest had begun four days earlier, when they intercepted a cell phone message from a Dr. Story to a colleague at Oxford. Jasso had been dispatched to the Falklands immediately by private jet. He had booked a room at the Malvina House Hotel, waited for the *Captain Fallow* to arrive, talked to the crew, studied plans the Group had obtained from contacts at the admiralty, and made his move the next night.

As heists go, this one had been relatively effortless. Jasso knew that daytime on the vessel was used for repairs and provisioning, after which most of the crew went ashore. The watch at night was lax: no one, neither thief nor stowaway, had reason to board a geological survey ship that was about to head back into the cold, unwelcoming Southern Atlantic.

There had been no problem finding Dr. Story's cabin. Jasso had taken care to stay on the port side, where there was no moonlight and the shadows were long and deep. If he had been caught, that too would have been easily taken care of. Jasso was publicly, aggressively opposed to drilling in these waters in general and on the Patagonian Shelf in particular. It was a useful cover story for a man who spent so much time on Group business in that region, from the Humboldt Plain in South America to the Agulhas Plateau in Africa. If he had been detained by seamen or law enforcement, he would have claimed that Falkland Advanced Petroleum was not only harming the environment, they were recklessly destroying submerged historical treasures. The company would have wanted nothing more than to be rid of him. At worst, he would have had to turn over the relic. It would have ended up in a local museum from which, one day, it would disappear.

But he had not been caught. The artifact was his.

As soon as the jet was airborne, Jasso set his tablet on the table beside his scotch and established a Skype connection to New York. In less than fifteen seconds the thin face of Chairwoman Flora Davies filled the screen. Her eyes were alert, expectant. She smiled when she saw Jasso's grin.

"You did it."

He raised the glass to himself.

"Show me," she said. "Please."

Jasso hefted the camera case to his lap and opened it. He removed a pair of rubber gloves, slipped them on, and withdrew the swaddled artifact. He placed the face of it in front of the red eye of the camera. Though it was probably just the glow of the computer screen, the object seemed luminescent.

"It's a symbol," she said.

"It appears so," Jasso agreed. "Something I've never seen."

"Nor I. It's beautiful," the woman remarked, leaning forward. "Turn it around."

Carefully rotating the object, he showed her the reverse side. Seeing the markings facing him, in the dark, they really did have an inner radiance of their own.

"The finger of God," he said.

"What?" she asked.

"Jehovah on Sinai, writing the tablets," he said. "I was just thinking—the markings are still visible even away from the light."

"That's the metal content reflecting ambient light, I would suppose."

"Maybe," he said. "But I'll bet this is what the tablets of law may have looked like to Moses after they were cut from the rock."

She smiled. "A theological side, Mr. Jasso? You?"

"I'd describe it as more poetic," he said.

"Either applies," she said.

Jasso did not disagree. He was not a religious man. He believed in the aspirational power of human beings, not in the interference of gods and demigods. Still, the impact of religion and mythology on what every civilization dreamed of and strived for could not be ignored.

"Excellent job," she said, sitting back. "Thank you."

"An honor, as always," Jasso said.

He closed the tablet and nestled into the seat. His eyes yearned

for sleep but he wanted to savor the moment a little longer. The artifact's presence weighed heavily in his left hand. It was probably just
his imagination, but it seemed to have the faintest vibration, like a
tuning fork. He switched on the overhead light and brought it closer
to his face.

"What kind of metal are you, I wonder."

If it was of meteoric origin, it would be iron, but it seemed lighter
than that. Silver? Aluminum? Magnesium? It had the look of those
metals, but in a form unlike any he'd ever seen.

As he stared at it, the artifact had an almost mesmeric quality. It
was something like watching a gyroscope: you couldn't *see* it moving,
but you felt somehow that it was.

Or else it's the scotch, he thought, snapping the spell.

Quickly wrapping the object, he put it back in the case and pulled
off the gloves. Shutting his eyes and drifting swiftly into sleep, he
dreamed of high ocean waves rushing over him in forceful, endless
succession. He saw lights through the breakers: orange and flickering
specks that formed strange, unfathomable shapes. But they were lost
in the waves before he could make them out and they were different
each time they appeared. Were they taunting him? So visible yet so
remote . . .

He woke with a jolt as the aircraft jerked violently.

"Seat belts!" the pilot announced over the intercom.

Half-asleep, Jasso fumbled for the strap as the sole attendant
weaved her way over.

Just as she reached him the plane tilted and she was swept backward against one of the seats on the other side of the aisle. Jasso
reached to help her but was restrained by his own belt and grabbed
the sliding camera case instead. The attendant slid into the seat and
fastened her belt.

Hugging the case to his chest, he was again aware of the low
buzzing he had felt when holding the artifact. He looked out the
window and noticed that the aircraft was flying very low, just about

five hundred feet from the ground. It was dawn and the flaming sunrise obscured his vision, yet what he saw was unmistakable. Well over a dozen albatrosses were flying dead-on toward the underside of the jet, their eight-foot wingspans batting hard as they struggled to achieve the jet's height. He had never known the birds to seek this height or speed and was about to remark on the abnormality to the flight attendant when the birds began to drop, either exhausted or asphyxiated.

And then the world itself suddenly vanished.

The interior of the jet, the sky, and the low clouds seemed to depart, and in their place an explosive flash of red blinded him. His nostrils were filled with a smell like burning plastic, or was it sulfur? And his breath felt thick, tasted noxious on his tongue. His mind turned like a spinning top, his body seemed to liquefy, and his eardrums rumbled. The last rational thought he had was that one of the birds had been caught in the engine and they were plunging to earth. But there were no whining turbines, no rush of air, no impact—

"*No!*" he screamed in his mind.

"Mr. Jasso!"

The flight attendant's voice was at the far end of a tunnel.

"Mr. Jasso!" she repeated.

His shoulders were being shaken and his head bobbed in circles as he fought through the sensory chaos. Like poured molasses the plane began to come back into focus just as it thumped to a hard landing on the tarmac. He was aware of the rear-mounted jets roaring to help brake the aircraft, felt himself being pressed against the seat, saw the calm white of the cabin spread out in front of him . . .

The flight attendant was hastily undoing her belt.

"Wait, who had my shoulders?"

"Are you all right, Mr. Jasso?"

"What? Yes, yes. I'm fine," he said.

But he wasn't. He felt nauseous, panicked. The vinyl of the

camera case felt hot, no doubt from how tightly he had been clutching it.

"I'll get you some water," the woman said.

"No, I'm all right. Weren't you affected?" he said, starting to get paranoid.

"By what?" she asked. "The turbulence?"

"I don't know," he said. "You didn't hear anything? See anything? Birds?"

"At this altitude?"

"That's what I thought," he said, more to himself.

"No," she said as the jet slowed and steadied. "I wasn't looking outside. Perhaps a cloud formation, a trick of the sunlight?"

"Maybe."

"Mr. Jasso, you look pale. Would you like to have a doctor meet us at the terminal?"

"No, I'll be fine," he said. "It was just . . . overwork, I guess. It will pass."

She accepted his explanation with reluctance and went to the cockpit. The engines had slowed to a dull hum. Jasso thought he heard the woman ask about damage. The pilot said he was going out to check the aircraft when they refueled but didn't think he was going to find anything. The engines and flaps seemed fine.

Jasso drained what was left in his glass and sat very still as the jet taxied toward the refueling area. It seemed impossible, but . . .

But the birds . . . they weren't an illusion. They seemed to be throwing themselves at the jet.

Was there something in the artifact that had . . . something in the stone, the metal? Perhaps it had interacted with particles in the air, with the electronics of the jet.

He looked at the case, which sat blank and unrevealing on the table. It was somehow menacing in its faceless simplicity. With sudden urgency he reached for the flap and threw it back, taking out the cloth-bound artifact.

The only thing trembling was his hand. The stone was very still. It was also cool. Whatever had begun in Port Stanley was apparently over.

Replacing the relic in the case and closing it, he gestured for a second glass of scotch and stared at the sleek new terminal in the distance. It looked like a flying saucer, a low, inverted white bowl gleaming red in the new day.

CHAPTER 11

The morning broke slowly across Caitlin's consciousness: a bright thread of illumination along the horizon, then flashes of yellow-orange light on the crests of waves, and finally the dawn itself. She had dreamed, she knew that, but remembered her dreams vaguely. Dark skies, gray water. And red. Somewhere there was red.

She swung herself out of bed and padded in to wake Jacob, who was instantly revved, talking nonstop about his zoo essay. He was still bubbling as she dropped him off at a birthday party. Caitlin asked a favor from one of the attending parents to shuttle Jacob to a second party later that day—the usual Saturday birthday deluge—then let herself into her office to catch up on work. She left a message for the Pawars to call her and let her know how Maanik was doing. By noon she still hadn't received a return call and she was beginning to worry. She considered calling Dr. Deshpande to see if he'd heard anything but she didn't want to push his boundaries on confidentiality. She called Ben instead. She'd sent him some stills from Maanik's video after she'd noticed the arm movements the night before, but his only reply was to ask her to meet him on his lunch break from the peace negotiations, which were continuing over the weekend. Ben specified that she should meet him at the UN and not at the Pawars' apartment building.

Did the Pawars not want to communicate with her? Now she was really worrying.

She was given a day pass to Ben's office, a glorified closet-space on the fifth floor. He barely resembled himself. His face was dark and he kept rubbing the bone beneath his left ear, an old stress tell from their undergrad days. He said hi to her and that was all as he scooped up his tablet and hurried her out of his office, down a couple floors, and into a slightly larger workspace with a desk and a couple of chairs.

Shutting the door, he said, "This is one of the rooms they keep electronically secure. I was lucky to get it."

"What's going on, Ben?" She was starting to feel uneasy.

"Nothing about Maanik. Well, not exactly."

"You've lost me."

"At nine fifteen this morning the ambassador suddenly announced a thirty-minute break and disappeared into his office alone. He was visibly distracted, uneasy, very off."

"Had he received a call from home?"

Ben shook his head. "Honestly, I think everything just piled up on him at that instant. Maanik, post-traumatic stress from nearly having been killed, and ratcheted-up expectations from both sides. Full disclosure—he's had anxiety attacks in private now and then. It's a freakin' pressure cooker in there. And it got worse when he left. The Pakistani delegation basically lost it, started trumpeting that this was a 'diplomatic illness' for nefarious purposes."

"Maybe that was just posturing," she offered, attempting to calm Ben from his own anxiety.

He shook his head. "One radical openly theorized that the ambassador was buying time for India to move its civilians out of major metropolitan areas in preparation for a strike. Meanwhile, most of the Indian delegation also flipped out. They think the ambassador's toying with them in some way, and they weren't really sure he was on their side to begin with."

"Which he isn't. He's on a third side."

"Huh?"

"He's on the side of compromise," Caitlin said.

"Oh, right. Anyway, he was calmer after his break. I know he prays at times of stress, and maybe that's what he needed. But when the talks started again it was like we'd been set back three days' worth of negotiating." Ben shook his head and drummed his fingers nervously on the table. "Caitlin, I'm afraid they might really do it this time. I think their atomic trigger fingers are finally overwhelming the instinct for self-preservation."

Caitlin put a hand on his shoulder and breathed deeply. For a moment they sat in silence. Then Ben gathered himself and flipped open his tablet.

"So, I'm thinking we need some good news about Maanik for the ambassador just as fast as we can find some."

"Okay . . . ," Caitlin said, trying to catch up with his still-manic thought process, "you have something in mind?"

Ben opened the screenshots Caitlin had sent him. "I think you're right about the arm movements. If this is a coherent language, they're part of it. They may serve the same function as the diacritical marks in written Hebrew. Some of those marks change the letters, words; some serve as punctuation; some represent abstract concepts like numbers."

"Wait, are you saying what I think you're saying?"

"Yep."

"When did you study the video?" she asked.

"Let's just say it wouldn't let me sleep."

"No wonder you look like crap."

"You look good too."

They smiled at each other.

"Okay, I'm with you," she said. "But Hebrew diacritical marks are simple. Lines, really."

"Right. I'm not sure what purpose these gestures serve, yet. They might be emphasis but I kind of doubt it; they're elaborate."

"Could they be parts of words, like prefixes and suffixes?"

"Maybe, maybe, but look here." Ben jumped to a screen grab Caitlin hadn't made. He had caught a moment when Maanik was lying on the floor, her mouth open to speak, her hands resting calmly beside her. "This was when she first dropped those unfamiliar sounds into English. Her arms were still. The gestures only started as she sped up." He switched to one of Caitlin's screen grabs, where Maanik was still lying on the floor but her hands were in the air. Her left hand was angled away from her body; her right arm was starting to arc diagonally across her torso. "See? They could signify something we would ordinarily express through the subtleties of body language."

"We?" Caitlin said. "That would suggest there's a 'them' in this equation."

"I know, that's crazy." He rubbed below his ear. "But these expressions of hers have patterns and they're not like any I've ever seen. Maanik's not just riffing, Cai. What's more, it's going to be tough even separating discrete words from her stream of speech, since she barely stopped to take breaths. It's like when we hear a foreign language that seems to be a wild, racing babble to us but not to the speakers."

"And you just suggested that those speakers are . . . what?"

"Cai, I really have no clue. Not from what little I've seen and heard here. Maybe it's some kind of schizophasia or glossolalia—"

"But people with schizophasia tend to use recognizable words, and Mrs. Pawar would have picked up on any kind of religious chant."

"I'm not saying it has to be those, exactly, but something like them. I just don't know. This could be terra incognita. I've got a program that should help with transcription. I'll get to it tonight, let you know what I find out."

He shut his tablet, stood, and before she could say anything, he leaned in and hugged her, briefly but close. She had wondered why he had brought her over here when he could have said everything on a phone call from this same secure room. This was why. The hug. She tried to imagine going home to an empty apartment every day after hours of frustrating peace talks. The sudden sense of loneliness over-whelmed her.

"You know, they're lucky to have you," she said. "You may think being a translator makes you invisible, but you're fighting to stay cool and grounded and I know everyone in the room is benefiting from that, whether they're conscious of it or not. You're doing a great job."

He let go before either of them felt awkward and guided her from the room without further conversation.

Before leaving, Caitlin detoured across the newly renovated lobby to an exhibit: *Photographs of Hiroshima and Nagasaki, 1945–1946.* They were, in the oldest sense of the word, god-awful. She felt tears rise, looking at the dead or screaming people, the swaths of burn blisters, whole torsos stripped of skin, ears burned away, blinded eyes. And then there were the famous photos of human shadows on walls, caught in the atomic flash.

How, how, how, Caitlin wondered, *how can anyone see these and want to repeat history?* These images weren't just about nuclear bombs. They were about the unthinkable, lingering pain and horror caused by every war in every era. In them was an implicit warning that the next big conflagration would be exponentially worse. *Yet here we are, rocketing toward it.*

Her blurred vision was caught by one particular image, a young girl curled over her dead baby brother. Caitlin was surprised by how much the girl looked like Maanik. Caitlin wiped her eyes. A sign warned that this was a place for solemn meditation, nothing else. She checked that the security guard was facing away, then snapped a pic-ture of the photograph with her phone.

As she left the lobby, more than anything in the world she wanted to put her arms around her son. But he was at the second birthday party and when she sent him a text—*I love you, kiddo*—there was no reply. Caitlin forced herself to return to her office and attack her back-log of paperwork instead of joining him at the party.

Four hours later, there he was, on a massive sugar high, bright-eyed and huggable.

Caitlin took him to a Ping-Pong club as a special treat for no particular reason—but after only half an hour, she received a phone call from the Pawars. They were in her neighborhood and were hoping to visit her, would that be all right?

Even as she was assenting, Jacob's hands were already rising to his hips in defiance. No doubt he recognized her apologetic shoulders and the sidelong glance that always signaled a change in plans.

"One more game," he signed when she ended the call.

She shook her head and smiled. "So you'll play as slowly as you can?"

He couldn't help snickering; she'd read him right.

"Fifteen minutes," she said. "And I'm sorry. I wouldn't cut us off if I didn't think it was important."

He just shrugged and served an extremely fast ball, which she missed.

"I don't want to go," he signed. "You have to sweeten the pot."

She chuckled. "Where on earth did you pick up that phrase?" she signed.

"I read it. Don't change the subject."

"All right, what are you thinking?"

"Extra hour of TV."

"No way."

"Okay, we order dinner."

His reply was so fast she laughed. Her kid was learning to set her up.

"Okay," she signed, feigning resignation, "but you pick the restaurant."

"No, I pick the restaurant!" Then he giggled as he saw how she'd gotten him.

On their way home, they turned the corner onto their block and walked into the light of the setting sun. Suddenly Caitlin felt a strange pressure against her chest again, a profound sense of being watched, and that whatever was watching her was smarter and faster and fiercer. She grabbed Jacob's hand, walked briskly, looking around for someone, something.

It's just me, she told herself unconvincingly. *It's just the exhibit and Maanik.*

She was suddenly distracted by the sight of a black sedan parked outside her brownstone apartment building. A tall, blond man with an earpiece and an arm cast nodded when he saw her, though she didn't know him. He opened one of the back doors and Ambassador Pawar stepped out, followed by Mrs. Pawar. They stood together, composed and elegant, icons of stability despite everything they were going through.

"Hello," Caitlin said, offering her hand to the ambassador and his wife in turn. She introduced Jacob, who signed his welcome. The Pawars caught on and dipped their heads toward him, smiling.

"Thank you for seeing us," the ambassador said pleasantly.

"Is everything all right?" Caitlin asked, not willing to wait until they got upstairs.

He responded with a half smile. "There is a saying, '*Durlabham hi sadaa sukham.*' It means that one cannot have happiness alone."

Caitlin smiled back.

Upstairs, with Jacob ensconced in his room poring over menus, Caitlin seated the Pawars in the living room. She offered them tea, which they declined, stating that they only intended to stay a few minutes.

"How was your day?" she asked generally, but meant the ambassador.

"Taxing," he replied.

Caitlin turned to Mrs. Pawar. "Maanik?"

"There have been no further incidents," the woman said. "I've instructed Kamala in what to do. She will call if there is a recurrence."

"I see," Caitlin said.

"The blackberries," the ambassador said. "It is somewhat disturbing that one can have that much power over a child. Over any human being, though I confess I could benefit from a cue like that in my professional life."

Caitlin smiled.

"Maanik did agree to the cue," Mrs. Pawar reminded him.

"Yes, I would not have done it without her consent," Caitlin said, trying to reassure them. "And believe me, if she ever feels an urgency to communicate that is more important than calming down, she can and will ignore the cue."

The Pawars seemed surprised by that.

"So she is not helpless," the ambassador said.

"Not in that sense, no."

"Then our real daughter is merely locked away somewhere?" he asked.

"In a manner of speaking, that's the case with many of the kids I see. But we frankly don't know yet what Maanik is experiencing."

Mrs. Pawar pressed her palms together and the ambassador suddenly seemed to be searching for words—or courage, she couldn't be sure which.

"Dr. O'Hara," he said slowly, "I know that our daughter needs help—help we must continue to provide as quietly as possible. This is not an easy thing for a father to do, to weigh his responsibilities against the well-being of his daughter. Yet it must be done."

The ambassador hesitated. Caitlin sensed that he was about to take a considerable leap of faith—or rather, a leap of science over faith.

"Dr. O'Hara, I would like to ask that you continue to work with Maanik, at our home, by whatever means you deem best. I do not pretend that simply because I can turn my daughter off"—his voice caught and he cleared it—"that somehow she is healed. That is clearly not the case. I would like you to find the cause if you can—within the parameters of our home."

"Do you believe the problem *is* psychological?" Mrs. Pawar asked.

"As opposed to a head trauma?" Caitlin said. "I believe so. There are no swollen areas or cuts, no sensitivity to sound and light, no irritability or confusion, clearly no issues with balance—in short, nothing to suggest even a mild head injury."

Both of the Pawars seemed to exhale as one.

"Then please continue," Mrs. Pawar said. "Please."

Caitlin was moved. She took a breath and said, "I'm very grateful that you feel this way and I will be honored to continue treating Maanik." She reached forward and each of them grasped one of her hands. "Thank you for your trust."

Mrs. Pawar clasped her hand more firmly before she could withdraw it. "I am afraid," she said. "I do not wish to put that burden on you—"

"It's no burden at all," Caitlin assured her, squeezing the woman's hand gently. "As I said, this is what I do. First there is some research I'd like to complete. I will call tomorrow."

The ambassador put a comforting arm around his wife as they rose. He left Caitlin with a grateful smile as she saw them out the door.

After they left, she ordered Indian food as per Jacob's instructions and they watched TV. She checked her e-mail every two minutes, hoping to hear from Ben. There was nothing. She decided not to call him.

Late that night, lying in bed, Caitlin found herself thinking of the photo exhibit. She thought of Maanik, of the child in the photograph at the UN. She reached to the wall and drummed on it with her fingers. For the first time, she was initiating it instead of Jacob.

After a pause, she felt and heard him drumming back. It made her smile. And then, as if a witch's spell had been broken, she plunged into sleep.

CHAPTER 12

Croix-des-Bossales Market
Port-au-Prince, Haiti

Dr. Aaron Basher hurried after the seven-year-old girl, one arm wrapped protectively around the emergency medical kit slung from his shoulder. The ground was slippery with thin mud, discarded plastic wrappers, and the overflowing sewage that covered most of the city. He kept one eye on the little girl, her steps purposeful though her feet flapped in the tattered shoes of a man, shoes that sloshed muck onto her toes with every step. She turned, flashing her "Lollipop Guild" T-shirt, which, like most apparel for the residents of Port-au-Prince, had been rejected by American thrift shops, sorted in Miami, and shipped to Haiti semi-legally.

If irony were clean water, this would be a paradise, Aaron thought, not for the first time.

"She was waving her arms around," the girl pattered, "and she was saying something, nothing we know, and most of the women say she got a spirit but other women say no, she got the devil. She was talking so fast, it's very important to her, she even drop one of the phones she shown us!"

A fresh wave of stench pushed away the exhaust fumes that saturated the city. As he covered his nose with his sleeve, Aaron heard a woman screaming nearby. The ragged, shrill terror of the cry sent a chill over him. This was not a daytime sound, nor was it the kind of desperate shout that accompanied the attacks and assaults that regularly befell the populace after sundown.

"Then she start to scream," continued the little girl, gliding over the thickening trash and looking proudly around at the collection of small children who were now trailing them, curious what the white man in his scrubs was going to do.

They turned a corner into an open patch of ground between several of the market's long, open-sided, orange-roofed sheds. This gap in the sheds, like others, was nearly filled with garbage, full of plastic bags with food skins and peelings, the occasional animal carcass, and human waste from when someone couldn't wait for one of the few portable toilets. It was all rotting in the tropical noon sun. Yet the screams, more hideous than the smell, dominated his attention.

The screamer was a young Haitian woman, definitely under twenty, wearing a yellow T-shirt that said "Twerkin' for the Weekend." She was not desperately thin, as many Haitian women were, so he guessed she was getting regular meals from somewhere and probably was not a member of the poorest poor. She was standing barefoot in the mud, her hands raised slightly as if in supplication or protection, or both, and her whole body was rigid. She was staring up past the sheds at the sky, mouth agape.

No one was touching her but all the ladies who sold the food in the market were watching. Aaron heard the word "*fou*" many times over and knew they were saying the young woman was psychotic.

He placed his hands on her arms. She didn't move them. He pressed a little. She resisted. He released them and placed his hands on her face. She didn't register his presence, even when he pulled gently at the corners of her eyes to see if she would look at him. Nor did she stop screaming.

Aaron had been trained to respond to post-traumatic stress disorder but this was different. He'd been in Port-au-Prince for five years, having arrived three weeks after the devastating earthquake, and he'd seen things that had kept him up vomiting at night. But he had never seen anything like this young woman. This was fresh trauma happening *now*. There had been no storm or earth tremor. There were no traces of blood on her body.

He balanced his medical kit on a stack of calabash gourds and rifled through it, wondering what the hell he had that he could use. He wasn't equipped with the effective sedatives of wealthy countries.

Well, he thought, *when in doubt, eliminate pain, even if a source of pain isn't evident*. He loaded a syringe with codeine and slipped the needle into the young woman's bicep. She showed no reaction to the pinch.

He stood back for a moment and, out of habit, looked at his kit to make sure no one was edging near it to steal something they could use . . . or sell. He realized that most of the children gathered in the square were watching a couple who were both aiming horizontal smartphones at the girl, shooting video. Half of Haiti now owned ordinary handsets but smartphones were still prohibitively expensive. Aaron did not have time to be disgusted by the couple. He suddenly noticed that he could hear motors and horns from the road again, and a cheerful music station from a hand-crank radio nearby. The young woman had stopped screaming.

"*C'est la fils avec vous?*" Aaron asked the couple, remembering that the little girl had referred to the young woman as having a phone.

"*Mais non, non*," the man said with an American accent, reinforcing the denial with a wave of his hand.

The woman put away her phone, tugged at his arm. They held trinkets from peddlers, had probably been walking through the market and sought to capture the drama of a native in distress. Aaron wondered what had been lifted from their pockets while they indulged themselves. He didn't feel sorry for them. They could have offered *something*, a donation for medicine.

He turned his attention back to the young woman. She was still staring at the sky, but now her physical behavior had changed. He could not say it was a more comforting sight. With her head tilted back and her mouth dropped open, she appeared to be holding her breath. Her arms were waving back and forth slowly with her hands curled in clawlike shapes. She seemed to want to move her legs as well but her feet were rooted to the filthy slop on the ground.

What now? Aaron thought anxiously. He pawed through his kit again—bandages, dressings, ibuprofen, nothing that was going to help.

The crowd of whispering women parted. Some moved aside willingly, others grudgingly. Aaron watched a few of them make the sign of the cross, and some sucked their teeth, a severe insult in Haiti. Others nodded respectfully toward an approaching figure. Aaron suddenly smelled a cigar, somehow able to penetrate through the stink of the garbage.

"Mambo," some of the onlookers said, explaining and introducing the woman who stepped out of the crowd. The Vodou priestess looked dismissively at the American doctor.

About fifty years old, she was not wearing a hand-me-down American T-shirt but a threadbare, short-sleeved ivory blouse; a skirt that had once been a pale pink; and a thin white kerchief tied around her hair. Her elbows and hips were sharp with undernourishment, and her strong cheekbones would have been envied in another world. Her eyes, tough and fierce, regarded the young girl.

Be respectful, Aaron thought as he stepped aside to admit the woman.

"That girl is drowning," the mambo said in clear English.

Aaron was speechless. After a moment he said, "I don't understand."

"You better hurry," the mambo said. "She got ice-cold salt water in her chest."

The woman raised a cigar to her lips and stared at him.

Aaron wrenched his eyes away and looked at the girl. He glanced from her arms to her neck to her open mouth, and, yes, if this girl had been in water, those hands might have been trying to claw to the surface. His mind shoved the thought away hard but . . . He looked at her face and, by god, her lips were turning blue. Her ears too. She was trembling all over and her arms were slowing down.

This girl has hypothermia. In Haiti.

Aaron waved at several women to move cabbages and stalks of sugarcane off a sheet that was spread beneath them on the ground. He turned to his kit and pulled out two packages and ripped them both open. As soon as the sheet was clear he put his hands under the girl's armpits and dragged her to it as gently as possible. Supporting her body, he laid her down. He pulled a crackling silver Mylar emergency blanket from the larger ripped package and spread it over the girl to keep her warm under the scorching-hot sun. Then he checked for anything in her throat that might be obstructing her breathing—there was nothing. With one desperate glance at the mambo smoking her cigar, he interlocked his hands and leaned on the young woman's chest to perform CPR. He ignored his brain, which demanded to know what the *hell* he was doing.

After five pumps he pulled a piece of plastic from the smaller ripped package and placed it over the girl's mouth so that he wouldn't infect her with anything he might be carrying. He placed his mouth over hers to breathe into her lungs and was shocked to feel that her lips were warm. He pulled away, second-guessing everything, but the blue of her lips was unmistakable. Exhaling deeply into her, he then moved back to her chest and pressed on her heart, two, three, four, five, inhale . . . exhale into her, back to the chest . . .

Suddenly the girl spasmed and hacked, hard. If they had been on a beach, by a swimming pool, in the flat bottom of a boat, a spout of water would have arced out of her mouth. Here, there was nothing. And yet, when she lay back down, she was coughing and breathing hoarsely exactly like someone who had been drowning only seconds ago.

"Good God," Aaron murmured. He turned to the mambo, a look of awe and confusion on his face. "Thank you," he said.

She tapped the ash off her cigar onto the foul ground. "*Se bon ki ra*," she replied. "Good is rare." Then she turned and walked into the crowd as it closed behind her.

PART TWO

CHAPTER 13

Caitlin ceded her Sunday morning with Jacob to one of his school friends, who'd come over to plan a partnered science project. Determined not to resort to working, Caitlin found herself sitting on the couch watching TV—and the face of Ambassador Pawar as reporters' microphones bristled around him. Earlier that morning, the entire Indian delegation had, as a group, walked out of the United Nations building. Within minutes, the Pakistan delegation had followed. The talks had imploded.

Ambassador Pawar was holding fast to his diplomatic façade as he read a statement. "By no means does this presage a final decision on behalf of either country," he said. "We are simply cooling our minds for future discussions."

Caitlin hoped there was some truth to it, that the delegations had simply burned out. Yet as she inspected the ambassador's face, she saw a set to his jaw that she had only seen when he was speaking of Maanik's troubles. She suspected the disruption of the talks had been caused by something much more serious than exhaustion. She considered calling Ben, who had been silent since their discussion about the video.

Just then her phone buzzed. *Speak of the devil.* The text was from Ben but there was no message, only a video link. The owner of the video had posted it with a caption: "Crazy Haiti!" and a winking emoticon. Caitlin clicked the link and gasped. The first thing she saw was a young Haitian woman, her eyes rolled to the sky, her left hand angled away from her body, her right arm arcing across her torso—precisely the same gesture Maanik had made in her trance.

With a deep chill racing down her back, Caitlin watched the video all the way through. The familiar, unintelligible speech—it had to be speech—was difficult to hear on the recording. She thought she recognized two other gestures; then the young woman started screaming and a few minutes later the recording ended. Caitlin immediately watched it again, leaning forward from the couch and hunching over her phone.

What the hell is going on? she wondered. Two young women, geographically isolated, culturally unconnected, with the same physio-psychological symptoms? If there was a trigger, it had to be found. If there was more information that could help Maanik, she had to obtain it.

Just as she registered the silence behind her in the dining nook, she heard a sharp rap on the table. She turned to see both children staring at her in concern. Though his hearing aid was on, Jacob had knocked to get her attention.

"Mom, are you okay?" he said and signed.

"I'm fine," she signed back. "Everything's okay."

"Who's that screaming?" he signed.

Caitlin realized she should have muted her phone as she watched the video.

"It's a girl," she signed. "A client," she said, hedging.

"Are you going to help her?"

"If she'll let me," Caitlin signed back, and it wasn't a lie: she was going to have a session with this young woman even if she had to catch a flight to Haiti that night. Caitlin patted his shoulder and headed to her bedroom. Behind her Jacob rapped on the table again. She turned.

"Are you leaving soon?" he signed with a sigh.

She half-laughed and signed, "Knock before entering my brain, kiddo."

He laughed too. "I did!" he signed. Then he quickly resumed his work with his friend. He knew he wasn't allowed to press for details about her "kids," as he had once called them.

Caitlin's phone buzzed in her hand. A text gave a young woman's name—Gaelle Anglade—with an address in Jacmel, Haiti, and an international phone number. There was also a message from Ben: *UN Youth Development office says she's fine. Taken to hospital released within hour. English-speaker.*

That last was a little push. Ben knew Caitlin all too well. She sat on her bed, took a very deep breath, and tapped in the phone number.

"Allo, Anglade Charter Fishing," said a young woman's voice.

"Hello, is Gaelle Anglade there?"

"I am Gaelle," she answered.

That was unexpected. The young woman's voice was unhurried; Caitlin made sure hers was the same. "Hi, Gaelle. My name is Dr. Caitlin O'Hara and I am calling from New York City. Do you have a minute?"

There was a brief hesitation. "Do you need a boat?"

"Sounds like a *great* idea but perhaps some other day." Caitlin chuckled. "Gaelle, I have a patient who I *think* is experiencing the same thing that happened to you in the market yesterday."

Gaelle was silent for so long Caitlin said, "Hello?" to see if she had hung up.

"Are you a friend of Dr. Basher?" Gaelle's voice was cautious, thick with distrust.

"I don't know him."

"Then . . . you saw that video?"

"I did," Caitlin admitted. "It was a terrible invasion of your privacy and I'm sorry. I would like to help."

There was silence, but it was a connected silence. She had not ended the call.

"How?" the young woman asked. It was not so much a question as a challenge.

"My patient has had repeated episodes, and while I have treated them I am still searching for a cause. I believe that talking with you might help." Caitlin paused, then said, "I am concerned for you as well as for her, and very interested to learn if you too have had other episodes."

"I do not have demons," Gaelle stated. She seemed embarrassed.

"Of course not!" Caitlin replied. "Good lord, no!" She was well aware of what the woman would be up against in her culture, where Catholics, Protestants, and Vodou believers did not always live free of friction.

Caitlin heard the young woman speak away from the phone in Haitian Creole, talking to a male voice in the background. When she returned to the call, she asked Caitlin to repeat her name slowly and said she was looking her up online.

Caitlin obliged and heard typing. "You live in Jacmel?"

"Yes."

"May I ask why you were in Port-au-Prince yesterday?"

"I train women at the market to use smartphones. It is a combination literacy and technology program."

"Do you work for a phone company?"

"No, for my stepmother. She takes people out to fish. I am also studying to be a nurse. I would like to be a social worker so I find visiting programs to volunteer with. I have found your website, doctor." Her voice turned upward. "You are a psychiatrist."

"That is correct. I work with young adults."

"Do you think I am ill? Mentally?"

"Not at all. I believe that you had a reaction to something—"

"Like an allergy? Peanuts? We don't have food allergies in Haiti," she said with disgust. "We cannot afford to."

"I don't believe it was digested or airborne," Caitlin replied, as she would to a fellow professional. "It was something else."

"I see."

"I want to try and find out what it was. Gaelle, can I come see you? Can I meet you tomorrow?"

She heard the girl say, *"Pas bon, pas bon,"* but wasn't sure whether she was saying "Bad, bad" to her or to the person with her.

"Gaelle?" Caitlin pressed. She didn't want her to jump off the phone.

"No, thank you," Gaelle said defensively. "I had a CAT scan yesterday, in Port-au-Prince. There is nothing wrong with me. That is in the past."

"Gaelle, my other patient has had multiple experiences this past week. It appears the past does not always *stay* past. I'm afraid that what happened in the market *could* happen again. I just want to be sure. That's why I am willing to fly down."

The girl was silent. Caitlin remained patient.

"I am not sick," Gaelle repeated. "But I want to be a good nurse. I want to help you help your other patient."

Caitlin hadn't realized she was holding her breath until she exhaled. "Thank you. I couldn't ask for anything more. So you'll see me then?"

"I will."

CHAPTER 14

Gaelle and Caitlin set a time and place for the following day. Then Caitlin called her parents on Long Island and her father agreed to come to the city to stay with Jacob. She jumped online to reserve a flight to Haiti leaving early the next morning with a return late that night. After booking transportation to and from the airports, she focused on the final necessity, a guide and translator. She did not consider calling Ben or even the ambassador to help, as she knew that most Haitians hated the UN. They believed that one of its camps had introduced cholera to the country for the first time in a century. Thousands had died; a lawsuit against the UN was crawling through the New York judicial system.

She called Sharon Tanaka at the World Health Organization instead. Sharon was a tough nut with budgets but an excellent connector. She agreed to find a good person to meet Caitlin the next morning at a hotel conveniently located in Port-au-Prince and escort her to Jacmel.

Logistics settled, Caitlin reached for the top shelf of her bedroom closet, where she kept a go-bag for emergencies. She banged the wall accidentally as she did so.

Jacob banged back—gently, reminding her to chill.

She knocked back, chilled. The sense of urgency wasn't gone, but now at least it had a direction.

• • •

Waking from a dreamless sleep just after dawn—and a half hour before her alarm was to go off—Caitlin put her mind to rescheduling her appointments. Dr. Anita Carter was on call if any of her kids had an emergency. Caitlin sent Mrs. Pawar an e-mail with the video from Haiti attached, explaining why she was going. She added that if there was another episode and the cue failed, they should try to administer one of the sedatives during one of her more conversational phases, assuming she would progress through the cycle she had demonstrated. Caitlin would change her flight back if necessary.

Caitlin also took a minute to check the news online before Jacob woke. The headlines were in big, bold type, ugly and ominous. Indian and Pakistani troops were being massed along the Line of Control—a buffer between India's Jammu and Kashmir and Pakistan's Azad Jammu and Kashmir—as well as near the Zero Point, which lay between the Indian states of Gujarat and Rajasthan and Pakistan's province of Sindh. The reporting was frank, the editorials pleading, the faces in the photographs set in every shade of fear, whether they were citizens, soldiers, or politicians.

A *spark*, Caitlin thought. That was all it would take to ignite those long, fierce borders. Not necessarily a bullet there but a wrong word here. She was sure the Pawars would insulate Maanik from the news as best they could, but there was no way of knowing how much of her father's anxiety was being communicated subconsciously and whether that affected her condition. How could it not?

Jacob stalked behind her and put his arms around her. She turned and kissed his forehead.

"Morning, hon," she signed.

"I am a zombie," he replied with a mushy face.

"Then go make us oat brains." She smiled. "Get it? Brains . . . bran."

He acknowledged the joke with a grunt and shuffled to the kitchen to make breakfast.

Joseph Patrick O'Hara arrived shortly before seven. He was a big man with a pile of white hair and a chronic smile in his eyes. Jacob left the breakfast table to hug him around the waist while Caitlin kissed his cheek.

"Thanks, Pop," she said. "It's good to see you."

"Always a pleasure," he replied, rubbing Jacob's hair.

That tended to be the length of their conversations whenever he drove in from Long Island to "sit": she was always running late, he was always misjudging traffic, and they usually only spoke as she was racing into the hallway. Her father hugged her quickly as she headed to the waiting car service.

"I love you both!" she said at the door. "Jacob, you can stay up late but no video games, surfing the Web, or zombies after eight thirty. See you Tuesday."

Caitlin was on her tablet for much of the four-hour flight. Most of that time was spent answering e-mails from patients and colleagues. She also went to the UN Youth Development website, which had first noted the YouTube video of Gaelle Anglade. There were no other reports of anything similar, but Caitlin couldn't help thinking of the boy in Iran who had first exhibited logorrhea, then set himself on fire. There had been no mention of gestures with him but perhaps . . . perhaps she was being hasty. She wouldn't even know this case in Haiti was related until she saw Gaelle face-to-face.

The airport in Port-au-Prince was a modern affair and the van to the hotel in Pétion-Ville, a wealthy district south of the city, was an air-conditioned, scented bubble. "Real" Haiti would begin when she left the district.

The hotel receptionist pointed her to the roofed section of the courtyard near the pool. That was where people met guests, she said.

The wicker chairs and tables were in deep shadow compared to the brilliant sunlight outside. Caitlin stood looking around and saw a white man approaching who seemed vaguely familiar. He was wearing scrubs and had just been sitting with two Haitians who were dressed more for the Port-au-Prince markets than a Pétion-Ville hotel. The duo remained sitting at a table out of the sun as he came forward.

"I'm Aaron Basher," the white man said, offering his hand. Caitlin suddenly recognized him as Gaelle's doctor in the video.

"Caitlin O'Hara," she replied.

"Sharon Tanaka asked—actually, she insisted—that I meet you and take you to Jacmel."

"That sounds like her usual MO." Caitlin smiled as she followed him to the table. She did not ask about his companions. He would introduce them in his own way.

"New Jersey?" she guessed about his accent.

"West Orange." He nodded. "Go Jets," he added as a somewhat sour joke. A football stadium with plush skyboxes was the polar opposite of Haiti.

They reached the others, who were uncommonly still in their wicker seats.

"Dr. O'Hara, I'd like to introduce you to Madame Mambo Langlois." Aaron gestured toward a very thin, very formidable Haitian woman. He slightly emphasized "mambo" and gave the tiniest of bows.

Caitlin picked up on his cues: he was hoping she either knew what a mambo was or would notice his extra sign of respect. She bowed slightly and thanked the woman for accompanying Aaron. The woman did not rise from her chair or speak but she did offer Caitlin her hand. Caitlin accepted the handshake, which was something of a compliment from a Vodou high priestess.

"And this is Houngan Enock Capois, the madame's son." The Vodou priest was about thirty, with the same startling cheekbones as his mother. He was wearing mirrored sunglasses and an antique woman's ring on his right hand. It looked odd, almost ridiculous at first, until Caitlin realized the gold and emeralds were real in this poorest of nations. He barely shook her hand. His disdain was clear.

"So, let's get to Jacmel," Aaron announced with a sudden, pointed cheerfulness. The priest and priestess walked ahead, and Aaron managed to steal a second with Caitlin as he picked up her small suitcase. "They were waiting outside my house this morning," he murmured.

"Is that common?"

He shook his head. "They seem to 'know' things," he whispered. "Gossip, probably."

"Do they speak English?"

He nodded.

And then they were back within earshot, loading up the white four-door Land Cruiser Aaron had borrowed. Enock Capois immediately claimed the front seat, leaving Caitlin to sit with his mother in the back. Caitlin stopped herself from smiling. An assumption of hierarchy seemed almost quaint, but there was something preferable about sitting with the madame anyway.

With Aaron driving, the truck began the long climb up the hills outside of Pétion-Ville. Route 101 led south away from Port-au-Prince. It was a decently paved two-lane road lined with cobblestone gutters, sometimes concrete walls. Dark and brilliant greenery tumbled over the latter, backed by palm trees and a cloudless blue sky that seemed as flat and taut as a drum. But less than ten minutes later they began to see occasional pedestrians walking along the side of the road, carrying plastic jugs, plastic bags, bundled blue tarps, and car tires. If there was a universal sign of poverty, it was this: adults and children on the march, recycling, reusing, repurposing items that could barely buy them a single meal.

The mother and son seemed disinclined to talk and Caitlin decided there could be no harm in asking Aaron about Gaelle's episode in the market. That was, after all, why she had come.

Aaron recounted the incredible story—drowning on dry land, CPR, coughing up nothing—without editorializing. He had decided not to judge and Caitlin appreciated that.

"Gaelle mentioned that she had a CAT scan?" she said.

"Yes."

"I was surprised to hear one was so readily available."

"I snuck her in," Aaron said bluntly. "We usually need the machine Saturday nights or on Sundays. Gangs smash the solar-panel streetlights on weekends so they can operate in the dark, so all the blunt-force head trauma tends to happen then."

Madame Langlois spoke up: "People are angry."

Caitlin regarded her. "Which people?"

"All. You know the name of the market where the video was made? Croix-des-Bossales."

"The Slave Market," Aaron translated.

"We keep the name to remind us. Someone always wants to be the new master."

Her son reached up and turned Aaron's rearview mirror so that he could look at Caitlin without turning his head.

"You are a psychiatrist?" he asked. His accent was thicker than his mother's but his English was just as polished.

"Yes."

"I have been to college too," he said. "Do you teach people that they should not fear the world?"

"In a way. I help them to see that—"

"Is that what you are going to say to this young woman of Haiti?"

"I won't know until I—"

"Nature conspires against Haiti," he said. "World governments conspire against us. Our past conspires against us. She has a dark life ahead of her."

Caitlin heard Aaron mutter, "He's got a point."

"Is that why she's so agitated?" Caitlin asked. She glanced at the man's mother. "Has someone or some*thing* chosen her to express Haiti's pain?"

She had kept the question broad, hoping that they would narrow the focus. Aaron seemed to tense; the "something" reference opened the door to gods and demons, the personifications of centuries of fear.

Enock did not take the bait. He just sucked his teeth. Aaron kept his eyes on the twisting road and pedestrians.

The madame broke the short silence. "I heard Dr. Basher treated knife wounds from the Group Zero fight two nights ago."

Enock suddenly lost all interest in Caitlin. He pelted Aaron with questions about the victims, who apparently included some of his friends. Aaron gently restored his rearview mirror to its position as he answered that the wounds were not life-threatening, and gave Caitlin a warning look.

While Enock processed the information about his friends, the madame looked out the side window.

"Do you know that Vodou is currently illegal in Haiti?" she asked, clearly to Caitlin, though she was not looking at her.

"I thought it was protected in the constitution."

"The new constitution last year did not include this protection."

"I'm sorry. Religious freedom should not be optional."

"We have been attacked for dancing, for our rites. There have been stonings of Vodou priestesses."

"I didn't know."

"So you understand, with pressure descending upon us, we are . . . cautious."

Caitlin nodded once, twice. The woman was not apologizing, simply explaining her reserve.

"We are also proud," the madame added.

"I understand, and my concern for Gaelle is genuine," Caitlin replied. "Genuine and without judgment."

"But you do not believe in demons," she said.

"I don't believe in labels," Caitlin replied.

The madame nodded and stared out the window again. There were fewer houses along the road now, and most of them were shacks.

The rounded mountaintops, deforested over the past century, looked bare and hungry.

"May I ask," Caitlin said, thinking back to what Gaelle said and choosing her words carefully, "if *you* believe in spirits?"

The madame did not answer. Aaron's wary look in the mirror told her that was a yes.

Caitlin pressed on respectfully.

"What do you see when you look out there? Does it just look like a landscape to you, or is there more?"

The madame reached into her bag, pulled out a cigar, lit it, and smoked for a while. She said, "In Africa, elephants hear the footfalls of other elephants hundreds of miles away. They carry a map of the land in their minds far beyond anything we have. Pigeons, too. Plenty of other birds, other animals."

"Subsonic communication," Caitlin said, merging the worlds of science and magic.

The madame smoked. "Humans have this too. We don't use it."

"Do you?"

Aaron frowned at Caitlin.

"I see only my tired country," the madame said. "Only that."

A silence stretched into quiet. Caitlin allowed the motion of the car among the hills to lull her into a reflective state—*Observe and let go, tide in, tide out*—but she was hoping that somehow answers, or at least the right questions, would rise from these depths. The torment of Maanik and now Gaelle was never far away.

Just over an hour later they crested a hill and saw the Caribbean sparkling below them. The southern coast, dotted with beaches, was like a flute channeling Haiti's tired breaths, sweetening the sound. Fortunately and unfortunately, the beaches were being discovered by foreign investors. Jacmel already had several resort communities, including one that was painted aggressively white. Caitlin was sure the planners had thought of it as bright and cheerful, but to a people who built mostly with gray concrete, the paint was an insult. Yet tourists brought money for meals and education. The Anglade Charter Fishing office was tucked behind the slim, New Orleans–style columns of a pale green house. It would not have existed without the vacationers. Nor would Gaelle's education as a nurse.

The door to the office was open and Caitlin, first in, watched Gaelle stand up behind her desk as the little group strode in. The first thing Caitlin noticed was the slightly sunken look around Gaelle's hazel eyes. This young woman had not been sleeping well. Otherwise, her hair had been freshly braided and pulled up into a chignon, and she was wearing a pale yellow blouse. Everything about her and the office was tidy, tucked in, as neatly organized as a nurse's station in a hospital. And Gaelle's manner was purposeful, just shy of abrupt.

The young woman did not seem overly pleased to see Dr. Basher or the Vodou family, but she greeted them courteously and shook hands. A surprisingly tall, strong middle-aged woman with a creased face and worried eyes appeared from a back room. She had an air of reticence that had grown over her formidable physicality like a vine on a wall. Gaelle introduced her as her stepmother, Marie-Jeanne, and she was cordial to the madame and her son, slightly less so with the Americans. Caitlin quickly asked to sit alone with Gaelle in the small garden in the back. Marie-Jeanne agreed to mind the office for a few minutes and Aaron took the madame and her son around the corner for coffee. They went willingly, the madame giving a shrug as if to say, *Free coffee is free coffee.*

Gaelle made it clear by her proper, unrelaxed manner that she had no interest in small talk. Caitlin asked her some basic questions about her family's medical history, and Gaelle answered. Caitlin marked her answers in a small, unintimidating notebook.

"I want to make sure you understand," Caitlin went on, "that you don't need to feel embarrassed or ashamed about our talk."

"This happened through no device of my doing," Gaelle replied frostily. "What have I to be ashamed of?"

"I was not referring to the incident," Caitlin said. "I meant my questions."

Gaelle seemed embarrassed by her own defensiveness. She softened a little. "Please ask the questions you need to help your patient."

"Thank you again. You said your mother died a few months after you were born. You were raised by your father?"

"Until I was sixteen, four years ago. Now he lives in the Dominican Republic. He works in a hotel."

"Why did he leave?"

"The money is a little better there. I encouraged him to go."

Caitlin smiled. It had no effect. "Dr. Basher explained to you what happened in the market? That you showed symptoms of drowning and hypothermia?"

Gaelle nodded once.

"Have you ever come close to drowning?"

"No."

"Do you go out with your stepmother on the fishing boat?"

"Rarely. I have my work and my studies. I have little free time."

"Do you ever swim in the ocean?"

"As I said, there is little free time."

"What about when you were a child?" Caitlin pressed. "Might something have happened then?"

"Dr. O'Hara, I am from a town in the mountains where we walked for an hour to get our daily water. We moved here in 2012. An organization offered to establish fishing businesses for Haitians."

"So you were inland during the 2010 earthquake?"

"Yes. I was not near the tsunami that struck Jacmel. I only saw trees falling, shacks collapsing onto the people inside them." She closed her mouth, lips pressed tightly together.

"Gaelle, has anything happened recently—anything upsetting?" Caitlin was thinking of Maanik and the assassination attempt.

"Life is not easy here," she said. "That is upsetting."

"I understand," Caitlin said. "I was asking about anything specific. Something that made you fearful, afraid?"

Gaelle took a moment. Her pinched expression did not suggest someone who was trying to remember something. Rather, she seemed uncertain about what to share.

"There are gangs who come out at night, from Port-au-Prince," she said. "We go inside to escape the biting insects—but then the other hunters, they know where to find us."

Caitlin felt a wave of anxiety rise as she imagined being afraid to walk in the town at night, being afraid of strangers.

"Were you hurt?"

Gaelle shook her head brusquely.

"Threatened?"

"They touch, they push, they grab," she said with disgust in her voice. "Sometimes too much. That is not new. I am all right."

Gaelle was not all right, and Caitlin hurt for her while resenting her own helplessness. But the psychiatrist accepted that she wasn't getting anywhere with this conversation. And worse, she sensed that Gaelle was pulling up the drawbridge. She had to try something more direct.

"Gaelle, are you familiar with therapeutic hypnotism? Using a trance to access your subconscious?"

"A little. I researched psychiatry online last night."

"Because . . . ?"

"I like to know things," she answered evasively.

"So do I." Caitlin smiled.

The girl sat stony-faced. She did not want to bond.

"Gaelle, I have been using this technique with my other patient. I would like very much to try it with you."

Before she even made the request Caitlin knew that Gaelle would say no. This young woman had fought for control in a country that afforded little. Structured time and a structured mind were as close as she could come to feeling safe.

"Before you answer," Caitlin jumped in, "I want to explain that I am not asking this lightly. If I thought there was any other way to identify the cause of your episode, I would suggest it. This is emergency psychiatric medicine."

Gaelle stared at her, placed her chin in her hand. "Do you believe that I am mentally ill?"

"I told you over the phone, I do not," Caitlin said emphatically.

Gaelle stared at her a little longer, then stood. "I will discuss it with my stepmother. Please come back in a half hour."

CHAPTER 15

Caitlin spent the time watching waves slide across the beach. She had always enjoyed going to Coney Island or Jones Beach as a kid, but back then the ocean was an adventure. Now it was a mystery. She remembered her dream, the black wave rolling toward her.

Is that the ultimate paradox of life, she wondered, *that the universe should become less clear with age?*

Yes, she decided with a last, admiring glance at the sea as she dusted sand from her butt. She looked at a grain among grains on the tip of her index finger.

"You were here before we were," she said.

Caitlin did not brush the sand away but left it, like a second skin, and headed back to the pale green house. Now, away from the fresh sea breeze, she was starting to sweat through her blouse. The afternoon heat surpassed 90 degrees, typical for October in Haiti. Sunset and stronger winds from the Caribbean would provide some relief in the evening, but then mosquitoes and fleas would become plentiful. The universe had a cruel sense of humor.

A dozen people had clustered on the street by the Anglade office, not too close to the veranda. They were all Haitian and were loosely divided into two groups, those staring mutely at the house and those who were chatting with each other. Word had apparently spread about the Anglades' visitors, but was it Caitlin or the Vodou clergy from the city who were attracting the attention? As soon as one person in the gathering saw her, they all turned their heads, fell into a stony silence, and watched her approach. There were no smiles, only cautious eyes and defensively lifted chins.

A man in a priest's collar called to her in French or Creole, she wasn't sure which. She replied only, *"Excusez-moi."* Although she heard him start again, Caitlin didn't break her pace toward the door. It was not the time to engage with anyone else, not now.

The door to the office was open, in keeping with tropical etiquette. Madame Langlois, her son, and Aaron had arrived before her. Houngan Enock had been speaking fervently to Marie-Jeanne; he stopped when Caitlin entered. The madame was perched in a corner holding her blue tarp bag on her lap with the patience of ages. Aaron was on his cell phone in the room behind the office. He was talking to the clinic and hydrating with a two-liter bottle of water.

As Caitlin made her way across the room she watched Gaelle, who was sitting at her desk in a semblance of normal working life, a cup of jasmine tea losing steam in a saucer nearby. The young woman was drawing on a small notepad and Caitlin leaned in for a closer look. She saw crescent marks in the shape of triangles, grouped into one large triangle. The symbols meant nothing to her but she didn't have long to examine them. Gaelle moved the notepad aside and pulled a brochure over it. Gaelle's guard was back up, and Caitlin thought better of asking about the drawing she had just hidden away.

"Is everything all right?" she asked instead.

Gaelle nodded.

"Have you had time to think on your own?" Caitlin did not emphasize the last three words but her meaning was clear. "This is *your* decision," she added.

Gaelle shook her head and seemed about to speak, but Houngan Enock interrupted. "We do not value loneliness in Haiti, doctor."

"What does that mean exactly?" Caitlin queried, restraining her increasing defensiveness.

"What I said. We are here to help her with this important decision."

They heard an upswelling of noise from the street. Caitlin looked through the window. The group outside had increased in size and intensity.

"You are certainly bringing a lot of 'help,'" Caitlin said quietly.

Gaelle gave her the ghost of a smile. *At last, a connection*, Caitlin thought.

Gaelle's stepmother spoke in Creole. Gaelle translated for Caitlin. "She is saying, 'Don't blame our visitors. Since the video was on the Internet, we have been seeing many strangers around. Some Haitian, some white.'"

Caitlin spoke up. "Have they said anything to you, Gaelle? Done anything?"

"Only talk," the girl answered unhappily. "It doesn't matter."

"Yes, it does. You should not have to live with that." Caitlin cautiously moved a hand across the desk toward her. "Please let me help you."

"So they can talk more?" Enock challenged.

"So I can help you stop an incident like the last one if it happens again."

Gaelle looked at Caitlin, then at her desk, and shook her head slowly. "I must say no, doctor."

"But why?"

Gaelle's stepmother said something quickly, made an axe-like gesture with her hand. Gaelle translated, though it was unnecessary. "The decision is made."

Enock smiled and placed himself on the edge of the desk, between Gaelle and Caitlin. He began to dig in his own plastic bag and pull out small boxes and bags. Caitlin tried to catch the madame's eye but she was watching her son impassively.

Caitlin stood and stepped to one side. It was becoming clear what was soon to happen.

"Gaelle, is it your wish to seek help through a Vodou ceremony?" she asked.

They heard a sudden chant from the people in the street and then several voices rose in a Christian hymn. Marie-Jeanne and Enock began to speak quickly in Creole but Gaelle cut them off.

"No, *I* will go," she said emphatically.

Gaelle stood and glided toward the door with elegance. From the window Caitlin saw her approach the Catholic priest. There was no sign that he was of special significance to her but she was respectful and unafraid. The people nearest the priest shot the young woman suspicious looks.

Aaron, now leaning on the doorjamb of the back room, spoke to Caitlin. "People are on edge," he said.

"Clearly."

"It's not just this," he said. "In early November there is usually a severe spike in violence in Port-au-Prince. It's the Vodou holy days. Grave robbers desecrate Vodou territory, throw rocks at their holy people, that kind of thing. Sometimes there are riots, though I think it's really all a vent because of the poverty here."

Caitlin understood his point immediately: anything could spark off this crowd. Especially if they thought someone was possessed. That was why Gaelle had been so quick to deny it when they spoke.

"And there is white bias," Enock snapped. "They come here and tell us that we are primitive yet they have no knowledge of our faith. Frightened people spread outrageous lies—that it was Vodou that caused the earthquake, that we bargain with devils. We do not do this 'black magic'!" He shot the accusation at Caitlin personally.

"I would never say that you do," Caitlin replied.

"Your questions in the car were . . . superior."

"I never meant—"

"No. Your kind has been like this!" He threw his chin angrily toward the crowd and the priest. "Your arrogant manipulation of reality is more black magic than ours!" He slammed a jar of red powder onto the table next to him. "We look farther into reality. You . . . you just twist it."

"How?" Caitlin asked, trying to stay focused and understanding.

"You peck at it, like chickens at meal. You study the pieces instead of the whole. That is not a cure! That is"—he took a moment to search for the word—"what you call dissection. It is autopsy."

Against her will, Caitlin's temper started to rise. But she kept her mouth shut.

"From what I know of Vodou," Aaron said to no one in particular, "it's a way for people to gather, bring up their problems, share food, dance, and feel that they matter—that they're part of something bigger."

"Your explanation is like the surface of the sea." Enock scowled, moving his hand like rippling waves. "It is just what the white outsider sees."

"You misunderstand me," Aaron said. "I think all of those things are essential for our souls."

"I tell you, you know nothing," Enock sneered. "Either of you."

"Then educate us!" Caitlin said.

Marie-Jeanne said something quickly to Enock that stopped him in his tracks. Enock paused and then casually translated for Caitlin.

"She says she knows what caused Gaelle's *fou* in the market."

All eyes snapped to Marie-Jeanne. She was rubbing her forehead and staring at the ceiling.

Enock continued translating. "You do not need to hypnotize Gaelle. She will tell you. Three days ago a tourist fell from Marie-Jeanne's boat. Marie-Jeanne dove in and rescued him but she nearly drowned herself. When Gaelle heard of this she was very upset."

Caitlin said nothing. She felt as if she'd been hit in the chest by one of those large breakers on the shore. This could not be a coincidence.

They heard voices rise in a hymn from the street. Caitlin looked out the window and there were thirty-five or forty people outside the house. Gaelle, still in the middle of them, turned from the priest and entered the office, frowning.

"They are children, sometimes," she said. "Fighting, fighting, fighting about the business of others."

Caitlin heard but did not process what Gaelle was saying. Her mind was still on what Enock had translated. "Gaelle, I must talk to you. I came here initially to help my patient in New York, to learn—"

"No!" the girl insisted before she even sat down. "Everything stops now. No confession, no hypnotism, nothing. I am not sick, except of all this nonsense!"

"You're absolutely right," Caitlin said, with sudden inspiration. She had to convince Gaelle, had to show her what was at stake. "This is not illness. It's an *assault* of some kind." She pulled out her phone and scrolled through her files.

"What are you saying?"

"Please, I can show you . . ."

Caitlin found the iconic picture of the girl from Hiroshima and handed the phone to Gaelle. A shade of empathy and fear crossed the young woman's face.

"Who is this?" she asked.

"That is a girl who just survived a nuclear bomb. The look on her face, that intensity of suffering, is exactly what my patient in New York is experiencing. And what I believe you have experienced too."

Enock, Aaron, and Marie-Jeanne all looked over Gaelle's shoulder. For a moment Caitlin thought Gaelle might weep. The young woman handed the phone to her stepmother and spoke in Creole.

Enock stood peremptorily. "You are simply manipulating her. Sympathy is not a revelation," he stated. "Nor is it action. I will show you both."

He grabbed the small jar he had slammed on the table, then moved two chairs to clear a space on the floor and closed the door to the veranda. The crowd outside immediately responded to his actions as if they knew what was coming next. Their tones of disapproval rose into almost a chant.

But what *was* happening next? Caitlin thought she had tapped into something with Gaelle, that she was getting somewhere, but was this silence the girl's only response? Was she going to submit to Enock?

The Houngan began tapping red powder out of his jar in a long line down the floor. Caitlin caught a very faint, familiar scent. It was cayenne pepper. Enock finished the first line and started tapping out a second one perpendicular to the first.

Caitlin was moving to confer with Aaron when Madame Langlois stood up and, handing her blue tarp bag to Caitlin, turned her fierce eyes on her son. In Creole, she snapped at him. He answered back defensively. Caitlin thought she recognized the word "papa" and asked Aaron about it.

"Papa Legba is the *loa* that guards the gate between our world and theirs," he whispered in her ear. "No spirit can come through without his approval."

"I don't understand," she whispered back. "Was Enock going to try to contact him?"

"I don't know," he admitted.

The madame suddenly marched into the back room and ordered her son to follow her. Enock huffed but turned and shoved past Aaron. Leaving the door to the back room open, they exploded into an argument in Creole. Gaelle looked slightly relieved.

"What's wrong?" Caitlin asked.

"He was going to trace the Papa spirit's symbol on the floor," the girl explained. "His *veve*."

"Why did Madame Langlois stop him?"

"It is always done with flour or cornmeal, not pepper. She is asking why he has so much cayenne in the first place. It's expensive. He is saying it is more powerful." Gaelle paused and listened. "She says that the power comes from the one who invokes, not the powder. Using cayenne will make him weak . . ." She searched for a word. "Forget- ful."

Despite the drama of the moment, Caitlin could not help but smile. Theirs was like any family squabble in any corner of the world.

"You're brave," Aaron said.

Caitlin raised an eyebrow.

"Holding the bag of a Vodou priestess." He smiled.

Caitlin had forgotten the bag, rapt as she was in the debate in the next room. Through the open door, she saw the madame lift her son's hand with the ring, then fling it down. Caitlin wondered if this argu- ment would make Gaelle more or less inclined to listen to the Houn- gan's advice, if the madame might allow her a little more leeway.

Suddenly, Caitlin's eyes lowered to the blue tarp bag. She had felt it *move*. It had been infinitesimal but definitely real. There it was again, a little more lively this time. She gripped the bag tightly to keep from dropping it.

"Madame," she breathed, with no sound behind her breath.

Madame Langlois looked in on Caitlin, sized up the situation in a glance, and entered the room immediately. Enock followed but she pointed at him with one finger and he sat in the nearest chair. Retriev- ing the bag, the madame hefted it twice gently, like a grocer judging the weight of a bag of grapes.

"This is very interesting," the madame murmured to Caitlin. "Damballa is active in your life."

Caitlin did not know who or what "Damballa" meant and did not feel disposed to speak. She remained absolutely still.

"He protects the weakened," the madame continued. "This is why I brought him."

Caitlin noticed that she did not say "the weak" but "the weak- ened." It was an interesting distinction. The woman placed her bag on Gaelle's desk and reached into it. Slowly and with both hands, she brought out a clean white bag that looked like a hotel pillowcase. Its end was twisted, curled over, and secured with white ribbons.

"Enock," the madame said.

Her son stood quickly, looked around, and seized the bottle of water Aaron had been drinking from. He took the saucer from Gaelle's cold cup of tea and poured a few tablespoons of water into it. Then he placed the saucer near the madame and went back to his seat.

As Madame Langlois unfastened the white ribbons, Caitlin felt cold fear grab her throat and heart.

"Fear is respect," the madame said, as if from a distance.

She opened the pillowcase and slowly, almost lovingly, pulled out a tightly coiled snake.

Caitlin was barely breathing.

"The serpent is in pain," the madame told Caitlin. Then she leaned toward the reptile and murmured, "Damballa is grateful for your sacrifice."

Caitlin could not pull her eyes from the snake. It was not very big, and its scales were a chalky gray with copper spots shaped like a leopard's. She remembered from one of Jacob's projects that a snake only coiled tightly when it was very afraid. She saw the faintest of trembles across the snake's skin. Had that been what she felt through the bag? But the bag was too thick . . . The madame held the snake near the water but it made no move toward it, no flick of the tongue to sense its surroundings.

"Why is it acting like this?" Caitlin asked. "Are you torturing it?"

"These tiny hands cannot harm her," the madame said. "She is doing Damballa's work."

Madame Langlois slowly, stealthily stepped to Gaelle. The girl was crying silently and she craned backward as the snake neared her. Suddenly red liquid oozed from the snake's eyes, nostrils, and mouth, dripping onto the floor. Caitlin felt bile rise in her throat. Some snakes, she remembered, could bleed from their orifices at will, in the presence of a predator. This snake was terrified . . . specifically of Gaelle.

Jack London flashed through Caitlin's mind.

The madame stepped away from the girl but the snake continued to bleed. She pointed at Caitlin's left hand. "Place your fingertips on her."

"Me?" Caitlin said, mortified.

"Yes, you who knows so much."

Caitlin tentatively lifted her hand and saw that her palm was literally dripping sweat. She thought about holding off, posing some of the myriad questions that flashed through her mind, but warily and somehow irresistibly she rested her fingertips on the snake's outermost coil—

Suddenly Caitlin slammed backward on her heels and the world turned red. She was choking, suffocating on clouds, thick, billowing sulfur. She struggled for breath, tried to scream. She felt every major and minor muscle in her body tense and twist, as if she were the snake holding itself tight. And then she felt *presences*. That was the only way her brain could describe it. Shades, wraiths, something ephemeral but *there*.

People? Robes filled with wind? Red flashes of fire and lightning, illuminating sharp spires of pale rock.

Everything turned then, twisting in circles, hoops within hoops. And in the center was a terrible face with huge eyes. Its massive mouth gaped at her in a horrific smile. She flung up her right arm against it and all in a second the robes and the wind, the fire and rock, all of it seemed to ram through her arm and out of her hand—

Across the room, Gaelle fell hard against the wall. *Was she thrown?* Suddenly Caitlin could see again. She could see Gaelle against the wall, her whole body spasming. Her arms flailed sideways as she shouted unintelligible words. And then she started screaming and screaming.

Marie-Jeanne shouted and dove for her daughter, attempting to cradle her in her arms. Aaron followed, trying to support her head. He was shouting at the madame, "Stop it!" Outside fifty voices rose, some in angry shouts, some in desperate songs. Some pounded on the front door. Caitlin looked behind her at the faces pressed against the window, shouting. Then she noticed the madame. The old woman was choking.

Almost unconsciously, Caitlin stood and hurried to the madame's side. She placed a hand on her back at the base of her neck. The woman was freezing, goose bumps rising from nape to shoulders. Incredibly, the madame was still holding the snake in her right hand. Forcing her fingers into the woman's mouth, Caitlin worked it open, feeling for an obstruction—but there was none. Then suddenly the madame inhaled deeply, filling her lungs, then coughed, clearing her throat. As if this was an everyday occurrence, she nodded in thanks. She rose to her knees and bowed over Gaelle. Gripping the serpent tightly in her right hand, she placed her left hand on the girl's ankle. A tremor passed through the older woman's body like an earthquake but her right hand held the snake steady.

Then, abruptly, it was over.

Gaelle, curling away from all the hands around her, compressed into a fetal position against the wall and cried. Someone shoved the front door open and rushed into the room. It was the priest. He did not touch Gaelle, and he did not pray over her, only spoke quietly to her. He was serving as a buffer against the eyes and mouths that hovered just outside the office.

A half hour later, a calm settled over the Anglade Charter Fishing office. It had been hard-won. There had been an epic shouting match between the crowd and two policemen, and another among the Catholic priest, Marie-Jeanne, Enock, and Aaron, all of whom disagreed about what Gaelle required next. Even the madame had raised her voice in outrage at one point, but in this she was with Caitlin: the two women had conspired by joined will and physical interference to move Gaelle out of the office into the back room. Caitlin settled the young woman onto a makeshift bed of waterproof boat cushions.

As Gaelle was shifting from tears to exhaustion, the madame

entered the room to place the snake back in its pillowcase and set it on a shelf where Gaelle would not see it. Caitlin smoothed the girl's hair and forehead and wiped her cheeks until she fell asleep.

"She will protect," said the madame, indicating the snake, then Gaelle.

Caitlin nodded. She did not understand what had happened, what role the snake had played, but there was no denying that there were powerful forces at work. She had endured nightmares after the encounter with Maanik and they were of a piece with the visions she had experienced here. Whatever the agent, it was strong enough to leap from one subconscious mind to another.

Right now, more than anything else, Caitlin wanted to curl up and sleep too. She knew the urge came not only from exhaustion but from fear. She just wanted to pretend none of this had happened. But she knew sleep would not be possible, not logistically or practically. Even now, when she closed her eyes, the memory of that manic face she had seen jerked her awake.

"You are okay," Madame Langlois said to Caitlin.

Caitlin wasn't sure whether the woman meant she was healthy or acceptable. Either way, she thanked her. Then she looked her in the eye and said, "I feel bad for the snake."

Madame Langlois nodded. "Me too. There are alternatives."

"Are they dangerous? To either Gaelle or the snake?"

"No. I will make a *wanga*, what you call a fetish. It will do the job of the snake. I will do that today."

Caitlin slowly nodded. Whether it was household gods in ancient Egypt, totems in Native American lore, or Catholic icons, she had always understood that people thought inanimate objects had great power. Like the placebo effect, their beliefs could change their minds and actions, thus changing their situations. But maybe there was more to it. She had felt the power through the snake, and she had seen the madame wrestle with that power and manage it. If the madame also wrestled power into an object . . .

But you don't believe any of this, her rational side was telling her. *Snakes don't intercept energy any more than frogs cause warts or pulverized eye of newt can make someone fall in love. That woman was squeezing the poor creature, choking it, putting on a show that caused Gaelle to react. And that caused* you *to react. The power of suggestion, that's all this was. You brought back your nightmare because you were in a receptive, weakened state.*

Maybe so, Caitlin told her brain. *But maybe not.*

Tentatively she asked, "Can an inanimate object handle that much . . . whatever it was? Energy? Pain?"

"It will take some doing," the madame admitted, then unexpectedly smiled in a very tired way. "I will stay here with her. And if it must be, I will take some." She shrugged. "That is the responsibility. That is the job."

Caitlin smiled, closed her eyes, and rested the back of her head on the wall. From outside she heard people, tourists most likely, asking questions in a hodgepodge of languages. They reflected the confusion she felt. There was only one thing she knew for certain: like the universe itself, the scope of this mystery continued to confound, deepen, and expand.

"Doctor," Madame Langlois said.

Caitlin opened her eyes to see the madame tearing a sheet of paper from a small notepad. She held out the page—it was Gaelle's drawing of crescent triangles. "Take it," the madame ordered. "This is not of Vodou."

CHAPTER 16

Caitlin gasped herself awake on the plane.

The hum of the engines just outside the window had a soothing effect as she eased herself back . . .

From what?

The nightmare face from her vision in Haiti had violated her mind with startling ferocity . . . and contempt. She'd been dreaming of domestic familiarity: feeding Jacob's fish while he was away on a sleepover. Then the awful *thing* appeared, leering with its hideous grin and lifeless gaze, burning like a brand into her brain.

The late evening flight from Haiti to New York was nearly empty and she had full privacy in the dark. As much as she flew, Caitlin didn't really like it; she wished there were some way to ride outside the plane, with real air instead of this canned stuff, and a big, unobscured view. She turned to the side and brought her feet up on the seat next to her, curling into herself as Gaelle had curled against the wall.

Caitlin's breathing was shallow and quick, panicked, and she was shaking; she felt as though she were wearing a heavy winter coat zipped tight to the throat. She tried tapping the sides of her eye sockets with her fingertips and running a slightly cupped hand down her breastbone, slowly, to focus on clearing her airway. Neither worked and she felt like she might start to cry. Caitlin had participated in too many street-corner arguments with dates, colleagues, a stalker, and decades of cab drivers; and Jacob, when he was little, had not been shy about calling attention to himself in restaurants when he felt frustrated. Over the last ten years Caitlin had become much more self-conscious about public displays.

Still shaking, she gently rested her head in her palms. No tears came. The magnitude of what she had experienced overcame her: *How do I help these girls? Are their experiences related—and if so, by what conceivable mechanism? What am I missing?*

And then there was Vodou.

An eccentric woman and a fussy, arrogant son. A charmed snake, or was it a possessed snake or drugged snake? The entire thing could have been smoke and mirrors, the madame or her son working some kind of trickery while Caitlin was distracted by Gaelle. Even the vision, that face, may have been induced by a combination of suggestion and a burned or powdered drug that Caitlin had smelled or ingested. She had not applied any kind of scientific methodology to the experience. The data was useless.

This is too much for me, she thought. *I'll give it to someone else, I'll refer Maanik to some other kind of expert.* Maybe what she needed, what they both needed, was exactly what the madame had provided: a figure of faith, not reason.

Yet another part of her was trying to get through with a message. *You have a choice.*

It was the same choice that she had elucidated for every one of her clients at some stage of their therapy, because it was a fundamental part of being human and alive: you had to choose between being afraid and being angry.

Fear was a natural reaction, but if she chose to dwell in it, it would cripple her. She had to stop it before she spiraled downward. However, she was not naïve. For all kinds of evolutionary and biochemical reasons, positive thinking and "Go, Caitlin!" pep talks alone were not going to do the trick here. They didn't have enough force to generate the necessary escape velocity.

So she chose anger. Not a knee-jerk, arrogant fury that could backfire and tie her in knots, but a clear, decisive, protective instinct. Whatever the cause of these episodes for Maanik and Gaelle, whatever she had felt herself, it was resulting in a certain torture, and that was unacceptable.

She sat up straight and turned on her seat light. Lowering the tray table in front of her, she pulled a pen and a few printouts from her bag. Flipping the printouts over, she prepared to write on their blank backs. What did Maanik and Gaelle's episodes have in common? What did they possess that she *was* familiar with, that she *did* have practice in treating?

Start with what you *experienced*, she thought.

Freud believed that dreams were comprised of manifest and latent content. The manifest content was immediately recalled on waking and was thought to mask the true meaning of the dream: the forbidden, subconscious elements.

She found herself not writing but drawing. Before she knew it, she had accurately re-created the huge face and terrifying smile that had manifested in Haiti and woken her just moments ago. Now it was in front of her. Her mind had been throwing all kinds of words around to describe it—"otherworldly," "evil," "alien." But the salient point was that the visual was real. Here it was, right before her.

What are you? she demanded.

Suddenly the hair rose on the back of her neck and she felt cold all over. The fear was back—the same flavor of fear she had tasted outside her office building when she was certain she was being watched. Her skin tingled, prickled all over. She adjusted herself in her seat and peered slowly around the dark cabin. The hum of the engines was the only thing that felt safe and sane. The dark was the exact opposite. One of her professors once remarked, "Young people and animals are instinctively afraid of the dark. What right have we to say they're wrong?"

They were not wrong. The stillness and blackness about her felt like just a few shallow breaths from death. Her reading light gave scope to the darkness everywhere else; specks of starlight revealed the vastness of the night outside. The hints of light were like a map to Caitlin: the breadth of what she knew measured against the expanse of what she did not know. That in itself was terrifying.

Maybe someone *was* watching. Maybe it was the flight attendant. Maybe it was this face from the Vodou-induced trance.

Caitlin at this moment rallied her anger and chose not to care. They, whoever they were, could watch all they wanted as long as they didn't interfere. She had work to do. She studied her drawing again and pulled out Gaelle's sketch to compare them. The triangle of crescents looked almost Celtic, not at all similar to this. She put away the sketch and stared at the nightmare face again for several minutes. She could not shake the feeling that there was something familiar about it. She closed her eyes and combed through all the cultures she had experienced through travel and research. It didn't seem like a mask, nothing like the horned, fanged Hannya figure of Noh theater. Intuitively she felt it was something carved. The Easter Island statues? No, that wasn't it. The mouth wasn't the same. This mouth had lips indicated by a line curving around eight or nine thick, oval teeth. Somewhere in Hawaii? In New Zealand, something from the Maori?

Tiki figures, she recalled with a jolt. They had large mouths and eyes very similar to this. She whipped out her phone; took a photo of her drawing, wincing from the bright flash; and texted it to Ben with a message: *I saw this in connection with Gaelle. Long story. Polynesian influence?*

Then Caitlin did what she had previously avoided. She walked herself through the trip from the time she got off the plane, making detailed notes on everything that she could remember, without gloss, without explanation, and with only momentary hesitation when she reached her experience of the force that had thrown Gaelle against the wall. What could she even call it—energy? The Vodou push? She wondered if an electrical force could possibly account for it. It was worth researching later. She wrote until her hand cramped, until she was done. Folding the pages carefully, she numbered them in case they fell, then tucked them away before once again attempting sleep. Her mind would gather strength; it would not feed her dream demon, not if she could help it. She turned off the light.

Her last thought was of something she'd seen through the window of the Land Rover heading back to Port-au-Prince—a patch of new trees planted on one of the mountainsides. The government had recently announced it was going to replant Haiti's decimated forests. Caitlin hoped that the madame and her son would see it on their way back to the city and trust that fumbling, faulty human beings did sometimes create solutions.

• • •

Caitlin arrived home at two in the morning but her father was awake to open the door, allowing her to walk into a bright kitchen and a hug. She dropped her bag on the kitchen table and sat down.

"How is he?" she asked.

"Fine, fine," Joe said. "A little quiet, maybe."

"When?"

"Earlier tonight," he said. "He just kind of stared out the window for, oh, two minutes or so. I left him. He snapped out of it."

Caitlin felt a shiver. Two minutes. That's about how long she was in her bizarre trance.

Her father chuckled. "I'll tell you, though. He crowed like Peter Pan when he got me to eat kale."

Caitlin returned to the moment. "Eat it and like it?"

Joe grinned. "It was better than I expected. Don't tell your mother."

Caitlin chuckled. She opened her bag and sorted through it, separating items she would leave in the bag and items to put away.

"Cai, why don't you unpack in the morning? You look like you need as much sleep as you can get."

She shook her head and kept sorting.

"How did things go down there?" he asked.

She stopped, looked at him sideways. "Dad, what's the weirdest thing that's ever happened to you? Something that didn't have an explanation."

"Hunh." He sat back and thought, staring around the room much like Caitlin did when she needed to think. He was a tall, broad-shouldered man with close-set Irish blue eyes and a sort of permanent youthfulness. "Well," he said, "to be honest, it was you."

Caitlin stared at him in surprise.

"You had your own personality from the day you were born," he went on. "Well, maybe the day after you were born. You were always such a watcher, big eyes studying everything, and with very little to say."

"Mom said I was always quiet."

"Quiet but not—what—not drowsy or dull. You were always alert. I could see something in your eyes. To your point, the question you asked, I don't know where souls come from but I know they exist. I saw yours."

Caitlin felt tears in her eyes, the tears that had refused to come before.

Her father placed a hand on her shoulder. "What's on your mind? Did Haiti get to you?"

Caitlin shook her head. He stepped back. He knew not to pry, and she was relieved when he changed the subject.

"I remember you loved ghost stories when you were a kid," he said. "You read every one you could get your hands on. I always wondered whether you'd seen one."

Caitlin laughed. "Really? I remember the mythology books, Edith

Hamilton. Oh, and Nancy Drew and the haunted lighthouse or farm-house or something like that."

"Oh sure. We stopped letting you read them when you had night-mares."

She turned back toward him. "I had nightmares?"

"Normal kid stuff," he said. "That's what the doctor told us. We ended up giving all the books away and they stopped."

It was Caitlin's turn to say, "Hunh." She placed her papers on the "to put away" stack. Her drawing of the face was on top and Joe picked it up to look at it. He laughed.

"Where in the hell did you see this?" he asked.

"Do you recognize it? I think it's some kind of Polynesian tiki fig-ure."

He grinned. "It's not often that I get to tell you you're wrong."

"What do you mean?"

He patted her hand and held up the drawing. "This is from your ancient past, kiddo."

CHAPTER 17

Flora Davies, the forty-year-old chairwoman of the Group, was locking the airtight door of their basement on Ninth Street. The founder of the Group, Otis Davies, had purchased this grand mansion on the corner of Fifth Avenue early in the twentieth century. Named the Global Explorers' Club, ostensibly it was a home for travelers who came to the city and needed a place to rest before leaving. Here they could relax among fellow adventurers, swap tales, study maps and rare books in the library, or leave treasures they had found to be collected at some future date. Treasures that the Group examined thoroughly. Statues, vases, tablets, and other finds that might have writing or images, carvings, or paintings that fit their particular interests served the Group's highly secret need. It had proved a worthwhile arrangement. All the results of the Group's efforts, previously scattered throughout the world in bank vaults and secret warehouses, were now consolidated in this basement.

Flora emerged from the side of the building and walked up the steps to the quiet street. She was heading to her apartment with the intention of getting some long-overdue sleep before Mikel arrived with his latest artifact from the Falklands. Other members would be arriving within hours to study it, and there would be much to do.

Each new find was a key, and this particular key could well be the one that exponentially expanded what they knew, confirmed what they suspected, and ultimately narrowed their ancient search.

At this moment, however, Davies's mind was not on the artifact. She stood at the top of the steps that led from the well of the basement door to street level and looked south toward the park. Something was wrong. She heard voices in the park, which was not unusual even at this hour, and dogs barking, which was also not uncommon. What she could not understand was why she didn't see the towering white marble arch that was built to celebrate the centenary of George Washington's inauguration as president. It was gone.

At a fast clip she walked toward the park where the Washington Square Arch used to be. As she neared it she realized she was wrong; the arch was there. Only it wasn't white. And it wasn't marble.

Through the center of the arch she saw a dozen or so students backed well away, standing by the fountain toward the south. They were looking, pointing, taking photos and cell phone videos—not that they would convey the real-time creepiness of a nearly eighty-foot structure covered bottom to top with rats.

When Davies realized what they were she stopped dead in her tracks and gasped. There must have been hundreds, even thousands. She had never seen, never heard of anything like this. Her first thought after her brain unfroze was that it was some kind of stunt, something concocted for a reality show or a guerilla cinema project by film school students.

That has to be it. They couldn't be real, could they?

Suddenly spots of white appeared beneath the undulating carpet. First small and then larger, unevenly shaped patches. The students on the other side began to scream and as Davies started to realize that the rats were leaving their perch in great heaving swaths, someone jokingly cried, "Stampede!" The creatures raced in all directions, with one tidal wave of them rolling unswervingly toward her. A charge of dark gray fur pushed down the center of Fifth Avenue and along both sidewalks. She stood transfixed, not so much with fear or revulsion—though she felt both as the rats rushed over her feet—but because the rats were real, there were no cameras, and though her heart was racing, her mind was working harder still, trying to figure out what on earth was going on.

She turned protectively toward the club and that was when the real horror struck.

The concrete recess outside the basement door was overflowing with pile upon pile of the surging vermin. Were they trying to get in the door? They were squealing, scratching, and tearing at each other to get higher still as they formed a roiling triangle in the doorway. Under the streetlight she could see tufts of fur floating upward and the occasional streak of blood. Those that could not get into that small area flowed into the garden that fronted the structure. All the rats that couldn't fit in the stairwell were facing in one direction, aligned as much as possible to the north and south.

Davies got as close as she could without making further contact. With shaking fingers she retrieved her cell phone from her shoulder bag and began shooting video. The rats' activity was inexplicable indeed, but what challenged and distracted her was that this behavior was not entirely without precedent.

As lights flicked on in surrounding apartments, people rising to check out the shouts coming from the park and the strange thumping and scratching taking place right outside their doors, Davies switched off her video and stepped into the shadows.

She thought back to the call she had received from Mikel when he landed in Montevideo. The field agent had mentioned something strange—a flock of albatrosses that had flown directly at the plane from the north.

Davies put her cell phone away and walked up the vast stone steps to the front door of the Global Explorers' Club. There would be no sleep tonight.

CHAPTER 18

Under orders from Joseph P. O'Hara, Caitlin was allowed to send exactly one e-mail about the drawing before she went to bed.

"That's it, little lady," he'd said in a voice she recognized from those old, old days when he let her make a phone call or have a Scooter Pie before retiring.

She had to tell Ben, and she had to tell him now; it couldn't wait. Caitlin took her tablet into the bedroom, sat cross-legged against the headboard, prepared an e-mail with attached notes from her trip and a photo of Gaelle's sketch, then wrote:

> You might think I'm crazy but forget Polynesia. That's not what I drew. Dad recognized it: a Viking longship. The teeth are either circular shields on the hull or people sitting inside it; the eyes are the tall, curved carvings at the prow and stern. He's been dabbling in genealogy and our Irish roots are all mixed in with Scottish and Norse. He hit a few museum collections online and he saw a brooch design very similar to this. Gaelle sketched a symbol too—see the jpeg—that seems Celtic to me. Could the ship be connected to Gaelle's almost drowning? I know that sounds nuts and you're probably too busy to meet but call if you can tomorrow. I mean today. Tuesday. Thanks. —C xo

Caitlin set the tablet on the floor and crashed. Her mind and energy and body had all hit a wall and she had no trouble sleeping through the night.

She awoke feeling rested but restless, with a readiness to prowl through this mystery. Her father dropped Jacob off at school on his way out of the city and Caitlin looked over her work schedule. There was nothing until noon, after which the day was packed. To her surprise, Ben had not only called early and left a message but had time to meet. She called him back as soon as her "lads" were gone.

He picked up on the first ring.

"Hey, Cai."

"That's not good news, is it? That you have free time?" She didn't really have to ask; his solemn voice said it all.

"No, it's not," he said. "The highest-level diplomats haven't come back to the table. They've sent their lower-level people—trusted staff, essentially—to sort of act as placeholders. They can't say much so they're taking a lot of breaks."

"So the world is closer to the brink?"

"I wouldn't say closer," Ben replied. "More like the cliff could give out with just one good sneeze. I'll tell you more in person," he said cautiously. "So please, let's talk about something we can actually work out."

"Roger that, and I have to say I'm really glad you can meet."

Ben laughed, somewhat wryly. "Is that a crisis in your pocket or are you just happy to see me?"

"Both." Caitlin laughed and said good-bye.

She slugged down some coffee her father had made and headed out. It was one of those blessedly mild days that late fall in New York sometimes delivered. Caitlin appreciated the transition from the heat of Haiti so she texted Ben suggesting they walk. He readily agreed.

Sitting in the cab for the short ride over, she saw the already infamous "Rat Pack" video on the backseat monitor. It was creepy, and the speculation was that Con Ed's working underground replacing cables had caused the rodents to leave their "homes." What was even creepier was the army of pest control personnel descending on stately Fifth Avenue, bagging dead rats and setting traps.

Caitlin met Ben with a warm hug that momentarily pushed his long, drawn expression into something like a smile. They strolled north from the United Nations through the small park in Turtle Bay. The sunlight glittered on the East River and they unbuttoned their coats.

"Anything new with Maanik?" Caitlin asked.

"She had a small incident," he said. "Hansa found her talking to the dog in the middle of the night. What was strange was that he seemed to be listening. When Hansa tried to get her back to bed, Maanik started sobbing and flailing a little. But your cue worked."

"How are her parents doing?"

"I didn't speak with Hansa but the ambassador's emotional state has shifted. He's less anxious but he seems more . . . 'sad' is the only word that fits. A part of it has to be the sense that he's failing the peace process, but I also think he feels as though he's failing his daughter. He said something about having to take some kind of action before she's stuck like this for life. I told him you were making progress." Ben looked at her. "Are you?"

"Maybe. I've got so much to share with you—"

Ben put a hand on her arm. "Before we get to that, I . . ."

Caitlin sensed he was struggling with something and put a warm hand on top of his.

"I feel guilty for putting this on you." Ben looked at the pavement.

"Go ahead. Seriously. You know I'll keep it confidential."

"Okay. There is a rumor—and I want to stress that it *is* a rumor— that some countries are considering shutting down their embassies in India and Pakistan and flying out their employees. Countries that include us, the UK, and Japan."

"Oh my god," said Caitlin.

"God?" Ben said. "You see *God* in this? *Anywhere?*"

Caitlin didn't answer. The question made her think of her vision, of millennia of prophets and shamans and mystics who had visions, of the ivory-tower debates about the difficulty of distinguishing between profound faith and dementia. She got back on topic. "The cliff you talked about on the phone. It's that close to crumbling?"

"It might be a brinksmanship maneuver, but those have a catastrophic tendency to take on a life of their own. It could be politicos testing the water to see how everyone reacts, whether the Indian and Pakistani delegates will come back to the table given the right impetus." He exhaled and rubbed the bone below his ear. "I just don't know."

"What do you think?"

He hesitated. "I think it's a ploy."

"Is that what you would say to me anyway, to keep me from worrying?"

"No, Caitlin. I would never play you."

"Okay." She pressed his hand again. "You know those Magritte umbrellas that look black to everyone else but underneath they're blue sky and puffy white clouds? We're going to stand under one of those. Because if I don't ignore what you just told me, I won't be able to focus."

He nodded and half-smiled. "I just felt like one of your patients getting a safe-haven visual."

"You were." She half-smiled back, then jumped into a description of her trip, ending with the conversation with her father. "So, his crazy idea that my drawing invokes the Vikings—when I say it out loud it seems to lose some weight but, Ben, he was one hundred percent certain."

"It's not so crazy," Ben said. "My linguistic programs broke down the snatches of language we have and I did some comparing. Part of what came out of Maanik's mouth seems to be rooted in Old Norse."

Caitlin stopped and gaped at him. Finally, at least some of the pieces were coming together. She allowed herself a big smile.

"Don't get too comfortable," said Ben. "There's a strong strand of Mongolian as well."

"Oh. But Mongolian and Norse had no connection, at least not that I know of."

He shook his head and laughed. "None at all. Nor the snippets of Japanese. This kind of discovery could make history in certain circles. Last night, when I confirmed all those languages, was the most exciting night of my life. Thank you, Cai. You made it happen."

"What every woman loves to hear!" She grinned and realized she was flirting. She blamed it on his infectious enthusiasm and switched back to professionalism: "Can you give me specifics?"

He spoke slowly and deliberately to make his point. "This hybrid language should not exist, but it does. And it makes sense. The hand gestures are superlatives but they apply to nouns as well as adjectives. So for example, if I say 'hergha' "—he rolled the r and sort of hacked out the second syllable—"it means 'fire.' But if I say it while doing this"—he made a circle with his hand, the palm facing his torso, then pushed it to the side exactly as Maanik and Gaelle had both done at different points—"it means 'the biggest fire,' a conflagration."

"Can we sit down?" Caitlin could hardly believe what she was hearing. She needed a bench to take it all in. She shook her head not just in awe but in relief. Seeing her old friend perform the gesture without an accompanying fit of screams and scratching was profoundly comforting.

"You are amazing," she said.

"Eh, it's just good software." He grinned, shrugging away the compliment. "I only have about twenty-five percent of the words translated, and we don't have that many to begin with. Nouns have been easiest. What's most interesting to me is that the word for 'fire' and its superlative appear very near the word for 'sky.' "

"Do you have any idea why?"

"Well, I'd like to be cautious about interpretation but I doubt the proximity is accidental. This shows up in ancient China as yin-yang, with the sky being the 'fire' force and earth being a 'water' force. But in this language, the superlative for 'fire' also appears very near what I think are the words for 'arm' and 'pain.' So maybe . . . ?" He urgently patted his forearms as if he were putting out flames.

"God, *yes!*" Caitlin exclaimed when it had soaked in. "If burning sparks were falling on my arms and wouldn't go out, burning deeper into my flesh, I might try to scratch them away, like Maanik. All right, so in the broadest of terms, what kind of causes do we have for fire in the sky? Either it was manufactured means—firebombing or a burning building—or there was a natural cause. Lightning? A volcano? A meteor?"

"All of that is possible," Ben said. He repeated another gesture they had seen in the videos: pointing his left hand away from him at an angle while crossing his body with his right hand. At the same time he said, "'*Ogrusse.*' That seems to be the superlative for 'water,' meaning 'the *biggest* water,' and it appears very near the word for 'sky' too."

"You mean they're interchangeable? 'Sky' and 'water'? Because they're blue?"

"I don't think that's it," he said. "I took it to mean water that touches the sky."

"Like a tsunami?"

"Again, still guesswork, but that's a possibility."

Caitlin thought back to Phuket. "You'd have to be sitting on the beach to see it quite like that, rolling in from the horizon."

"If we're talking about recent tsunamis, yeah. But what if this is a mega?" He extended his arms as if he were holding a barrel. "One big mother?"

"How big are we talking?" she asked.

"In living memory?" Ben replied. "Lituya Bay, Alaska, July 9, 1958. An 8.3-magnitude earthquake along the Fairweather Fault caused a landslide that pushed a hundred million cubic feet of earth and glacier into the narrow inlet of the bay. The result was a wave that rose 1,720 feet. That's the tallest mega-tsunami of modern times, and I stress 'modern times.' There's a whole lot of history that happened before we started keeping records."

"Apparently," Caitlin said. She shook her head, not quite able to process all of this. Partly from gratitude, partly for comfort, she hugged her companion. "Thank you, Ben. I have no way to say it enough, thank you."

"*Thurstillalotlfttoworkt*," he said into her collar.

They laughed at his muffled voice and she pulled back.

"There's still a lot left to work out," he repeated. "I was hoping you would bring back a video or something with more language from Haiti, but it doesn't sound like you had a chance?"

Caitlin deflated. "No. I brought back stuff but I don't know what it was."

"More writing?"

"No," she said.

"Caitlin?"

"The Vodou vision I had there, and then the nightmare on the plane. When I was hit with—with whatever it was, I felt heat, I saw fire."

"Power of suggestion?"

"Well, sure, maybe. But from whom? The madame and her son didn't say anything about fire. I mean, I was choking on sulfur, Ben. What would do that except a volcano?"

"But you weren't around a volcano then. Or ever, were you?"

"I was around a caldera, once, in Southern California."

"Right, dormant for how many thousands of years? How about incense, was there any of that in Haiti? Anything that could have suggested that smell?"

She shook her head.

Ben took a deep breath. "So, a volcano. How? Where?"

"What about *when*?"

"No." Ben shook his head. "Not buying where you're going."

"Honestly, I don't know where I'm going but stay with me. We know that both of these girls experienced something—nightmares, visions, hallucinations, whatever you want to call them. And we know that they didn't experience these things at any other time in their short lives. All they seem to share, what stands out, is that both have a parent or stepparent—in any case, a close adult figure—who recently experienced a near-death incident."

"And the suicidal boy in Iran that you mentioned, didn't he have a relative who just died?"

"Yes, a brother who was executed. So these physio-visual-linguistic reactions are being triggered by family trauma, even if there is no direct bloodline."

"Which tells you what?" Ben asked. "Other than some kind of post-traumatic stress being a possible trigger. Where's the physical volcano? Where's the water that touches the sky? You're saying you all experienced some part of that. Where?"

"That's just it," Caitlin said. "I don't know."

"What else could it be, then? Genetic imprinting? Vodou? Aliens?" Ben said.

Caitlin slumped. She thought for a moment, then shook her head slowly. "Yeah, I'm not there either," she said. Then she started to get excited again. "But hold on. You just said genetic imprinting. What if it's something similar? Jung talked about genetic imprinting—feelings, ideas that were passed down from our ancestors. Maybe these three family bonds are creating a portal into that collective unconscious."

"But we're not just talking about vague feelings or even ideas. Maanik and Gaelle seemed transported, almost totally."

"And me," Caitlin said.

"To where? A volcano somewhere in the past?"

"Not just the volcano, the Vikings too," she said. "A lost language." Then she murmured, almost as if it came from her unconscious, going with the flow: "No, not genetic imprinting. That's too specific, individual-to-individual, and Gaelle wasn't related to her stepmother, at least not genetically. What about racial memory, Ben? Group experiences."

"You mean like past lives?"

"Honestly, I don't know what I mean," she said. "Because there's something the girls and I share, *my* Viking ship and the Old Norse factor in *their* language."

Ben shook his head no. "That's tenuous at best. And really, really specific. Besides, where do the Mongolian and Japanese fit?"

"I don't know, but my point is we are dealing with something way older than any of us that has somehow manifested itself here, now."

"I don't know, Caitlin. If you're going to consider racial memory and past lives, what's to prevent you from considering future lives or—"

"You're right." Caitlin nodded.

"Cai, I wasn't being serious."

"But I am! Ben, *what if*? What if these phenomena—or just a single big phenomenon—are somehow free of time constraints? What if there is some kind of communal stream that's carrying images and language—information—from 'somewhen' to 'now' and we're here to receive and pass it forward?"

"Why you four?"

"I don't know," she admitted. "I need to look up Pompeii, I remember there were eyewitness reports—"

"Pliny the Younger," Ben said. "Chilling stuff. One of my schoolmates did a translation for his thesis."

"Atlantis," she muttered.

"Cai, don't."

Caitlin was only half-listening. Her brain was free-associating all over the map and through all the calendars that were and ever would be.

"Time to reattach your wires to the ground," Ben said. "This is beyond speculation."

"I'm fighting myself," she said.

"Huh?"

"One of my professors always said that guesswork is part of the scientific method and if you skip that step, you just keep living in the same box that was handed to you at birth. I never really liked that intellectual bungee jump—but here I am, doing it!"

"And heading for the rocks," Ben said. "You remember what your sophomore roommate used to call you?"

"'The girl with rivets,'" Caitlin said. "Yeah. I like things to make sense. And this thing doesn't seem to, does it?" Then she added almost dreamily, "But it must."

Caitlin's phone buzzed with a text. It was from Mrs. Pawar: *My husband suggested I send this to you. It's from Maanik.*

Caitlin tapped on the attachment and a triangle made of triangles made of crescents filled the screen.

"Oh no. No."

She turned the phone to show Ben.

"Jesus," he breathed. "That's impossible."

"I'm going over there." She stood, already tapping a reply to Mrs. Pawar. "I've got a couple hours before my first session."

Caitlin started walking toward the Pawars' building, then turned and spoke as she walked backward. "Thanks, Ben. Thanks for everything."

"You're welcome," he said. "For everything."

CHAPTER 19

Caitlin stood in the hall outside the Pawars' apartment door for an unusually long moment. The corridor was thick with the same still, unwelcoming atmosphere as the last time she was there. And then a click on the other side of the peephole: someone had lifted the cover to look out. When the door opened, Caitlin realized why Mrs. Pawar had used it. The wife of an Indian diplomat would not allow most outsiders to see her in a housedress with no makeup. The woman clearly wasn't eating or sleeping enough. When they'd first met, stress had penciled dark smudges around her eyes, but these past days had hollowed her cheeks. Caitlin was mildly shocked by her appearance.

"I'm sorry you had to wait," the woman said.

"Don't worry about that," Caitlin answered, stepping into the apartment. She waited until the door was shut before asking, "Is Maanik all right?"

Mrs. Pawar locked the door behind them. "The blackberries finally worked," she replied, with no sign of being relieved.

"Finally?" Caitlin asked. She noticed Kamala standing sentry several paces back. Caitlin guessed that Mrs. Pawar was beginning to micromanage the household, trying to control anything she could in the face of a nearly uncontrollable threat to her daughter.

"Just after I sent you Maanik's drawing, she began running around the room, shrieking," Mrs. Pawar said as they walked down the hall to Maanik's bedroom. "She could not hear me. Or would not, I do not know. Finally, her father managed to restrain her and I was able to use your cue."

"I'm sorry you had to go through that," Caitlin said. She gently took the woman by the arm and slowed them down. "Tell me something, Mrs. Pawar. Have either you or your husband been having nightmares?"

"To have nightmares one must sleep," the woman replied, stalwartly fighting tears. "Our world seems to be coming apart. There is no haven—not abroad, not in this city, not in our home. No, Dr. O'Hara, there have been no nightmares."

"I understand," Caitlin said. She released Mrs. Pawar's arm and they continued toward the bedroom.

Proximity and a familial relationship clearly were factors in what was happening. Whatever nightmares Caitlin had experienced as a result of being with Maanik and Gaelle had come from a connection made through hypnosis . . . or possibly Vodou. Forces that operated on a subtle, subconscious level—but even accepting that, she could not even begin to see how such forces could generate the same symbol from two very different hands.

In Maanik's boldly colored bedroom, the rich scent of flowers and harsher smell of chemical fragrance failed to mask the stale, stagnant air. Caitlin spotted an air freshener incongruously plugged into a surge protector also feeding Maanik's computer. About a dozen small bouquets were arranged around the room, most of them including stuffed animals, which suggested they had been sent from Maanik's friends. Doubtless they'd heard she was going to miss a week of school and realized something more unusual than flu was going on. Perhaps the Pawars were claiming stress from the attack on the ambassador.

The ambassador was sitting on his daughter's bed with his arm around her shoulders, at once comforting and protective. Her freshly bandaged right wrist rested in his open palm. Her left hand rested on the back of Jack London, who was curled up and snoring. The ambassador looked up as Caitlin approached. He nodded courteously but he did not have a smile in him. Maanik was asleep, breathing through her mouth with a slight rasp. In contrast to her mother, she looked as though she had been eating: her cheeks had a healthy color and her face seemed fresh. But there was a shadowy quality in her brow, a pinching of the eyebrows, that showed distress even in sleep.

"Thank you for coming," the ambassador said as he gently withdrew his arm from his daughter. He stood, passing the responsibility of propping up his daughter to his wife, and shook Caitlin's hand. She could see he was hiding his unease better than Mrs. Pawar, out of necessity. "I feel so helpless."

Caitlin impulsively placed her right hand on top of his. "Mr. Pawar, we *are* getting there."

He glanced back at the spent form on the bed. "I wish I could believe that."

Caitlin persisted. "I just spent time with a young lady who has a condition similar to your daughter's."

"Were you able to help her?" Mrs. Pawar asked hopefully.

"I was able to learn from her," Caitlin said. She searched through the photos on her phone and held up Gaelle's sketch. "She drew this too."

After taking it in they shook their heads in shock.

"That's what this phase is about," Caitlin continued. "To *learn*. There is no easy explanation for why both girls are experiencing similar symptoms or why they both drew this symbol." She put away her phone. "And there may not be a quick and easy fix for Maanik. I sometimes work with a high school for children from war-torn countries. They saw terrible things before America offered them political asylum. They experienced trauma as intense as your daughter's and it takes months, sometimes years, before they find ways to be teenagers again."

"I do not want to hear that," the ambassador said, as if his wish could somehow sustain him.

"I understand," said Caitlin, "but I will tell you this—you are lucky because Maanik has your support and the support of everyone around her, *and* she is a fighter."

The ambassador looked at the floor. "Understand this too. I don't want my daughter to be a fighter. I want her to be my daughter."

"Of course. That's *my* goal as well," Caitlin said patiently. "Which is why I have several important requests to make."

"What kind of requests?"

"First, I would like to hypnotize Maanik again."

Mrs. Pawar reacted instantly. "No! My daughter is not a laboratory animal!"

"We cannot protect her, Hansa," Mr. Pawar said evenly. "We can only love her, and loving her means taking the next necessary step." He looked back at Caitlin. "All right."

Mrs. Pawar tensed when she heard his pronouncement but said nothing.

"Thank you," Caitlin said. "I won't do it now but it does need to happen imminently. And for my second request, I would like Ben to be present during the hypnotism. He is known to you and, more importantly, to Maanik, and his linguistic skills could prove invaluable."

Now the ambassador's eyes sought his wife's support. He received it in the slight softening of Mrs. Pawar's expression.

"I trust Ben like a son," he said to Caitlin. "You may ask him."

"Thank you again."

The ambassador's brow lifted slightly. "Have you finished with your requests?"

"Not quite," Caitlin said.

"I admire your resolve," he said. "Perhaps you should take my place at the negotiating table."

"Ben would tell you, sir, that I never give up."

He finally smiled. "I've missed hearing such a hopeful expression."

Caitlin smiled back warmly. "Hold the applause until I'm finished."

"With?"

"Request number three. Jack London."

The ambassador looked at her as if she might be pulling his leg. "What about him?"

"I want to try something. Now. It will just take a minute."

The ambassador opened his hands in a gesture of approval and sat with anticipation in the desk chair. He and his wife watched as Caitlin approached Maanik's bed. She scooped her hands gently under Jack London. The dog opened his eyes and gave her nearest fingers a few licks. Carrying him, she walked around the end of the bed to Maanik's right side, where she was leaning against her mother. Caitlin held the dog close to Maanik's right hand, which was resting in her lap. Instantly, the dog snapped his teeth at Caitlin's hand, at the fingers he'd just been licking. Caitlin moved in time to avoid more than a nip but had to drop the snarling dog. He landed on the bedspread in an aggressive crouch, barking loudly at Maanik's hand, then leaped from the bed and ran around to the other side. He stood there shaking and barking, but also trying to edge closer to the bed and to Maanik. It was a strange tug-of-war, as though invisible hands were pulling him in two directions.

The dog seemed about to jump back onto the bed when Mrs. Pawar raised her voice and Jack London froze. In rapid Hindi directed at her husband, she seemed to be arguing vehemently. Mr. Pawar started to argue back but checked himself and spoke in a low, calm voice.

Caitlin turned away to give them a semblance of privacy. She patted the bedspread near Maanik's left hand. Jack London eyed her warily but soon jumped back to the place where he'd been sleeping earlier. He huddled against Maanik's side and nudged his nose under the girl's palm.

Caitlin heard a sigh from Mr. Pawar.

"I'm sorry," Caitlin said.

"Do not be," he told her. "How did you know he would respond like that?"

"I noticed him acting skittish last time, and in Haiti I saw animals reacting strangely around the other girl," she said. She considered mentioning the rats in Washington Square but decided they had enough horrors to face, and there was hardly a shred of connection to the incident anyway.

The ambassador sighed sadly. "My wife wants to have him put down."

"I would strongly argue against that," Caitlin said quickly. "We don't know what the connection is but it should not be broken." She gestured at the restored tableau of mistress and pup. "My point in trying this little experiment is to show that there's a little light here, a little bit of understanding. The dog is ahead of us, reacting to something that we don't comprehend yet. But there's hope that we can learn."

The ambassador's eyes were a bit brighter than they had been before. "I'm not sure what you mean but it is good to know that *you* think so. Now I must return to the United Nations. When will you come again?"

"This evening, if I can arrange it."

"We will see you then," he told her.

The ambassador grasped his wife's hand and lingered just a moment as she squeezed back. Then he left the room.

"Excuse me," said Mrs. Pawar. "I must give my husband something before he leaves."

The woman started to stand, handing Maanik's weight over to Caitlin. As the door closed behind her Caitlin carefully maneuvered the girl into a horizontal position, with Jack London adjusting to the new arrangement to stay close to her left hand. Placing Maanik's head gently on her pillow, Caitlin glanced down—and jumped back.

Maanik's eyes were open and regarding her. They were clear, alert, steady. Incredibly steady, like little machines that had suddenly locked onto her.

"Hello," Maanik said softly. "I surprised you."

"A little," Caitlin admitted.

"You surprised me too." A faint smile tugged at the girl's mouth. "But I'm too tired to scream."

Caitlin laughed nervously. "I guess that's a good thing. Do you know where you are?"

Maanik nodded.

"Where?" Caitlin asked.

The girl looked around. "It is not the Taj Mahal, so it must be . . . my bedroom."

Her parents had said she had a sense of humor. Caitlin was glad to see that it had returned intact. "Right. And do you know who I am?"

"I think so. Dr. O'Hara?"

"Caitlin," she said, nodding. "And I'm happy to properly meet you."

"Me too," Maanik said.

"I'm unused to speaking like this with you," Caitlin admitted. "I've only met you during emergencies." Honesty, she'd always found, worked best with teenagers.

"I can try scaring you, if you like."

"How would you do that?"

Maanik hitched up one side of her face and stuck out her tongue. "Howsh thish?"

Caitlin laughed. This was the easygoing girl she'd seen in the theater video. "How do you know about me? *What* do you know about me?"

"My parents said you are a doctor. A psychiatrist. Will I be cured soon?"

"Workin' on it," Caitlin said. "Can I get you anything? Food? Water?"

"I'm good," the young woman said. Her left hand sought Jack London and began rubbing him behind the ears. He seemed normal, unperturbed. "How are my parents? Are they here?"

"Your mother's in the living room. They're doing very well under the circumstances."

That seemed to bring Maanik down and Caitlin didn't want that. She also didn't know how much time they might have, whether this period of lucidity would last for an instant or endure. "Hey, are you up for a few questions? I have so many."

"I'll try to answer them," Maanik said. "I'm a little confused."

"Totally understandable. Me too." Caitlin pulled the desk chair to the side of the bed and sat. "Let's try this for starters. Do you remember what happens during your episodes?"

Maanik sat up, preparing to speak. "I remember nothing. I know about the screaming and scratching because my parents tell me. Oh, and"—she held up her right arm—"because I'm wrapped like the Mummy."

Caitlin laughed. "So you don't remember doing that."

"Not at all."

"Or speaking?"

"Speaking?"

"Not the way we're talking now," Caitlin said. "More like—acting."

"No."

Caitlin didn't see the benefit of complicating Maanik's grasp of the situation by mentioning other languages.

"You're usually awake when the episodes begin," she said. "What does it feel like when you—"

"Start to lose my shit?" Maanik cut in, eyeballing the door to make sure her mother couldn't hear.

"You're not wrong about that," said Caitlin, enjoying the girl's spunk.

Maanik looked away and continued patting the dog, whose eyes were shut. "It's weird. I just, kind of . . . go away."

"Go away how? Do you mean like falling asleep?"

"Not exactly."

"Do you feel dizziness or do you sense anything different, visually or with any of your senses?"

"Well . . ." Maanik frowned in concentration. "It's like I disappear.

No, that's not right. It's like first I am in pieces, small pieces, and *then* I disappear."

"I'm not sure I follow. Small pieces?"

"My ears are listening, my fingers are feeling, my nose is smelling, my eyes are looking, but they are not connected. It's sort of like every part of me is candles stuck in a cake."

"I like that description." Caitlin smiled. "Go on."

The girl suddenly grew solemn.

"Maanik?"

She was looking at Jack London. "Candles."

"What about them?"

"Flickering." She rolled the dog over with her left hand and rubbed his belly. He snorted in his sleep.

"What is it?" Caitlin pressed her. "What's wrong?"

"I don't know," Maanik said. "I just felt this sadness."

Caitlin reached out and held the girl's hand. "Do you want to talk about it?"

Maanik didn't answer. The silence that settled on the room reminded Caitlin of the quiet in the hallway, unfriendly and oppressive.

"Maanik—can you hear me?"

The girl was staring at the dog.

"Are you worried about Jack London?"

She didn't answer. Tears were now dropping onto the bedsheet. They were tears of sadness, great mourning. She turned away.

"Maanik?"

"My arm," she said in a low monotone.

Caitlin leaned in a little closer. She was trying to look into Maanik's face, to get the girl to see her. "What about your arm?"

"My left arm," Maanik said. "It's gone."

"That's not true. You're petting Jack London with it. Your arm is fine."

"No."

Caitlin let her pause, sensing that something else was coming.

"My arm is bloody and ripped off and a terrible mess." She began to squirm a little. "The animal . . . is dead."

"Maanik, listen. What you're seeing is not real."

Maanik didn't seem to hear. "I am disappearing, like pieces of paper in a fire."

"That's a dream," Caitlin insisted quietly. She shifted onto the bed and put her arms around the girl. "You're right here, in your apartment, in your room, with me."

"No. It's happening right now. *Help me!*"

"What's happening?"

Maanik's mind seemed to be searching for the right word. "The end," she sobbed. "It is the end."

CHAPTER 20

From the corner of her eye Caitlin saw Mrs. Pawar appear in the doorway. Caitlin put up a hand to stop her from coming in.

Maanik's arms started to rise and words spilled from the girl's lips—not English, not Hindi. But Caitlin thought she could still see some of Maanik left in her eyes. They were pleading with her. Jack London leaped from the bed and began spinning and barking.

The girl was no longer capable of answering questions and Caitlin did not want to lose her again. Reaching out, she touched Maanik's left ear and said, "Blackberries."

Like strings had been cut, Maanik went limp. Her eyes closed and she relaxed into sleep. Freed from whatever thrall he had been in, Jack London sat on his haunches and howled.

Caitlin heard Mrs. Pawar breathing heavily in the doorway.

"What just happened?" she asked.

"I don't know," Caitlin replied. "Maanik woke, seemed all right, and then relapsed. Please, you've got to promise you won't do anything to the dog."

"Why? What has he got to do with this?"

"I don't know," Caitlin said, "but I am becoming certain that he's important. Please?"

Mrs. Pawar nodded tightly.

Caitlin crossed the room unsteadily. There was a wave of guilt: had *she* done something to send Maanik drifting away? Had she crowded her? Had her proximity triggered a panic attack?

It was the mention of candles that got to her. That seemed to transfix her.

Was fire a metaphor for "gunfire," the transformation of something foreign and terrifying into a concept she could understand?

This was not the first fire reference Caitlin had heard since she'd been introduced to Maanik. There was Ben's interpretation of the language: fire, arms, pain. There were the flames Caitlin had seen flashing in the vision with Gaelle. And there was Atash, the boy who had set himself on fire in Iran.

Or is this a dead end? she wondered. Fire was not exactly uncommon.

"Doctor?"

Caitlin snapped from her reflection. "Yes?"

"May I ask what you are thinking? I feel so helpless."

Caitlin turned to her. "Of course. I'm sorry." She looked into the woman's tired eyes. "Mrs. Pawar, how does your husband cope with stress? I mean the mechanism."

"He prays."

"In the apartment?"

"Sometimes. He must be seen in public, to show himself as a humble man, and he goes to a temple here or among Indian-Americans on Third Avenue. However, he prefers to pray in the living room."

"In 'the peace of many choices,'" Caitlin said.

Mrs. Pawar brightened. "Yes."

"Then you'll understand, perhaps, what I'm about to say. When we pray, we close our eyes. We relax our bodies. We access a spiritual side that is driven by faith, not logic. I believe your daughter has done something like that, only much deeper. She spoke to me briefly about how she thinks she 'disappears.' Maanik may have created what she thought was a safe place for herself inside, except her fears got in there with her. They have become real things made of fire, loss, physical pain."

"My poor girl—"

"Mrs. Pawar, if this *is* a self-induced trance, I must get 'in there' and bring her out."

The woman nodded as Caitlin spoke. There was a hint of hope in her eyes.

"I'm coming back tonight, with Ben," Caitlin said. "In the meantime, I want you to do something for Maanik."

"Anything."

"Look after yourself. Feed yourself well, take a nap if you can, take a walk, even if it's just to take Jack London around the block."

"But the way I look," the woman said. "If I meet someone I know—"

"Chances are pretty good that anyone you run into around here has been impacted by the situation in Kashmir. They will understand and respect your privacy."

Mrs. Pawar agreed and Caitlin checked her watch. She had a twelve-thirty session and could just make it. Excusing herself, she hurried from the apartment into the corridor. While she waited for the elevator, she registered that the atmosphere seemed different than before. The sense of omen seemed closer.

Exponentially closer.

Rushing to her appointment, Caitlin left a message for Ben telling him to clear his schedule for the evening, then grabbed a cab. Her mind scanned what she recalled about the Iranian boy. His brother was executed, he set himself on fire, he was hospitalized. She looked him up again in the newsletter. Logorrhea; no suggestion of a language or gestures, but then this was Iran. Even medical information didn't exactly get out intact.

Had Atash been trying to mimic some kind of pain *he* was feeling, expressing it as fire, or was it another cause, something deeper and not voluntary? Or was he simply rebelling against the murder of his brother? Caitlin tried to do a search online to see if he was still alive but the cab ride was too short. She was then thrown into several straight hours of sessions with clients. Taking advantage of a short break in the late afternoon, she looked up the rat infestation at NYU. It seemed to be centered around an old mansion on Fifth Avenue, an exclusive club for world travelers. There were no teenagers on the premises, as far as her quick check could determine before her next client.

As her appointments rolled through the afternoon, Caitlin's regulars appeared to be doing surprisingly well. Most of them had been relying more heavily on group therapy in her absence, groups she had set up months ago. After her final client, she read a text from Ben saying he would meet her at the Pawars' apartment.

Before she left the office, Caitlin called on her colleague Dr. Anita Carter, who filled in for her when there were emergencies. African-American and originally from Atlanta, she had a classic New York approach to problems: acknowledge them, solve them, file them, and go to dinner. Caitlin seriously envied her uncanny ability to compartmentalize.

"Just a heads-up," Anita said. "You've got a couple of bean counters who've expressed displeasure about your recent period of unavailability."

"Let me guess," Caitlin said, "Lauren from hospital admin and Phil from CUNY."

"The lady's not just a healer, she's a psychic!" Anita said.

"I'll bet they used those very words, too," Caitlin said. " 'Period of unavailability.' "

"Why say 'absence' when you can use something big and formidable? Just throw a little oil on those troubled waters, will you?"

"Yeah. I'll e-mail them, explain that these clients are exhibiting a desperate level of trauma."

"Suicidal?"

"I don't think so," Caitlin replied, "but they are highly unpredictable."

"Well, remind Lauren and Phil about our liability unless we commit our assets—namely you—to the problem, and they'll back off," Anita said. She fixed Caitlin with a knowing look. "Want to talk about any of it?"

"Maybe later," Caitlin said, unable to reveal who she was treating. "I'm beat, I'll tell you that much. How's everybody else doing?"

"We're in a pretty quiet phase right now," Anita replied. "There's still a couple weeks before the stress of December exams hits."

"So you haven't seen anything out of the ordinary?"

Anita shook her head. "Anything specific on your mind?"

"No, I was just wondering."

"Lady, you never just wonder. What is it?"

Caitlin made a *You got me* face. "The tension between India and Pakistan. It seems to be knocking people off balance."

"A couple of the kids mentioned that, but there's so much hyperbole on the Web it's tough to know what's a real or a passing fear. A celebrity dies in a car crash, kids are afraid of cars for a day or two or three. Speaking of which, when you have the time, I want to talk about setting up focus groups on shared Internet and social media paranoia."

"I like the idea," Caitlin said. "Shared angst."

"It's like terrier frenzy," Anita said. "One dog gets upset, so another dog gets upset because *that* dog is upset, making the first dog even *more* upset."

"Right, you have two Jack Russells," Caitlin said. "Do they do that a lot?"

"Every time the doorbell rings," she said. "Funny thing is, for all its problems I bless the Internet every day, no exaggeration. The more cases I read, the more analysis that's offered, the more I feel we can help people."

Caitlin thanked her again for her help and began walking home. She was glad to hear that Anita's dogs weren't behaving out of the ordinary. She had enough trouble worrying about people without adding more animals into the mix. She kept wondering, though, about what Anita had said in relation to mass anxiety.

What's that word for when a group turns this way and then that at the same time?

"Flocking," that was it. Coming together in a group, banding for mutual protection from a danger, from fears that linger like a low, slow hum.

Like Neanderthals in their caves, she thought. *Our brains have evolved but our bodies are still locked in the Pleistocene.*

Caitlin suddenly felt as cold as if a deep winter wind had raced down the street toward her, but it wasn't from thoughts of the Ice Age. It was an idea gleaned from what Anita had said. Banding together in a group happened not just in person but also through computers and phones and Wi-Fi. What if millions and millions of teenagers had flocked to the Internet and social media over the past twenty years not just because it made them feel like masters of their caves, carving their universe into manageable pieces. What if there actually *was* an external threat, barely sensed, that was causing them to flock like birds? What if Maanik and Gaelle and possibly Atash and who knew how many others were the first to semiconsciously pick up those signals?

My god, she thought. Were they *that* close to the cliff, as Ben had said? Was Pakistan the imminent threat? Was it a big enough threat for the type of global reaction she was envisioning? Or were they reacting to something else? Something bigger?

And if so, what on earth could that be?

CHAPTER 21

Motahhari Hospital, Tehran

Atash Gulshan had been taken off the ventilator the day before, so the hospital room was unusually hushed. Now and then the corridors echoed with a rattling instrument trolley. Outside there was little traffic; it was one of the high-pollution days when only hospitals and banks stayed open. A sickly yellow-gray smog filled the window, partly obscuring the trees of the courtyard below.

The room had only the one patient. Two female nurses in blue uniforms and black scarves were changing the dressings on Atash's legs. They worked silently, hoping not to be noticed and caught up in yet another argument about women tending to men. This relatively small hospital had not fared well against the national shortage of male nurses, yet the women's service to Atash still provoked a debate with the male doctor whenever he visited. The end of the argument was always the same, the doctor shaking his head and saying, "For the brother of a criminal, I suppose it doesn't matter who ministers to him. Change the bandages."

Atash had received no visitors, no flowers, no bright quilt, no photographs, no other touches from home. He was an embarrassment.

One hour ago Atash had been given enough pain medication to prepare him for this twice-daily routine of circulation stimulation and rebandaging, leaving him in a waking dream state. His body was bolstered on all sides, propping him up and nearly immobilizing his upper body. The blanket was pulled up to his torso, covering his catheter tubes but leaving his legs exposed for the two nurses. The nurse working on his bandaged left leg was slowly manipulating his ankle joint so that he would have some chance of retaining full range of motion if he ever walked again. The nurse working on his right leg was removing his bandages. On his right foot and calf were fourth-degree burns. What scraps of skin remained were black. His heel had burned away to the bone and his calf muscles were raw shreds. Atash had burns on 90 percent of his body; it was a miracle he was alive.

"To suffer for the sins of his brother, that is why he lives," a visiting cleric had murmured after inquiring who he was. The only compassion the young man received was from the two women who shouldn't have been touching him.

• • •

Atash was barely aware of the miracle of his survival. In his waking dream he was running after his older brother, Rashid—no, somehow he was hovering above and behind him as Rashid was running a military-style parkour training through the city, sprinting hard, climbing walls, flipping over stairs, leaping fountains, all the while pursued by police.

"Don't run, Rashid!" Atash called. "It will only make things worse!"

But Atash already knew what the result of the trial would be. Homosexuality was the official "crime," but drug trafficking and sedition would be added on to create the impression that homosexuals were all thoroughly debased.

Suddenly, the stocky figure of Rashid stopped running. He turned to Atash, who was now on the ground, facing him. He seemed different somehow. The air around them quickly filled with a kind of smoke, rolling in like a haboob in the desert. Only this wasn't sand or smoke. Atash's throat and eyes began to burn as if the air were misty with acid.

"Brother!" he cried, squinting into the haze.

Was that Rashid? It had to be. That's who he had been chasing. Atash moved through the thickening clouds toward the indistinct shape.

"*Rashid!*"

The figure moved toward him in silhouette against the fog. Atash gagged on the choking sulfur, heard high winds rushing past his ears. He reached toward the figure even as the smoke swallowed it. "Come! It's urgent now! We have to go!"

"Go where?" the other said in a voice that was like a sour song, melodious but off-key.

"Back," Atash replied. "Back to the courtyard!"

His brother was yelling a reply, but while Atash heard the words, he had no idea what they signified. Something about boats . . . the sea . . .

"What are you saying?" Atash demanded. "I don't understand!"

His brother was now entirely lost in the smoke but Atash could still hear his voice—*a* voice, shrill and frightened. "I am saying that you and the Believers, you're insane!"

"And you're blind!" Atash shouted back. But this time it was not his own voice he heard. It was higher, fairer.

"Blind? Your *glogharasor* are blind!"

His brother had shouted a curse—it meant "stupid sacrifices." Atash did not know how he knew the meaning, but he did.

The figure suddenly appeared again through the smoke, only it was definitely not Rashid but somehow was still a brother. His skin was pale, his features unfamiliar. His layered attire was billowing in the strong wind, fastened to his chest with a strangely curving silver brooch. The figure picked up a bag like a seaman's grip and grabbed Atash's hand.

"Come!" the figure shouted. "Now!"

Atash grabbed the nearest heavy object, an ice pick that stood on end like a candlestick holder, and bashed it across his older brother's head—but lightly, only enough to knock him out. Then he picked him up under the shoulders and dragged him backward through the streets. But—Atash looked around—this was not Tehran. It was the flaming hell of someplace else.

As he lumbered backward Atash could see that his brother was bleeding from the wound on his head. Somehow he knew where he was going. It was a short haul to a courtyard through the sooty vapors and stench, made easier by the empty pathways. Ash fell, clogging his nostrils and drying his throat. He paused to pull a scarf of some kind in front of his mouth. Atash heard screams and running on other streets but then he saw *them*, lit by the fire in the center of the court-yard, ringed by very tall, dark, rectangular columns. The Believers were forming the sacred circle, white and yellow robes turning and turning. Their arms were moving up and down and around. Atash pulled his brother over and made as if to join the circle, but a tall man stepped forward and put out a hand, stopping him.

Atash had forgotten the oil. He laid his brother's head and shoul-ders on the smooth cobblestones, then ran into the nearest house and pawed through the stranger's shelves. He found some, ran back to the courtyard, and, uttering words that were familiar even if their mean-ing was not, he poured the oil all over his brother and then himself. He picked up his brother and continued into the circle of whirling robes—

But it was too late. He was struck in the face and chest by a wall of heat so powerful, so intense, that it knocked him onto his back and rocked the columns around him. He felt the oil sizzle on exposed areas of his flesh and then everywhere as his body ignited. He heard his brother wake from unconsciousness with a piercing shriek, heard cries ride the air like specters of those already dead. His eyes—what they could see before they melted—could not process the chaos and scope of what lay behind the superheated shock wave.

• • •

The nurses looked up at the small sounds coming from their patient.

"He is talking in his sleep," one of them said quietly.

"I wonder what his thoughts could be," said the other.

"Regret, I would think."

"Perhaps he is discussing the secret to igniting cold sunflower oil."

"Do not even begin to ask that question."

"But it's impossible—"

"Quiet! Do you want to attract accusations of black magic?"

The curious nurse hushed, and the nurses continued their gentle work in silence.

CHAPTER 22

Before sitting down to dinner, Caitlin did some prep work for the session with Maanik. There were still some matters she had to resolve in her own mind.

The day's events and her return from Haiti had been disorienting, yet she was surprised by how normal dinnertime with Jacob seemed. Ordinarily, whenever she returned from being away her son overwhelmed her with questions about where she had been and who she had seen and what she had done. She had always assumed that this was more than just his way of reconnecting. It was his way of feeling as though he hadn't lost her for those few days, that she had somehow been collecting information and experiences to bring back for *him*.

Tonight, however, Jacob was utterly uninterested in Haiti. Caitlin even tested it, dangling a few unfinished sentences about her trip, but he never took the bait. He just kept up a steady monologue about *Twenty Thousand Leagues Under the Sea*, which he was reading for school, and how he was going to use the novel as the basis for an essay about endangered animals.

"The Mexican walking fish is so doomed," he said with a fervor that caused him to half-speak, half-sign in order to get it all out. "So are big creatures like manatees and orcas."

"Do you have a favorite?" Caitlin asked.

"I love them all," he said. "I was wondering, would Captain Nemo be an ocean conservationist if he were alive today?"

"Honey, he was never actually alive—he's a fictional character."

Jacob rejected that thought with a shake of his head. "Every fictional character is based on someone. My English teacher told us that."

"Oh?" Caitlin said. "Winnie-the-Pooh?"

"He was a real teddy bear," Jacob said. "Just not alive."

He had her; that was true.

Her son was no different than on any other evening. She realized as she considered it that she had been expecting him to be different because she herself had been through so much. But he wasn't the one who was adrift. She was, and he was the anchor.

Over ice cream, Jacob was telling her he wanted to read the second Nemo adventure, *The Mysterious Island*, when Caitlin impetuously interrupted him.

"Hey, do you want to do an experiment with me?" she signed.

He shrugged like a bored teenager but curled up one leg and leaned forward at the same time, interested. She hoped it would be a few years before he discovered the "too cool for school" attitude.

"Okay, we're going to hold hands for one minute," Caitlin signed.

Jacob opened his eyes wide, rolled them, and pretended to die in his chair.

"Don't worry," she signed. "It's nothing mushy. I just kind of want to see what happens."

"Can I be timekeeper?" he signed, and she handed over her phone. Then she explained that she didn't want him to do or think anything in particular while they were holding hands, and she wouldn't either. They were just going to see if anything happened on its own. He nodded—the suggestion seemed remotely interesting—then tapped her phone and signed, "Go." She held his right hand with her right hand.

Nothing happened on her side. She still felt unsettled. Jacob got restless but only in the way a ten-year-old fidgets as a minute ticks by. When the phone beeped she asked if he'd felt anything and he said no.

"Okay," she said. "Again."

"Last time?" he asked.

She shrugged noncommittally.

This time when he started the countdown, she held his left hand with her left hand.

Again, nothing happened in her heart, her mind. Jacob's attention strayed to the phone and she had to stop him from playing with it.

After the beep she said, "Once more, please."

He huffed but set the countdown, and she picked up his left hand with her right. Nothing happened for a few seconds. Then Jacob suddenly focused, like the time he'd seen a hawk fly by the window. She wasn't sure what he was focused on—he seemed to be looking at the table rather than at her hand—but she recognized the stillness that settled into his body, the serious expression on his face. She felt nothing in her hand or anywhere else but clearly something was happening for him.

Suddenly Jacob broke their connection. Not violently but with some urgency, as if he'd touched a hot pan handle. He leaned across the table and put his hands on her cheeks and held her head. Staring at her face he said, "Mommy . . . ," as if he was affirming it was her.

"I'm here. Are you okay?"

He moved his hands away to sign but held her firm with his gaze. "I'm sorry," he signed. "I'm not big enough to help hold it."

The look on his face showed the feeling of his phrase.

"Hold what?" she asked. But he was sliding off his chair and not looking at her. He gave her a hug and went to his room. Caitlin was about to follow when she was interrupted by the arrival of the sitter, Theodora, who would watch him when she went to the Pawars'.

After letting the sitter in, Caitlin poked her head around Jacob's door; her mind wouldn't drop the conversation. He was doing his homework and held up a drawing of Captain Nemo he'd made.

"That's lovely," she signed. And it was. Nemo's beard in particular was enchanting, drawn as though it were a frozen white wave.

"Jacob, before, what did you mean by 'hold it'?" she signed.

Jacob tapped three fingers near his mouth, then made a stretching motion with both hands: "water" and "big."

Caitlin felt a chill. She positioned herself to make sure he could read her lips. "Do you mean the ocean?" she asked, as she repeated his signs for "big water." Jacob visited the ocean several times a year with his grandparents on Long Island.

He nodded.

She relaxed a little. "Did you see the ocean when you were holding my hand?"

He shook his head no.

"Then how did you know it was the ocean?"

"It was really big and it was moving."

"Moving—like waves on the beach?"

He shook his head again. "I have to work now, Mommy."

He turned back to his schoolwork like a mini-Caitlin. She lingered a moment in case he decided to say more. When he did not, she bent over and gave him his good-night kiss, which he returned. Nothing about the event seemed to be bothering him and for that she was relieved, but his reaction still unnerved her. Why would he mention a wave? Had he somehow tapped into her visions?

Halfway down the stairs, heading out of her apartment, Caitlin remembered how she had once described psychiatry to Jacob: helping people hold their problems in the light until they solved them. Maybe he had simply sensed her preoccupation with the traumatized girls and went to a place where *he* always felt calm—the ocean.

The ground was shifting under Caitlin's feet, more than it had when she was working with hundreds of people after the Phuket tsunami. Those were tragic multitudes; these were two girls, two individuals whom she knew and had spoken to. She was usually so balanced. If she suddenly wobbled, Jacob would surely feel it.

In the cab to the east side, Caitlin did some quick reading. Upon arriving at the Pawars' apartment, she asked for a few minutes alone on the balcony before she saw Maanik. Kamala showed her outside and shut the door behind her. Caitlin looked at the lights of apartments and streetlamps rippling on the East River, looked up at sharp clouds slipping past a full, bright moon. Despite the fact that Ben was about to arrive, she felt strangely alone. Maybe it was because their history was like a circus act. Sometimes they were hanging from the same trapeze, sometimes they were on opposite ends of the tent, and sometimes they were plummeting toward the net. Their relationship wasn't exactly something to hold on to.

Still, she was glad to see him standing before her when she went back into the apartment. He had a warm smile—a relaxed smile, for the first time in days—and a bag full of gadgets: video camera, backup sound recorder, and tablet.

"Good day?" she asked hopefully.

"Almost," he whispered. "The representatives huddled separately so I didn't have to interpret too much today."

They set up the equipment in Maanik's room and the girl watched them without comment; she seemed more distant than she'd been earlier, but not apprehensive. Resigned? Braced? It was difficult to tell.

Caitlin sat beside her and explained everything she was going to say and do as a guide throughout the session. Maanik listened without comment or acknowledgment. Ben crouched a few feet away, ready to turn on the devices and take notes on his tablet. The Pawars sat side by side across the room, on chairs from the dining room. Jack London hovered nearby but seemed more interested in sniffing the cuffs of Ben's pants than what Caitlin was about to do.

Caitlin kept one eye on the dog while she walked Maanik through the countdown to a state of hypnosis. The only change in Jack London's behavior was that he shoved his nose under a pant cuff and thoroughly inspected Ben's sock.

Maanik was also unperturbed. She slipped into a deep, relaxed state without resistance.

Caitlin had debated with herself whether to frame this to Maanik as simple hypnosis or as a "past life" session. The very phrase "past-life regression" still made her cringe a bit. However, she had looked up the process of regression and read about it again on the ride over. She was surprised to find that it was very similar to ordinary hypnosis. Still, Caitlin decided that actually saying the phrase "past life" would be too leading. She wanted Maanik to describe what she was seeing and experiencing unencumbered.

She began by asking Maanik to choose a peaceful location, somewhere she felt safe and at home. She would be able to return to this place any time she wanted.

"Have you found a spot?" Caitlin asked.

"Yes, I'm there," Maanik said.

"Tell me about it."

"I'm under a pink and yellow tent. It's swaying back and forth." She laughed. "It's on the back of an elephant."

Everyone chuckled.

"That's wonderful," Caitlin said. "You feel perfectly safe up there?"

"Oh, yes." Maanik sighed with contentment. "I'm in a line with men on white horses ahead of me and we're walking slowly through the fields toward the mountains. They're far away, though, we won't get there tonight. It's hot but we have a nice breeze. And I'm playing cards with my aunt. Round cards, all painted."

There was a quiet exclamation from the Pawars' corner. Mrs. Pawar said, "*Ganjifa* cards."

The ambassador added, "For teaching the Mahabharata, devised centuries ago."

Caitlin nodded but kept the focus on Maanik, who suddenly said dreamily, as if she were quoting, "The body is ashes but the breath is immortal."

Ben whispered to the ambassador, "From the Vedas?"

The ambassador nodded and Mrs. Pawar seemed surprised.

"The Upanishads," the woman said. She stared at her daughter and added, "Maanik has never studied them."

"She may have overheard me," Mr. Pawar said, but he didn't sound confident.

"All right, Maanik," Caitlin said. "Remember, you can come back to your tent on the elephant any time you want. Do you understand?"

"Mmmm."

"I'm going to ask now that you find the other place, the place you've been visiting. The place where you've been having so much trouble."

The smile dropped from the girl's face. "I don't want to," she said in the smallest voice Caitlin had ever heard.

"I know," Caitlin said. "I know it's a big favor to ask. But this is to help me help you. Can you be brave and do this for yourself?"

Maanik hesitated, then nodded. She swallowed hard and crossed her arms on her chest protectively. Caitlin could see Maanik's eyes moving under her eyelids as she looked around. Then her entire body jerked and her eyes flew open, but she was not looking at the room she was in. Her arms flung apart and just as quickly, she began slapping at her bandaged arms, hitting them in a way that made Caitlin shudder. She grabbed Maanik by the shoulders and leaned into her to stop the attack on herself. The girl was screaming again, silently, her mouth a wide O. Jack London suddenly started howling.

"Maanik, tell me where you are!" Caitlin said firmly.

The girl seemed to fight to regain control of her mouth. Her tortured lips pulled together and unfamiliar words spilled from them. She began gesturing with the wide circles and sudden slashes that Ben had identified as superlatives. Caitlin could see Maanik struggling to keep speaking, to make sense—as much as those words made sense—even as her eyes twitched rapidly in fear.

"Maanik, I know you can hear me," Caitlin said. "Please find a way to tell me where you are."

"I see tall posts," she said. "Pieces are coming off, falling around us . . ."

"Posts? Made of wood?"

"Stone. Carvings. There are waves beyond . . . I smell salt."

"The ocean?"

Maanik didn't acknowledge this but Caitlin thought she saw the girl's hair stir slightly, not as a result of any movement she made but lifted by something from behind. The window was covered by drapes and Caitlin could see no vents in the floor or ceiling. Maanik seemed to shiver. Her eyes narrowed and turned upward again.

"The sky! *It is on fire!*" she said.

"Is it sunset?"

The girl's head shook slowly. "I don't know." Her brow knit. "I—I don't *think* so."

"Please concentrate," Caitlin pressed. "Is it day or night?"

The girl's head shook uncertainly and then her face twisted into another silent scream, more painful looking than if she were crying aloud. Her body stiffened and her feet struggled on the bed.

Ambassador Pawar rose slowly. "Please, Dr. O'Hara. I know I agreed, but I insist that you stop this!" His voice was tight with grief.

"I'm sorry, but I want her to stay with this as long as possible," Caitlin said. "We must have the information."

"We?" he asked.

"Yes, *we.*"

"But it is hurting her!"

Caitlin turned as much as she could to look directly at him. He was on his feet. "Mr. Pawar, your daughter has been experiencing this trauma for over a week. If she were any other person exhibiting such severe symptoms with an unknown cause, I would have hospitalized her days ago. But then she would have been heavily medicated and I would have had limited access to her. I don't think either of us wants that, *or* the attention!"

Caitlin felt guilty using publicity as a lever but she desperately didn't want to interrupt this session. Not now. The ambassador was silent.

"Cai," Ben said, nodding toward the bed.

Maanik was moving like an eel, her body writhing, her mouth still opening and closing in wordless cries.

"We don't know how deep this goes," Caitlin said in a gentler voice, half-turning back toward the Pawars. "She can't fully express it. If we fail to understand Maanik's condition, I cannot, in good conscience, keep her in this bedroom much longer. But if there is a *chance* for us to understand, to heal her, we should take it."

The Pawars were silent, agonized.

"She is strong," Caitlin said, returning her full attention to the young woman. "I'm going to keep talking to her as long as I can."

She heard Mr. Pawar sit heavily behind her.

"Please focus, Maanik," Caitlin said. "Can you tell me if it's day or night? Look around you."

The young woman forced herself to use words.

"It is . . . night. The moon . . . so large! White light being eaten by the red light."

"The red light. Is it the sunset? Or is it closer? Fire?"

"Flame," she said. Her mouth made biting motions. "The dragon . . . red waves. So *maddening!*"

Maanik's eyes slid to Caitlin for just a moment but it was long enough to show she was still there, herself, however small. Then Caitlin saw her hands return to the gesture she'd made earlier, when Caitlin had handed her a pen and paper. The one thing she and Ben hadn't planned for. Caitlin felt Ben shove a tablet into her hands, a drawing app already open. Caitlin slid the tablet under Maanik's right hand and though the girl was shrieking again, she simultaneously drew several long, undulating lines on the tablet. Then she dropped it and attacked her forearms again, this time with her nails.

As Caitlin tried to restrain her, Ben snuck the tablet from between them.

"Maanik, go back to the elephant!" Caitlin shouted.

Maanik shoved her body back against the pillows but then just as suddenly, she relaxed completely. Her hands fell limp, her eyes closed, and she took a very long and solid inhale.

"Are you there, Maanik? Are you back in the pink and yellow tent?"

It was a long moment before Maanik answered.

"Yes," she said.

Caitlin saw a shudder pass through her, *all* the way through her.

"That's great, you are doing terrific work, Maanik."

"Yes," she said again. But she seemed to be repeating the previous statement, not responding to Caitlin's compliment. "Yes, I am here."

"I'm so proud of you—" Caitlin said, but then it hit her: *was* Maanik talking to her?

"Oh no," Maanik said, with a sudden terror to her voice. "It found me. It's coming here! Ashes!" Her body stiffened and she let out a scream so petrified and agonized that Mrs. Pawar gasped and Caitlin's eyes surged with tears. Choking on a sob, Caitlin leaned in, touched Maanik's ear, and said, "Blackberries."

The girl slumped back but it was an ugly movement, like all of her ligaments had been cut.

There was a horrible, horrible silence. The queasy hush that had always hovered outside the Pawars' apartment was now inside. Caitlin felt she could almost taste it; it was deadly. She turned at the sound of Jack London retching on the carpet under Maanik's desk, his small body convulsing. Even as Maanik began to breathe somewhat normally, Caitlin was still on high alert. She was afraid to look around, to give credence to something she was feeling: that *something* had come back with the girl.

CHAPTER 23

Caitlin remained with Ben as he dismantled his modest camera-and-tripod setup. Mr. Pawar hunched in his chair, rubbing his forehead with three fingers, while Mrs. Pawar sat on the bed with her sleeping daughter, having called for Kamala to take care of the vomit Jack London had left on the rug.

Caitlin was watching the dog closely. He had nearly slunk out of the bedroom but stopped just shy of the door.

What's going on with you? Caitlin wondered.

She realized that the dog was trying to stay away from where he had thrown up but he did not want to desert Maanik. When no stern words or rebuke came from Kamala or Hansa, Jack London returned to the room, beginning with the edges of the windows, sniffing thoroughly with his shoulders sunk in "guard" mode.

Caitlin was doing her own less overt analysis of her surroundings. The noxious air that had choked the area around the bed was easing somewhat. The closeness she had felt, as though something were pressing in on her, had also dissipated; she felt almost light now, the way she did when she took off her ankle weights after jogging. Caitlin suspected that Jack London had sensed the same. Still, he was very cautious about approaching the bed—and Maanik, who had been the epicenter of whatever the dog had experienced. When he eventually leaped up onto the bed and sniffed around the girl, he showed an aversion not just to her right hand but also to her head. It was just the tiniest recoil. Finally, Jack London curled up by Maanik's feet but remained on guard, staring at the wall behind her head.

"One good thing," Ben said in a low voice.

"What's that?" Caitlin asked.

"I'm sure Kashmir was pretty far from the ambassador's thoughts the last half hour or so."

Caitlin nodded. "Sometimes any break is a good break," she said quietly. "In the session, did you notice Maanik's hair?" She was trying not to lead his answer.

"I saw it move," Ben replied. "Like it was caught in a breeze that wasn't there."

She exhaled more breath than she thought she'd been holding. Ben smiled.

"I'll let you know if you're going crazy, Dr. O'Hara," he said.

"Good," she said, laughing a little, "because I'm starting to wonder."

"Cai, something definitely happened here, and like you said, it wasn't all in Maanik's head."

Caitlin and Ben left the bedroom and Jack London, who was still gazing at the wall but with his head resting on his paws. They were followed by Mrs. Pawar, who sat in the living room, clearly shaken. Mr. Pawar stayed with Maanik. Caitlin went over and sat with Hansa for a while, just listening—the woman needed to vent her worries, not just about her daughter but about her husband.

"You can't protect him from this," Caitlin told her.

"I know that. My hope is that he can handle it all without breaking." She looked at Caitlin with sad eyes. "He had no reaction at all, himself, to the attempt on his life. It is as if he has pushed that entirely out of his mind."

"For now, most likely he has," Caitlin said. "To him, these other concerns are greater." She smiled. "Trust me, there will be time for you to care for him."

"What about Maanik?" the woman asked. "Has this helped you understand?"

"I'm sure it has, I just have to sift through her answers," Caitlin said. "We'll be working on that this evening. I told you, we're going to figure this out."

"He is a caring man," Mrs. Pawar said, looking at Ben.

"Very." Caitlin beamed appreciatively.

Mrs. Pawar asked Kamala for water, then went to the window and looked down at the city. Caitlin implored Mrs. Pawar and Kamala to make sure that Maanik's bedroom was aired out with the windows open twice a day, not just with plug-in fresheners, and that Maanik should also sit twice daily on the balcony, bundled up against the cold. Mrs. Pawar started to object, indicating an overlooking terrace to the east, but Caitlin pointed to a Japanese folding screen and suggested they use that for privacy.

Caitlin checked on Maanik one more time and bade the Pawars a good night. It wasn't until Ben and Caitlin were in the elevator and nearly to the lobby that she allowed herself to ease from professional mode into her own mild release. She breathed through the slight queasiness and shakes.

"You okay?" Ben asked, noting her fingers' trembling.

"Will be."

But the feeling only grew as they stepped outside. A burning smell surrounded her, as if someone had lit a fire in a fireplace in one of the surrounding buildings. And then she felt eyes on her again, and a cold so thorough she shivered under her coat. She stopped just as they reached the sidewalk.

"Caitlin?" Ben asked. "What is it?"

"I feel like I'm being watched," she murmured. Somehow it was harder to tell Ben *this* than any of the other bizarre details of the past few days.

Ben looked around. Save for a few people walking their dogs, the street was relatively free of pedestrians. He glanced up at the lowest windows in the building. There was no one looking down.

"I'm sure it's some kind of emotional aftershock," she said. "Paranoia. Let's get a cab."

"On second thought . . . ," Ben said.

"What?"

"A security chief told me once that if you feel like you've got eyes on you, don't take a cab. You don't know who's driving it, and you don't know if they've been waiting for you out of your sight."

"But I don't think anyone's *actually* watching me."

"Doesn't matter. We're going to walk to the subway."

He put his arm around her and they headed north, then west. There was a mild crosstown wind and Caitlin didn't stop trembling until they reached Grand Central. They went through the main door instead of one of the side entrances. The turquoise vaulted ceiling and pale stars, the brass and opal clock in the center, helped her feel that she was standing on firm ground again.

"Better?" Ben asked.

"Much." She smiled. There were a great many people here, and shops were still open. It was all very normal, almost cheerful. She straightened; she hadn't realized that she had been curling into Ben's side. He pulled his arm away but not completely, leaving his hand on her back as they strolled to the subway entrance.

"Let's talk about something that has nothing to do with anything," Ben suggested.

His flustered tone made Caitlin laugh and he chuckled with her. It took about two seconds for Caitlin to snap back to the larger reality.

"Her hair," she said as they headed toward the subway steps. "That was just impossible. I mean, there's no other word for it."

"Cai, let your brain off the hook for a while," Ben said as he slid his MetroCard from its holder. "I know you want to drive straight at the problem, but we both know that if we don't give our brains a rest, a real rest, it fogs up the windshield."

"You are right, O wise one." She grinned. "Okay. I'll power down. You're taking the 6 home?"

"No, I'll see you home first."

"You don't have to."

"I know. But in case there *are* eyes on you, I'm taking you home."

Caitlin felt a rebellious kick against his white knighthood—and ignored it. She knew she had a much better chance of powering down if he was there, staying alert.

As they walked to the Shuttle train platform, Caitlin looked at all the faces around her, allowing herself to just see them, not read them. This kind of passive observation was primarily a right-brain activity, which is why it was so relaxing for her, but it also allowed a simple love of people to come forth, the admiration of human beings that made her so happy to live in one of the world's largest cities. Standing on the platform, she drank in the faces like fresh, pure water. And then, stepping onto the train and finding a pole to hang on to, she focused on Ben's face as he held on beside her—that sweet, studious, heartbreaker face, all in one. The face that had been with her through some of the worst events she had ever experienced.

The train intercom chimed and she heard the old, familiar recording, "Stand clear of the closing doors." Ben was looking down at someone's tablet over her shoulder, reading whatever she was reading. Caitlin reached up to Ben's now-stubbled cheek. He gave her a half smile but didn't look up, intent on finishing the page before the passenger scrolled to the next.

Too bad, Caitlin thought as she gently pulled his head down and kissed him. He did not mind the interruption. To the contrary, it was something he'd been waiting patiently for—not just tonight but since he first laid eyes on her. He gave her his fullest attention and suddenly they were sheltered in complete and quiet privacy. Their lips felt like fire and water and air all in one—until the train jolted and they bumped noses and laughed. But only for a moment, because Ben pulled her in close with one arm and kissed her twenty years deep.

Many long kisses later, they reached the door of Caitlin's apartment building. Ben hesitated on the sidewalk.

"Well, this is awkward," he tried to joke.

"You can come up," she said, turning his face to meet her eyes.

"You're sure?"

"Yes. But—"

"I know." He grinned. "We have to dial it back."

"Huh?" she said, before realizing what he had meant. "No. Maanik's drawing. I want to check it out *now*."

They both laughed as she led the way up the brownstone steps, her back burning warmly and steadily under his gaze.

Jacob was asleep and so was the sitter, who departed drowsily. Ben sat at the table and pulled his tablet out of his bag, bringing up Maanik's scrawl. Caitlin—who was immediately preoccupied again with the puzzle—realized she desperately wanted the drawing to mean something. Because she also knew that what she had told the Pawars was true: she could not justify leaving Maanik at home very much longer.

She and Ben huddled over the glowing screen. The drawing seemed unrelated to either the Viking longship or the symbol of crescents. Its wobbly lines seemed to undulate from upper left to lower right with something like a purpose, yet the lines themselves were as organically shaped as frost or the edges of a stain. Directional . . . textural . . . they appeared not to be casual.

But appearances are not necessarily reality, she reminded herself. They could be nothing more than random scrawls on which she was attempting to force pattern recognition.

"Thoughts?" she asked.

"Either too many or not enough," he said, tapping a few keys. "Two years ago, even a year ago, it would have been hell figuring out

what this might be. Now that image-search capabilities have im-
proved . . ."

He finished uploading the image and they watched an online
search begin. The "best guess" image that first appeared was an example of an irregularly shaped freckle—an indication of carcinoma,
which dampened their spirits. Ben slowly scrolled through the long
list of possible matches: children's drawings; several poor illustrations
of shorelines, which gave them pause; and a number of microscopic
images of skin cells. Then Caitlin stabbed her finger at the screen.

"Hold on. That. What is *that*?"

Ben tapped on the image and it filled the screen. It was a map, yel-
lowed and ancient. Ben placed it side by side with Maanik's drawing
and both of them felt the temperature of the room plummet as her
image fit easily into the shape of Antarctica, matching the ancient
map's outline with remarkable precision.

"The Piri Reis map," Ben read. "From the early sixteenth century."

"I've heard of it," Caitlin murmured. "It showed the contours of
Antarctica before it was covered with ice. Which is impossible."

"Right," Ben countered, "which is why it says here that's a still-
disputed claim. The best explanations are that the map shows something else altogether, possibly a combination of two or more maps
that were thought to be contiguous."

Caitlin didn't reply. Grabbing Maanik's file folder, which had been
at the top of her stack ever since she met the girl, she flipped through
its pages. Past the drawing she had made of the Norse longship,
through her notes on Haiti, down to the bottom, where she found the
drawing Maanik had made with her right hand, her nondominant
hand—the drawing Caitlin had thought resembled a steep cliff and
water. She showed it to Ben.

"What's that?" she asked.

"An iceberg," Ben said instantly.

"Drawn by Maanik during one of her earliest episodes," Caitlin
said. She put the paper on the table and they stared at the images.

Then Caitlin added the drawing of the longship. "The Vikings got as far as North America. Maybe they went even farther. To the south."

"To Antarctica?"

"Why not? Maybe not Vikings exactly, but their ancestors. We've been on this planet, and probably seafaring, for quite a while."

"Yes, but that's still a whopping great distance, Cai. From *anywhere* to Antarctica."

"Not necessarily," she said.

"What do you mean?"

"Continental drift," she said. "The landmasses were all closer, once."

"During the Triassic, yeah, maybe you could've walked from Australia. But there were no people then. No mammals, in fact."

"All right, what about—and we're speaking just for the sake of argument here—what if it wasn't Vikings coming south to find Antarctica? What if there were people sailing north *from* Antarctica?"

"Cai . . . ," he cautioned.

"What if ancestors of the Vikings lived there and sailed primitive longships away from the ice?"

"That's a very big 'if.'"

"Why?" she asked. "Because we haven't found traces of a civilization in the least explored continent on earth, where ice freezes and melts and shifts in a way that would stifle extended archeological research, hide any and all clues?"

"No, look at this." He pointed at text on the Web page. "The argument that the Piri Reis map shows an ice-free Antarctica rests on an assumption that Antarctica was ice-free around 4000 BC. Most scientists are sure Antarctica was covered by at least three million years ago. Humans were barely out of the trees."

Caitlin was silent.

Ben looked at her reflection in the tablet. He added quietly, "It also doesn't explain what any of that would be doing inside Maanik's head."

"No," Caitlin agreed. Her voice felt heavy, her words dropping like brass weights into the air. "But even you said that Maanik is seeing or channeling or experiencing something big."

"Yes. It's like a disaster movie of the mind," he said. "The operative words being 'of the mind,' a kind of waking dream. I'd even possibly, *maybe* buy a shared dream." He turned to look at her. "Why? Are you back on past lives again?"

"I don't know that I was ever there," she admitted. "I just don't know what else to think."

Ben shook his head. "Show me a Mongolian connection and I'll try harder to buy into it. The language definitely shows traces of Mongolian ancestry. But even so, Antarctic Vikings sailing north to Central Asia? That's a reach, Cai. About eight thousand miles of a reach."

"Yeah," she agreed. "Yeah. Fine, I've got nothing else."

"It was a good try, though."

"Sure, sure. A unified theory that explains everything . . . and nothing."

"Let's put it away for tonight," Ben suggested.

Caitlin gathered up the drawings and put the file folder away, trying to stop her mind from chewing on the problem. When she turned back to Ben, his focus had changed. He was sitting there looking at *her*, not at her analytical avatar, and he was sitting very still. She reached out with her right hand and picked up his left hand. Instantly she felt a waterfall surge through her body, vaguely channeled through her right hand. It brought a feeling of such immense relief, she laughed. Ben smiled and inhaled deeply, as if he had just downed a liter of water and was catching his breath.

"Jacob said he wasn't big enough to help hold it," Caitlin said.

"Huh?"

"The ocean."

"What made you think of that?"

"Nothing," she lied.

Ben was silent, choosing his words carefully. Then he said, "I have a lot of empty space. To hold things."

Caitlin stared at him, seeing all the countless moments he had been alone in his life. "You've got room for my slosh-over, you mean?"

He didn't have to answer.

She shook her head. "That worries me. Relying on someone, emotionally."

"Why? People help each other, Cai. It's what we do."

"Well, people do a lot of other things too, and some of them are pretty rotten."

Ben chuckled. "And you think *I've* got a problem with commitment."

"I never said that."

"Not with words," he said, smiling.

"Maybe we have complementary problems," Caitlin said slowly as she stepped to him, gently pushing his shoulders back and draping a leg over his lap to straddle him. Her back was to the table edge, her body molded into his.

"Even a crazy fit is a fit," Ben whispered.

She held her lips to his and they breathed together, deeply, as he laid his hands on her lower back and pulled her in tight. Ben was right: it was a crazy fit. But at the moment, it *was* a fit.

CHAPTER 24

The nocturnal world outside the Global Explorers' Club mansion was uncommonly still.

Earlier that day, pigeons had avoided the area just north of Washington Square Park. Dogs had not seemed eager to walk on lower Fifth Avenue; they hit the broad street and stopped, refusing to go farther. Cats that normally sat in the windows of buildings across the street avoided their perches altogether.

Arni Haugan had not noticed any of that. He had been working in the basement of his chaotic chemistry lab for fourteen hours straight, since just before dawn, when Mikel had arrived with the artifact. The Group's leading field agent had been delayed in Montevideo due to something about an albatross rookery and problems with the electronics of the private jet.

"You're getting as sensitive as people," the Caltech wunderkind muttered at his tablet as he waited for the results of a capillary electrophoresis test. Arni loved his tools; he just didn't always appreciate their temperament.

Like now. The computer insisted there was a problem with the current being carried by the borate ions, and the homogeneous electric field was unstable. Which meant there was a problem with the electrophoresis setup, the software, or both.

He grunted. It was time to stop. He would start fresh in the morning.

Arni shut the tablet and pushed back from the table with his usual cocktail of relief and frustration. Work was never done but it felt good to lay it aside for a while. He needed to plug back into the real world. The air in the Group's basement was rigorously filtered and purified as part of Flora Davies's war on dust—the "silent, corrosive killer of relics," as she described it—leaving the atmosphere with an almost electric perfume.

Arni was a synesthete, having always experienced one sense accompanied by another, especially colors with odors and sounds. The kids in elementary school used to call him "Nutso" because he used his Crayolas to illustrate what he smelled, heard, and tasted. This produced rhapsodic little works of art that no one understood but everyone responded to. His mother had always said that he should become an artist. She was one of the few parents, he suspected, who had ever regretted that her son elected, instead, to become a PhD.

Flora had found his synesthesia fascinating and potentially useful. He was convinced that this, not his strong but less-than-brilliant postgrad record, had scored him this job.

That, plus the fact that she needed someone willing to work in the opposite of an ivory tower, he thought. *A scientific wine cellar.*

The smell down here registered in his peripheral vision as straight, metallic, bright yellow lines. They didn't impede his work and didn't bother him until he'd put in over eight hours. Then they became constricting, like neon prison bars.

Arni had turned on a jazz playlist from his iPod to add a thin purple nebula to the yellow lines haunting his vision. Now he unplugged it, sending the basement into sepulchral silence. There had once been a pendulum clock rescued from a decommissioned train terminal, but when that died, Flora replaced it with a silent red display on the wall, like the countdown clock at Cape Canaveral.

Arni stretched, reviewing what his day's work had produced: little more than confirmation of what they already knew. He had shaved a slice of rock from one unmarked corner of the card-sized stone and hunkered over it with the light microscope to affirm that, yes, as the weight and location had suggested, it was a pallasite meteorite with a nickel-iron matrix and olivine crystals, and a bit of chromite as well. He had dug out a minuscule sample of the substance inside the carvings and run chemical tests, affirming that no, they still had no idea what kind of tool had made them. There was no trace of non-indigenous stone or metal, no hint of thread from a cloth or fur from a pelt that may have been used to smooth it. Arni admitted to himself that a dull familiarity had set in when he compared this object with the others in the Group's collection. Whether in stone or metal or clay or eroded alabaster or even rotted wood, the carvings were all alike in terms of relative size and depth. The only thing that altered between them was the arrangement of carvings.

Still wearing his latex gloves, he stowed the object in a large safe with the other eight objects.

"*Cras dies novus est,*" he said, quoting one of Flora's favorite Latin expressions. "Tomorrow is a new day." It always put an unapologetic, unbeaten cap on the day.

Arni flicked off the light. Just one stop in the locker room and he would be out of this sharp air and onto a nice, pungent uptown bus.

He e-mailed his friend Bewan to tell him he was on the way. Hanging up his lab coat, he pulled a new white button-down shirt from his locker. He was tired, but tired was the best way to enjoy Uranium, a throwback to the 1980s with disco music and black lights to make its cocktails glow. The sounds and tastes would become colors, unimpeded, and he'd finally relax.

Arni started to close his locker door and then stopped, going still.

The electronics. In the plane. In the lab.

A bloody *meteorite*!

Of all the tests they'd tried on the carved objects, they'd never checked to see if the objects were radioactive. There was no reason to.

Everyone knew that pallasite meteorites weren't radioactive—not enough to speak of. But "everyone knew" were words of death in scientific research. It wouldn't take more than a minute to grab a Geiger counter and wave the wand over the object.

Arni opted not to change clothes again. He returned to the lab, flicked on the lights, and found one of the Group's Geiger counters. He retrieved the meteorite and placed it on the worktable, then waved the Geiger wand in front of it. The count of ionizing events—evidence of radioactivity—was almost nonexistent. The Geiger produced a couple dull clicks at a limping, almost dead pace, generating one or two light brown spots in the corners of Arni's vision. Nothing to get excited about.

Arni heard a ring. Damn. His phone back in the locker room. No matter. It was probably Bewan saying he would meet him at the club, was already in line. Arni had to hurry. He gave the wand one last sweep. Suddenly, brown drops began pattering in Arni's vision like rain. He heard dull clicks at a rapid pace. The Geiger counter's needle was beginning to twitch toward the right of the gauge—even though that was impossible. An object couldn't suddenly *develop* radioactivity.

Then his synesthesia created a thin gray fog with black edges in his peripheral vision.

"Okay—that's just crazy," he said.

The gray fog was his unvarying response to recorded spoken voices, not the clicks that emanated from the Geiger counter.

"No," he said out loud. *These aren't clicks coming from the machine.*

They were dull, soft voices . . . coming from the *stone?* He moved closer, bent lower. There was no doubt about it. They were like voices on the wind—the chanting of angels came to mind. Arni practiced no religion nor believed in supernatural beings, but there the voices were.

He drew a sharp breath as the carvings began to pulse, not with his synesthetic lights but with an internal luminescence, ivory-white. The symbols were lighting up in a nonlinear order, each carving showing a soft visual pulse with every corresponding sound. The tones themselves were fractionally louder now. They reminded Arni of language tapes, native pronunciation slowed for the novice, but he immediately squashed that thought. The human propensity for personification meant that any unidentified sound resembling vocalization would automatically be interpreted as words and language. That was wishful, not scientific. He felt in his pocket for his phone. He had to record this—

His phone was in his locker. He reached over and rebooted his tablet. There was an audio recorder built in.

While it turned back on, Arni picked up the meteorite and turned it over, trying to see if there was a point of origin for the hum. He discovered that the stone was vibrating, but not in a way that could be producing the tone. The buzz was more like a mild electric current than a cell phone. It was not unpleasant to the touch; it was soothing, in fact. It made him *want* to hold it. The current seemed to magnify inside his body, as though triggering his own energy centers—the top of his skull, his forehead, his throat, his heart—

His thoughts suddenly felt muddy and something began throbbing behind his eyes, forcing itself forward. Something moving, something wholly *other*. Rust-red and swirling in a cyclonic cone, as if seen from the top, it was becoming thinner as he descended. Now, a landscape. A manufactured landscape of domes and spires incorporated among what seemed to be natural elements, long curves and slopes. The natural parts were enormous, making the artificial components seem like part of a train set or Christmas nativity—small. Very small. And nearly everything was white, as if the entire image was backlit or bottom-lit, somehow, as if light rays were extending up to create the image, yet no rays were visible.

Is this you or me? he asked the artifact.

Again Arni heard the voices. His orientation with the image changed. It tilted suddenly, in an uncanny lockstep with the sounds, so that Arni was looking up: specifically at a stone pillar about three stories high. It was tipped with something glinting green that made him think of the olivine crystals inside the meteorite. He looked around and saw that similar stone pillars circled the city . . .

And then the sky seemed to burst red again across its huge expanse. The landscape shifted, revealing a street, a route, at the end of which was white and blue in a riot of motion. This was *not* him, not his synesthetic response. The colors, the images, the sounds—they were all coming from the rock.

What are you? Arni demanded.

But he never got the answer, never saw what was at the end of the route. Suddenly his right brain and left brain ceased functioning together. His right brain continued to view the image. His left brain died, and he could no longer think to himself about what he was seeing. The right side of his body crumpled so quickly that he fell to the floor. Colors from all over the spectrum flooded his vision but he could not summon the ability to scream. Then just as suddenly, all the colors stopped, every sensation stopped, and he no longer felt his body touching the floor, no longer felt his body at all.

Arni experienced an overpowering urge to sleep. His eyes were shut but he still saw—for another moment. Then his medulla melted, and his corpus callosum, his thalamus, and his pons, and he stopped breathing even as his heart rate exploded.

Moments later he was dead, a trickle of blood and liquid brain dripping from his nose onto the collar of his new white shirt.

PART THREE

CHAPTER 25

Ben heard the soft buzz of his phone, reached for it, and grabbed air.

That potted plant wasn't his night table and the smell in his nose wasn't—

This wasn't his bed. In the dark, he saw the contour of a woman's bare shoulders and strands of hair.

He remembered . . . Caitlin . . . last night . . . as his phone buzzed again. *Where the hell did I leave it . . . ?*

He sat up carefully to avoid waking her and looked around, then down. The back pocket of his trousers on the floor was pulsing blue-white. He leaned over for it, snuck his phone from the pocket with two fingers, and sat in the bed so as to shield Caitlin from the glow as he read two texts. The first was sent at 3:02 a.m.: *Hangout asap.*

The second came a minute later: *Under fire now.*

The sender was Ignacio de Viana, a friend of Ben's from Uruguay— a civilian who, for the last year, had been one of the hundred UN personnel in Jammu, India. "Hangout" did not mean "let's hang out" and "under fire" was literal, no joke.

Ben texted back: *60 secs.*

He pulled on his trousers and eased out of Caitlin's room. Her apartment was chilly and dim, with the kind of hopeless illumination from streetlights through sheer curtains that made it seem like the night itself was drained, tired. Ben stumbled through the unfamiliar terrain, located his bag, and placed his tablet on the now-familiar dining table. Luckily he had only put the computer to sleep instead of shutting it down, so it was a quick jump to Google Hangouts. While signaling Ignacio for a video chat, Ben used the brief delay to turn on a program that would record the face-to-face call. He quickly pulled his earphones from his bag as well, to prevent sounds from traveling down the hall. Shivering, he threw a nearby afghan over his bare shoulders.

As the call connected, Ben jacked in. Machine-gun fire exploded in his ears and he jerked backward, his stomach in his throat. It took him a moment to realize that it was from the earphones, not the room.

Ignacio appeared on-screen but the camera angle was skewed, only showing part of his face and someone's living room. Gray smoke was spreading across afternoon sunlight. Ignacio was shouting in Urdu over his shoulder, "Get away from the window!" Someone shouted something back that Ben didn't quite catch. He would play it back later, enhance the sound.

When Ignacio finally brought the camera to his face, Ben saw that one lens of his glasses was gone and the other fractured. The young man's typically well-groomed hair was wild and matted on one side with blood. There was a red sheen on his scalp that indicated the wound was fresh and still flowing.

"Jesus Christ," Ben exclaimed. "Where—"

"Raghunath Bazaar," Ignacio yelled over the pounding of intermittent gunfire. "I don't know who showed up first, Indian soldiers or Pakistani, but they're *all* freaking insane, Ben. They're shooting civilians at random."

There was a loud pop outside the room and Ignacio dropped from the bottom of the screen. Ben heard shouts from the left and right sides, different voices, angry voices. There were more pops, then si-lence. Were they hit? Or had they just taken cover?

Ben watched anxiously as pictures fell from the wall across the room. Then the shock of a grenade blew into his ears. He recoiled and his hands flew up to yank the headphones from his ears. After a sec-ond, catching his breath, he replaced them.

"Ignacio, are you safe?" he shouted.

After a troubling delay, Ignacio called, "Yes." He repositioned him-self on the screen. "I'm across the street from the fighting, up the stairs. It's all across the street. Ben, you have to tell the assembly this is happening! It's like we're in bloody Afghanistan. No rule of law here. None."

"Where are the rest of the peacekeepers?"

"The main body is about ten miles away. Ten of us were making a routine tour when a bomb went off."

"Hold on," Ben said.

"I'm not going anywhere, trust me."

Ben texted Ambassador Pawar. Within a minute he had added the diplomat to the video chat. Ignacio's camera angled steeply as he stood up, keeping it in his hand. There was a glimpse of the silks of a sari, a woman pulling at his arm.

"Ignacio, I've got Ambassador Ganak Pawar, can you see him?"

"Yes." Ignacio coughed. "I'm told we have to go, the smoke in the room is getting thicker."

"Mr. de Viana, can you get to a safe place?" said the ambassador.

"The woman who lives here says they are going out the back, to the main road, where people are forming caravans."

Ignacio's camera swerved again and Ben heard a woman shout in Urdu, "The floor, the floor!" The camera dipped; Ignacio must have kneeled for cover again. A window came into view, showing the pock-marked onion domes of temples and shattered rooftops. Then the lens dropped to the retail shacks in front of the temples and the wide street. They looked as though they'd been toppled by an earthquake—

splintered, crushed by stone from an adjacent structure. Ben counted five bodies, wide, dark stains of their blood on the street, and others who were still crouched, wounded and screaming, in the doorway of a cinema. Six soldiers ran through the area, guns at their hips, ready to fire in an instant. One of them jerked to a stop, spun around, and shot his gun at second-floor windows above a shop.

"Pakistani and Indian soldiers both came in," Ignacio said. "Now they're shooting at each other."

Ben glanced at the ambassador's face in the corner of his screen; it was frozen with horror.

Out Ignacio's window, a pedestrian suddenly broke and ran for an alley but shrank in terror halfway, cowering next to a food stand as a soldier's gunfire shredded bowls of nuts and dried fruits just above his head. A bilious yellow cloud of spices flew into the air. Ben jolted as another bomb exploded in his ears. A section of a temple roof shattered before his eyes, blasting fragments and black smoke. The explosion had come from the inside. Terrorists, most likely—local instigators blowing up their own home so they could kill outsiders.

"My god," Ganak breathed.

Ignacio flipped his tablet to face himself but before he could speak his hands wobbled and the camera swung wildly, hitting the floor. Ben gasped. Had he been shot? But the picture remained, showing Ignacio crawling away from the window. He reached a woman lying nearby, grabbed her under the arms, and, still on his knees, dragged her jerking body through an arch into the living room. The woman was screaming, her stomach heaving, blood gushing from her mouth onto her yellow sari. They could see the red stain spreading over one side of her chest. Ignacio crawled back into the room and then he was facing the camera, yelling: "Get the UN forces here *now*! I don't have the authority—get the damned UN to order them to *move*!"

Then in the distance, another explosion. The picture dropped and the feed cut off.

Ben closed his eyes. He was perspiring, shaking as though he had a high fever. Globes of light were exploding behind his eyelids—physical memories of bombs at night high over Bangladesh in 2001. He heard his name from a distance, opened his eyes, and there was Ganak calling to him.

"*Ben . . . ?*"

"Yes," he said. "I'm here."

"I only recorded my portion—"

"I'll send you the full recording."

"Thank you. We must meet at once. Can you come to my office in half an hour?"

"Of course."

The men ended the chat without courtesies. The ambassador would already be moving to contact military officers. Ben e-mailed the video, then sat and shook, wiping moisture from his brow and eyes. He wanted the whole goddamned thing over there to end, *every* madness humans inflicted on themselves to go away.

• • •

Back in the bedroom, Caitlin jolted awake.

She swung her legs out of bed and only then remembered that her old friend Ben had been in that bed all night.

She pulled on a bathrobe and padded down the hall, pausing outside Jacob's room in case he was awake early. She heard nothing and continued to the living room, where she saw Ben sitting with his hands on the top of his head, huddled under her afghan in utter despair. *Is he regretting last night?* she thought, but then she noticed his tablet, his Google account open, and a blank video chat window.

"Ben," she said, and placed one hand on his shoulder. His breathing was deep and ragged as he forced it into a rhythm, trying to control himself.

"Jammu," he blurted. "Attack on a shopping center."

"Oh no," Caitlin said, sitting next to him.

"Sorry I woke you," he said.

"You didn't. Anything I can do?"

He shook his head and stood, dropping the blanket. "Another bump to the body count," he said harshly, and shoved his tablet into his bag with sharp, angry movements. "I've got to meet the ambassador. This thing is beyond out of control."

He hurried back to Caitlin's bedroom, miserable and urgent.

She gave him his space. She knew this side of Ben—this side of the work they did. She picked up the afghan and wrapped it around herself, trying to focus on anything other than what Ben had just told her. She had not heard from Gaelle since she left Haiti. Whenever she called, she got the Anglade Charter voice mail. And Maanik—Caitlin was barely keeping a handhold on the cliff of *that* trauma. She almost envied Ben's having a target to focus on: territorial carnivores fighting over land and ideology. What the hell was *she* battling? The session with Maanik had taunted rather than informed her. It was like she was searching for something cunning, cagey, that did not wish to be seen.

If I want to help these kids, if I want to sleep again, I need more information. Ben was dealing with his crisis by running toward it. She had to do the same.

There was another teenager Caitlin had not been able to contact yet. She brought up her phone's browser and searched for Atash. It took some time but she discovered an article written the day before about self-immolation in Iran. It referred to the boy who set himself on fire in a library. He was, it said, in critical condition at a Tehran hospital.

Still alive, Caitlin thought with a rush of exhilaration.

Ben came charging into the living room.

"I'm sorry." He glanced at her. "I'm sorry I'm handling this so—so crappy."

"You're not," she replied. "It's been a helluva few days."

He agreed with a grunt as he grabbed his coat and thrust an arm into it.

She struggled with herself, knowing that if she said anything now it was probably going to be seen as wrong—but it had to be said before she lost him to this crisis. "Ben, I know the timing couldn't be worse but I need your help."

"With what?"

"I have to get to Iran as soon as possible."

Ben's hands dropped from the coat zipper he'd been trying to close. He looked sad but when he spoke he sounded ferocious. "What are you *talking* about?"

"The boy who burned himself—he's alive."

"Okay—and?"

"You saw last night what we're up against. I have to see him."

"I need *you* to be alive, not kidnapped and imprisoned and God knows what. I'll find you a translator and you can call him."

"There's no guarantee the boy can talk. And, Ben, I can't see a nonexistent breeze over the phone."

"If he can't speak, if he's that badly burned, the likelihood of getting *anything* from him isn't worth the risk."

"You can't know that. I can find a way to safely navigate Iran if I have UN help."

"Not through me, Caitlin." Then, as though the sun had risen early, understanding washed over his expression. He turned to face her. "And not *from* me, either."

"Sorry?"

"You're running away from me."

She was surprised. "Ben, I swear to god, I'm not. I have to see this boy *now*. He may not live—"

"I said no," he snapped, giving up on the zipper, not meeting her eye as he grabbed his bag.

"Ben, listen. Last night I understood—no, I *felt* what could be possible with you. I felt the ability to hold more with you, to be stronger because it's more than just me now."

"Not buying. You're punching out like I'm an appointment."

"Please listen—"

"*No!* I will not help you go to Iran, Caitlin."

He left the room and headed through the foyer to the front door. She called after him, "I'm going, Ben. I'll find another way."

There was no reply but the sound of shoes on hardwood and the door shutting.

Caitlin strode to the dining table, picked up her cell phone, and called Director Qanooni of the World Health Organization.

CHAPTER 26

A couple hours later Qanooni called back from the Regional Office for Africa in Brazzaville, Congo. He was working through lunch at his desk. Caitlin told him there was a medical emergency in Iran and she needed to get there ASAP.

"The Country Office in the Islamic Republic of Iran has—how shall I put it? Insubstantial influence over the Ministry of Health."

"I am aware of that, Mr. Director, but the condition of a patient there may have a great impact on patients here and in Haiti."

"This must be serious," he said thoughtfully. "You called me 'Mr. Director.'"

"Sir—"

"And now 'sir,'" he said.

"—this *is* urgent," she pleaded. "I don't have time to file a formal request. Is there any way you can get me in?"

"Based on something so vague? No. If you can write something that can, perhaps, expand upon what little you've told me?"

Expand? she thought. *The minds of young people are being assaulted by a force that only animals and I can detect. Why don't I just say that? Or hell, why not just stick out my right hand and think it at him?*

Then a text from Ben arrived. It was just one word: *Done.*

Caitlin quickly talked her way off the call and phoned him.

"Ben—are you serious?"

"Very."

"Thank you," she said. "Thank you so much."

"You can thank Mohammed Larijani, a translator at the Permanent Mission. He's the one who's making it happen. He's telling the
Iranian ambassador that an American doctor needs to consult with
Iranian doctors. Very good propaganda for them. You don't mind
being used that way, do you?"

"Not at all." She didn't have time to work through the double
meaning his tone implied.

"I hope it's worth it," he added.

"It will be," she said as she went to her bedroom and began pack-
ing. "Ben, are you okay?"

"I'm fine. My friend in Jammu is alive, his girlfriend's in the hospital."

"That's good. But I mean—"

"I know what you mean. Have a safe trip."

"I will. Hey, Ben?"

"What?"

"A psychiatrist walks into an Iranian bar. She orders scotch with
crow."

Ben was silent.

"Not even a chuckle?" she asked.

"Not now. Not today."

"I'm sorry you feel like that," she said sincerely. "We'll talk when I
get back."

"I'll text the details of your trip. Mohammed thinks you can get on
the two o'clock Aeroflot flight. I have to go now."

She said thanks again and good-bye, ended the call, and did what
she always did when there was a challenge: looked ahead. She called
her father and asked if he could please come back to the city. He
agreed, of course. He always did.

Caitlin felt terrible all over. It was partly the ever-ready generosity of her father, partly the aftershock of what Ben had said to her, but she couldn't stop feelings of guilt from clouding her mind. Still, she had a job to do.

Jacob didn't help her self-regard. She had never taken two trips so closely together. She kept him home from school so they could have a half day together but he was furious throughout, making a point of ignoring her with abrupt turns of his back at first and then acting as if she were invisible. Finally, as her time to leave approached, Jacob simply removed himself. He sat in his room with his eyes closed and without hearing aids. If he sensed her coming into his room to say good-bye—and she suspected he did—he did not acknowledge it.

Caitlin had learned years ago that during these rare angry moments, any touch—tapping his hand or hugging his shoulders—would be akin to slapping him. It didn't leave her with many choices. But she could, and did, sit across his desk from him for several minutes so that he knew she was present. She kept her hands placed near him, not touching, so he could smell her hand lotion. And she noticed that his ankle was in contact with the leg of the desk, which had a slight wobble, so she knew he felt it as she wrote a note on his Museum of Natural History dinosaur notepad, which would be waiting in his line of sight when he opened his eyes.

I love you, Jacob, it said. *I'll Skype you as soon as I get a connection and I'll be right back. XOXO*

Her father gave her a big hug before she headed out to the waiting car.

"Don't worry about Jacob," he said.

"Of course I'm going to worry about him," she said, sighing.

"I mean it, Miss Caitlin O'Hara," he said as if he were reprimanding her thirty years ago. "You have to save all your worrying for yourself on this trip. I want extra caution from you, hear me?"

"I hear you."

"Zero risks. I don't care who needs help, you find someone else to help them."

"It's just one boy in a hospital bed. No natural disasters to run from." She tried to smile.

He kissed her forehead. "God, I hope so."

Just before Caitlin sat in the waiting sedan, Ben called with good news: she would not have to swing by the United Nations to pick up her papers. Not only would the Iranian ambassador's wife meet her at the airport, Caitlin was invited to ride with them and their staff on the state jet.

A smile spread across Caitlin's face. She thanked him again. He told her not to mention it. And meant just that.

She reached JFK and was met by a member of the mission staff, who advised her to put her head scarf on before they boarded. Caitlin reached into her carry-on and tied on her scarf—a present from Ben on one of their trips. He'd grabbed it from a nearby bazaar after she'd forgotten hers at the hotel, and the laughter they shared over its cheesy print had always trumped her vanity. She was then taken to the gate and across the tarmac to the waiting aircraft. The wife of the permanent representative of Iran welcomed Caitlin to join her fortuitously timed trip home to greet a new baby niece. After a period of courteous chitchat Caitlin curled into a plush fold-down seat with an eye mask and instantly slept. Exhaustion had finally caught up with her, and the thirteen hours felt like a gift.

She slept through the flight, a continuous rest for the first time in weeks, until the same staff member who had met her at the airport woke her.

"We will be landing within the hour," the young man told her.

With the hum of the jet engines sounding especially loud in ears still full of cottony sleep, and the kick of guilt already starting again in her gut, Caitlin navigated to the restroom with her carry-on bag. She changed into clothes she hadn't worn in years: tight jeans; a crisp, white Pink-brand shirt; and a bright red Yves Saint Laurent knee-length coat with long sleeves. She chose black eyeliner and mascara and a heightened but natural shade of lipstick, then applied them all a bit more strongly than she ordinarily would have. Finally she added short black suede boots with high heels and tied a red-and-blue Hermès Liberty scarf over her hair, carefully winding the ends around her neck. Ben's cheesy scarf would not be appropriate in Tehran. It did not escape her sense of irony that she was preening for a theocracy in a way she never had for any man.

When she reentered the cabin, the representative's wife, chatting on her phone, smiled and nodded approvingly. It was a small thing, but it felt good to have done something right.

Tehran's time was eleven thirty in the morning. Caitlin's concern about getting to Atash as soon as possible had made its way from Ben to Mohammed to the representative. The ambassador's wife informed Caitlin that her guide would meet them at Imam Khomeini International Airport and take her directly to the hospital. At their private gate she was introduced to a woman in a severe black and gold head scarf and designer sunglasses pushed back on her head. She introduced herself as Maryam, no last name, and spent little time coordinating with the representative's wife before ushering Caitlin through customs to a black sedan.

The windows of the car were smoked to near-opacity and Caitlin wondered during their half-hour ride whether she was supposed to pretend she was not really there, or that the city was not there around her. Maryam, sharing the backseat with her, only gave Caitlin's form a once-over before spending the rest of the ride on her phone in Farsi.

Caitlin glimpsed what she could through the windows and briefly mourned what she would not be able to do on this trip. Under any other circumstance she would have treasured the opportunity to see Tehran, a city she'd long hoped to explore. As it was, the driver used only expressways and the city didn't seem that different from any other. There were wider avenues than in New York, shorter buildings but with more massive proportions, something broader about the windows, fewer glass fronts. But she didn't have the time to move closer and really look.

The expressway passed near a boulevard that was crammed sidewalk to sidewalk with people. The color green was prominent in banners and she could hear the chanting roar from the gathering.

"A protest?" she asked, though Maryam was still on the phone.

"Yes," Maryam said. "Economic. The women bus drivers have not been paid in a month."

But to Caitlin's ears, the protest had sounded much more aggressive than that. She wondered whether here, too, people were feeling the tensions of a world on edge.

They merged onto a slightly smaller highway and greenery increased between the buildings. A handful of men and women stood together in a small park, moving slowly through a Tai Chi sequence. Caitlin was mildly shocked to see this Chinese practice in Iran, and the sliding and angular arm motions instantly reminded her of Maanik and Gaelle's movements.

A possible Mongolian connection right there, she thought as the sedan pulled in at the hospital. Connecting Mongolian to Chinese would certainly be a smaller step than tying Mongolian to Viking.

At the hospital, Maryam sat with her in reception while Caitlin quickly Skyped Jacob. Dressed in his pajamas and eating a Popsicle, the boy barely signed to her with one hand.

Finally she said, "Jacob, I want you to understand something. It's very important. The young man I'm visiting—he might die. That's why I had to come."

Jacob didn't say much, but he seemed to snap back to his usual, empathetic self and he blew her two kisses before ending the chat.

When the tablet closed, Maryam escorted Caitlin to Atash's floor. Their entrance to Atash's room was barred by a doctor who was not impressed with two female visitors—until Maryam held up a card that looked like an ID. The doctor did not miraculously develop a sense of courtesy, but he did walk away.

"I will also interpret for you," Maryam said as they entered the hospital room.

Caitlin had not expected the sight that greeted them. She knew the young man had suffered third-degree burns over three-quarters of his body and would be fully swathed in bandages. She knew he was being kept alive by an array of vascular tubes and catheters. None of that surprised her. But Caitlin had not anticipated his trying to turn toward her, from the shoulders, when she entered the room.

"Does he know you?" Maryam asked.

"No . . . ," Caitlin replied, a trace of hesitation in her voice, though she did not know why.

Caitlin did not approach the bed from the side but circled it, seeing if his movements would follow her. They did. Her heart ached for the boy and for his circumstances. She recognized the flowerless, impersonal feel of an unvisited room, an unloved person, an abandonment far worse than the burns that had immobilized him.

He was not only awake, he was murmuring. Maryam leaned over his head to listen.

After a moment she said, "This is not Farsi."

"Do you recognize it?"

The young woman shook her head once, sharply.

A wave of fierce energy rushed through Caitlin—she knew what was coming next, why she had hesitated when asked if the boy knew her. She had been here before. Not in this room, not with him, but with Maanik and Gaelle.

Atash's hands moved as much as the bolsters allowed him. His left arm trembled to the shoulder as the hand fought to point away from his body. His right hand moved up diagonally, just inches but enough for Caitlin to recognize one of Maanik's superlatives.

She pulled out her cell phone and held it up to record the gestures.

"No!" Maryam snapped.

"Please, this may help him! Someone else has to see—"

"No, absolutely." She was not demonstrative about her insistence, simply firm in a way that told Caitlin there was no point in arguing. She suspected this was a rule meant to benefit not the patient but the paranoia of a totalitarian regime.

She stowed her cell phone, leaned over Atash, and listened. There were the guttural consonants, the whirring of Asiatic "r"s.

"Ask him to speak in Farsi, please," she said.

Maryam leaned forward but before she finished the question Atash changed. His hands fixed rigidly and his utterances shifted in tone. The higher language disappeared, replaced by prolonged and very quiet grunts.

Caitlin felt her hands tighten helplessly. She knew the young man was in agony. She could only think of one way to communicate that might work, but both his hands were bandaged. She reached out with her left hand—the madame in Haiti had directed her to use her left hand with the snake; Jacob had sensed the ocean with his left—and lightly touched one of the only bare areas of Atash's skin, his throat.

Something exploded inside Caitlin's head. It was fast and heavy and pressed the sides of her skull outward, like the throb of a headache frozen painfully in place. Then it pushed through and was outside her body—pressure rolling around her, forcing her eyelids shut. She could not open her mouth to scream but she felt the cry in her throat.

She forced herself to open her eyes. The white of the walls, of the bandages, had been transformed into dark rock and ice—jagged towers of it coming into focus far behind the dark, rectangular columns that were in front of her. And a man, a pale young man, was communicating with hands and arms and strange but familiar words—leaning forward with urgency, begging, almost bowing with his pleading.

Caitlin couldn't understand. Her eardrums were throbbing from pressure that wrapped around her head, pressure that was closing her throat, blocking sound and breath.

The recent past, the present, her world and life were all out of focus. Wherever she was, whoever she was, whatever she was seeing, was rising before her with razor-edged clarity.

And suddenly the words became familiar. The columned structure, vast and high, was known to her. The buildings beyond, dark among patches of lavender and green foliage, were places she had seen. And farther away, those peaks that looked less like mountains than like explosions of ice—

She was looking through eyes that were not her own at a world that was not her own. The pale young man pleaded with her from the floor.

"Save my brother, save me! Please! Show us how!"

"I am no longer Guardian to him or to you," she said in the voice of an old man, unable to control the words coming from her own throat. *"You put your faith in things that have no true power. You have crafted your own fate."*

"We will repent, we will speak the cazh*!"*

"No," she replied sadly. *"You will die."*

The speaker turned away and the young man propelled himself up from the floor and ran away into the street. Her body hurried to join the other robed figures near the columns a dozen or so yards away, their arms raised toward the dark skies. Her sleeves heavy with oil, she lifted her hands to complete the prayer of *cazh* and let out a howling scream. Her hands were suddenly on fire, her fingers whirling to pieces in the air even as she signed a word, the only word she could manage, a superlative for "transform."

There was another scream and suddenly Caitlin was on the floor. Not a stone floor but a hospital floor.

"Dr. O'Hara!"

Caitlin opened her eyes to see Maryam's face hovering over her. Her head felt exceedingly light, her hands excessively warm, her brain extraordinarily confused. For a moment it was as if she had forgotten how to speak.

"You screamed," Maryam said.

"I—no. No."

There was no point in even attempting to explain. She wasn't sure she *could* explain, since she didn't entirely understand it herself. Caitlin pulled away from Maryam and shoved herself up from the floor, grabbing the railing of Atash's bed. She was reeling.

"It was Atash," Caitlin gasped.

"What are you saying?"

Caitlin fell silent. As with the snake in Haiti, she had been through something Atash was experiencing. She looked down at the young man. His fixed, red-rimmed eyes were staring at a corner of the ceiling. A tear was sliding down his cheek, and a line of blood trailed from his mouth down over his chin. She reached for his throat with her right hand, searching for a pulse . . .

"You'd better call for the doctor," Caitlin said sadly.

"What is it?"

"He's dead," she replied.

CHAPTER 27

Caitlin sat in reception again, a spartan room with religious symbols on the walls. Maryam was on her cell phone, sitting under a brass scimitar suspended point-up. An overhead light effected a glow.

Her hands and forearms heavy, Caitlin opened her tablet but stared at the dark screen. She knew she should Skype her father or Barbara, even Ben, but what she had witnessed—no, what she had *experienced*—had knocked her numb.

A part of her didn't want to stop the numbness. Atash's pain had joined Maanik and Gaelle's with a ferocious intensity and she felt guilty for not having come here days earlier when she might have been able to . . . do something. Maybe she could have worked with him in stages, used hypnosis, something to mediate between him and the vision. Now he was dead, and he had died in torment.

Then fear suffused the numbness. *Did his death in the vision cause his death in body?* If so, Maanik and Gaelle were in *mortal* danger. She began to shake.

A hand dropped on her shoulder but she did not respond. Then the hand turned her chin so that she was looking into Maryam's hazel eyes. They were softer than she had seen them before now.

"Dr. O'Hara, you must focus."

Caitlin nodded blankly.

"Doctor, I am not a woman who selects what she sees. I see everything. When your hand was on the young man I saw your head moving. Not like this." She nodded her head back and forth, then gestured at Caitlin's Hermès scarf. "Your head moved as if, beneath the scarf, your hair was alive."

Her words to Ben—about Maanik's hair justifying this trip—came back to her. So did a little bit of life. "Go on," said Caitlin.

Maryam stared at her. "You do not seem surprised."

"Strangely, no," she admitted. "Please, what else did you see?"

Maryam regarded her skeptically.

"Please," Caitlin pleaded. "It's all helpful information."

Maryam sat beside her. "When you fell backward, this came forward." The young woman touched a strand of hair that had loosened from Caitlin's scarf and was framing her face. "I watched it move as if a wind had caught it, but the windows were closed, there was no fan, no breeze. I am not an imaginative woman, doctor. I saw this."

"I believe you," Caitlin said. "There are things going on that I do not understand. That's why I came here."

"I know this now, so I am going to take you to see someone. We have enough time before your flight tonight."

Caitlin's mind cleared slightly. "Is this a polite way of saying that I am under arrest?"

Maryam smiled and discreetly looked around the room. "Doctor, if that were the case you would not have to ask."

The young woman pressed her fingers on Caitlin's palm. Caitlin noticed that the back of Maryam's hand was grayish, very wrinkled, almost blistered in places. It was a hand that, some time ago, had been badly burned.

"I was a girl during the war with Iraq," she said. "I was once a patient here."

Caitlin met her gaze and thought of the fortitude it must have taken for this woman to accompany her, whether by order or voluntarily, to return to this place of pain, sadness, and fear. Caitlin squeezed her hand gently. "Go on."

"There is more you should see while you are here."

Maryam rose and Caitlin followed her to the waiting sedan.

Forty-five minutes later they pulled up in front of a low, concrete apartment building. Caitlin followed Maryam into one of the apartments and was seated in a living room with sparse furniture and a flowered bedsheet for a curtain. She heard gentle clinks from what must have been the kitchen and became vaguely aware that Maryam was not beside her. Opposite Caitlin on the pale green wall was an elaborate design rising from the floor and flowering in red over the expanse—dots, starbursts, wheels like eyes, flourishing feathers. It was like a *mehndi* design, an adornment painted in henna on Hindu women's hands before a wedding.

And jasmine—she was suddenly aware of the strikingly familiar smell of jasmine tea as it wafted up to her. A cup and saucer had been placed on the low table. The aroma loosened the tension that had built behind her eyes, and unexpectedly, tears began flowing down her face.

"A cup of tears," said a soft male voice beside her after she gasped several long sobs. "In some cultures, there are sacred vessels that permit us to mourn."

Caitlin wiped her eyes with the palms of her hands and took a deep, shuddering breath.

"Is it always jasmine?" Caitlin asked as she composed herself.

"It is whatever it needs to be," he answered.

Beside her stood a small Indian man with graying hair, somewhere in his sixties. He had remarkably lopsided ears and a gentleness in his eyes that made him seem instantly friendly.

"I am Vahin," he said with a smile that warmed and comforted her.

"I'm Caitlin," she replied. She looked around. "Where is Maryam?"

"She is outside," he said, taking a seat in a shabby armchair opposite her. "The dear lady and I have very different business in this city but she . . . crossed lines, shall we say? She thought you and I should speak."

"I'm grateful to you both. What do you do, Vahin?"

"I am something like a clergyman to the Hindu community."

"Forgive me, but are you allowed to do that here?"

"We have a small community in and around the city," he said. "Iran allows us our religious freedom and India allows her resident Shia Muslims to visit Iran. It is a mutually beneficial relationship."

"If you like living at the stress point between two vastly different cultures," she said.

"Some of us have that calling." He smiled mysteriously. "But now, to your situation. Tell me what your tears told the cup. Omit nothing."

While Vahin sipped his tea Caitlin told him everything, not just about Atash but about Maanik and Gaelle, the Norse and Mongolian connections, Jack London's reactions, and her own glimpses of impossible visions. Vahin sat quietly throughout, nodding now and then, and occasionally dipping his head to one side.

"So," said Caitlin upon finishing, "how crazy does that all sound to you?"

"Not at all," Vahin replied. "You seem to feel that because you cannot rationalize what you have experienced it is therefore irrational. That is not the case. We do not blame words for being insufficient to express new ideas. We simply find better words. Do you know who put forth that idea?"

Caitlin shook her head.

"The Norse," he told her.

"Vikings," she said, starting slightly.

"Yes. They understood that the energy that binds us, one to the other, was manifest in each of us as thought . . . and thought as language. But it was what you would call a two-way street. If you changed the words you could change the way you thought about the energy." He rose and carried their cups into the kitchen, and Caitlin heard again the sounds of making tea. She decided to follow, and as she entered the room he smiled and continued. "In 1984, I traveled to Bhopal just after the Union Carbide tragedy. Do you remember that?"

"I do," she said. "The factory that accidentally released the poison-
ous gas."

"The factory was making a pesticide. The gas spread through the
slums surrounding the factory and thousands upon thousands of people died. It was most ghastly. I was part of the local clergy asked to
help relocate the orphans of this disaster. I kept track of my orphans
and visited them when I could over the years." He placed another cup
of tea in Caitlin's hands. "A fresh cup." He smiled. "No tears."

"Thank you." Caitlin smiled back as she followed him back into
the living room. This time he joined her on the couch.

"As to why Maryam brought you here. We have a mutual friend,
one of the children in my care who was in the hospital with her. For
many decades after the Bhopal tragedy, he spoke in tongues. It was
involuntary, in no way linked with any religious ceremony. And she
has heard me tell of another child, a young girl, whose arms would
sometimes flare in a rash that looked like a chemical burn. The girl
called it a *motu-cazh*."

His words caused Caitlin to start again. This time he noticed.

"You've heard that?" Vahin asked.

"The second part sounded familiar," she said.

"Well, I disagreed with a psychologist who was part of my group.
He argued that it resembled stigmata, a physiological expression of
psychological distress. I thought it was much more."

Caitlin drank her tea and waited patiently. Vahin seemed to be
searching for the words to express his thoughts precisely. Finally, he
leaned forward and set his tea on the table.

"Let me first tell you something that is clear to me," he continued.
"The left-hand, right-hand activity you mentioned. With your left
hand you collected enormous force from the snake, with the right
hand you pushed a girl against a wall without touching her. That is
the natural flow of things."

"To become superhuman?"

"No," he said patiently. "To be a conduit for the energy of the universe. The left hand receives energy, the right hand emits it. This is very old knowledge from Tantric Buddhism. It is similar to chi energy among the Shaolin monks in China."

He cupped his hands around an invisible sphere and pushed it toward Caitlin. A subtle sensation of warmth washed over her throat.

"I—I *felt* that," she marveled.

He continued. "Buddhism, Hinduism, the Vedas, Chinese Taoism, Tai Chi, the paganism that fathered the Viking faiths—the seeds of our minds were not planted in straight rows with walls between them. Every culture has discovered this same phenomenon of energy, both inside of us and surrounding us, all the while connecting us."

"You mentioned Tai Chi," Caitlin said, remembering the men and women from the park.

"Tai Chi is an example of great strength used to empower, not to destroy." He moved his hands in a way that reminded Caitlin of Maanik's gestures. "Movement stirs the energy inside our bodies and it also opens us to energy from the outside. When those two energies merge we are enlightened, uplifted."

"Are you talking about life energy or—the soul?" she asked, not entirely comfortable using the latter term.

"Both."

"Something that survives death."

He nodded once and pointed to the tea on the table. "When the leaves are gone, the scent remains in the air . . . and in the mind. It is rekindled, the memory is refreshed, when new tea is brewed. So it is with the soul. With death, the soul hovers until it finds a new body."

"Hovers how? Where?" Caitlin challenged. "Limbo? Heaven?"

"I prefer to call it the transpersonal plane," he replied. "As to where?" He paused and gestured simply "out there."

Caitlin sighed. "I have problems with that idea."

"Much of the world, throughout history, has embraced some form of that concept."

"I mean no disrespect, but there are still flat-earthers too," she said.

He smiled benignly. "Tell me why *you* reject it."

She collected her thoughts. "I don't believe in a cosmic score-keeper. That seems to be the general conception of God, with heaven as a reward for subjective behavior that changes from culture to culture. I also don't believe that a soul is a kind of immaterial flash drive where things get stored and then dumped into—"

She stopped herself.

"Yes?" Vahin smiled. "A waiting body? A body weakened by injury or trauma, a body hungry for strong, healing energy?"

Caitlin shook her head. "No. I don't accept it. That isn't what's happening."

"Self-immolation. A father almost assassinated. A stepmother's near-drowning. The loss of parents in a horrible mass poisoning."

"That's trauma and natural human empathy," Caitlin said. "I see it all the time. Obviously, *I'm* feeling it, yet I haven't suffered a trauma."

"Haven't you? Haven't you shared the traumas of these children?"

"As I said, empathy. That's not the same as experiencing it first-hand."

"In fact, your experience could in some ways be worse," he suggested. "You are collecting these experiences and internalizing them. They may be massing exponentially."

Okay, she thought. *He could be right about that.* Caitlin had always kept a strong emotional connection out of the doctor-patient equation. These kids had broken through that.

"But you are missing the point," Vahin went on. "You are trying to explain *away* before I can explain."

"I'm sorry," she said quickly, "I truly am. I'm being—well, I'm doing what I always do. Forgive me. Please enlighten me."

Vahin took a moment to consider his approach. "I believe that the common link between these children you have met is trauma, but not just their own trauma."

"What are you saying?" Caitlin asked. "That there is something else that links them?"

He nodded.

"Your transpersonal plane? The place that's all around us?" she guessed, still unconvinced.

"You doubt," Vahin said. "But accept, for a moment, the truth of what I say. Think of the bond those three children's souls would instantly share. Then multiply that by the countless souls you have not personally met. What else could cause them to experience that level of anguish?"

The suffering implicit in the nightmarish math of that prospect gave her a chill. "All right," Caitlin said. "Let's say for the sake of argument that there *are* traumatized souls somewhere else—let's call it your transpersonal plane. The assaults I've witnessed would suggest that these 'countless' souls are opportunistically seeking souls inside the bodies of traumatized youths."

"Correct."

"So assuming all of that to be true, why are these loud, aggressive souls getting stronger now?"

"That I cannot say."

Caitlin sat back hopelessly.

"But as you seek understanding," Vahin went on, "keep this in mind. These 'aggressive souls,' as you call them, may be from one event, souls that are already powerfully linked."

"One event? But where?"

"The transpersonal plane is boundless. Do not seek them somewhere else. Look for them some*when* else."

CHAPTER 28

Maanik and her mother stood bundled in their winter coats, watching the morning sun from the penthouse balcony. As the golden rays warmed their faces, the young woman said, "It feels almost like summer."

Hansa, shivering, hugged her daughter close, happy that she was feeling *anything*. This was an unexpected blessing after the difficulties of the last two days. Her husband had barely been home since the attack at Jammu. This morning when Hansa woke, he had already left again. Maanik had awakened early as well. Hansa found her lying on her side, absently stroking Jack London, and she had readily agreed to come outside.

"What do you think?" Hansa asked, looking across the long balcony, wanting to savor the time with her. "We could do some home-schooling out here, catch up on some of your homework."

Her daughter seemed to be smiling, her head tilted toward the sun, her eyes shut.

"Maanik?"

"Yes?"

"What do you think about that?"

Maanik moved slowly in her natural spotlight. "I'm sorry?"

"Homeschooling, out here."

"I like it," she replied.

Hansa gave her a little squeeze and began to rearrange the chairs, pulling a couple of large potted plants out of the way. She was startled to see how weak she had become and resolved to start her walking routine again.

"Maanik, how do you think I would do on your father's Nordic-Track?"

Maanik laughed.

"Do you think that's funny?" her mother asked, smiling. "Maybe when you're feeling better, you can teach me."

"It makes me tired."

"That machine? You can outrun your father."

"I'm going back to bed," Maanik said.

"Don't you want to stay out here a little longer? You look so happy here."

"I want to lie down." Suddenly, she sounded frail.

Hansa walked toward her. "Let me help—"

"I can do it."

The woman watched as Maanik disappeared behind the shining glass of the terrace door. Then she continued rearranging the furniture, in case Maanik missed the fresh air and chose to return.

From inside, Jack London howled. Hansa dropped the chair she was moving and ran toward Maanik's bedroom. The girl was still in the hallway, blocked by the barking dog, who, facing the open bedroom door, was making short, tentative bounds forward, then skittering backward as if trying both to attack the entry and avoid it.

"Jack London, quiet!" Hansa yelled.

He partly obeyed, his yelps becoming low growls. Hansa turned toward her daughter.

"No!" she cried.

Maanik's left arm had stiffened and her right hand had extended.

"Maanik, stay with me," she implored.

The dog began to bark again.

"Quiet!" Hansa yelled.

Kamala arrived, roused by the commotion.

"Take him away!" Hansa snapped.

Kamala edged around them, reaching for the beagle. Maanik made a swift, sweeping motion with her right hand in the air and without being touched, Jack London flew across the floor and hit the wall to their right. His howling turned into tiny frightened yips and he cowered low by the wall where he'd been thrown.

"Maanik!" Hansa grabbed at her daughter's left shoulder and spun her around.

Maanik's eyes were shut, her expression relaxed. She slipped from her mother's grip, heading toward the bedroom door.

"Don't go in there!" Hansa shrieked, and tried to pull her back, tried to turn her to face away from the bedroom. Maanik stiffened and shook her off. Hansa gasped as blood dripped down her daughter's wrists and along her fingers, even though her arms were still bandaged under her coat. Maanik's eyes opened and she began walking backward, lifting her hands and rubbing her forearms as she gazed stonily at her mother. Hansa followed her into the bedroom, reaching toward her child's ear, but Maanik jerked away.

"Stop!" Hansa cried, and again reached for Maanik's ear.

"You cannot take me back," Maanik said.

"From where? Please talk to me!"

"When she burns, I burn," Maanik said. "I have to go so it will stop."

"Go where?" Hansa pleaded. She was trying to think like Dr. O'Hara, trying to get information.

"Up," Maanik said. "That is the only escape."

"Up where?" Hansa asked, trembling as they moved farther into the foul air of the bedroom.

"Beyond . . . *fera-cazh*."

"Where . . . *what* is '*fera-cazh*'?"

Maanik's answer was a full-throated scream followed by the ritual clawing at her arms. Hansa tried to hug her but once again Maanik twisted out of reach, backing against the bed. Making a concerted effort to reach her ear, Hansa practically yanked her daughter's arm to her side—and was thrown back. Staggering, she saw a plume of smoke rising from the bed. Hansa circled, frantic, and only then saw that it was coming not from the bed but from the bottom of Maanik's nightdress, under her coat. With a hiss, another plume rose from near one of the girl's pockets. Maanik's hair was lifting into the air, rising not unlike the smoke trails—and Hansa realized she smelled burning hair. She violently slapped her daughter's hands aside, plunged her fingers toward Maanik's ear, and shouted, "Blackberries!"

Maanik wobbled on her feet but did not stop screaming or slapping at her arms. "Let—me—burn!" she choked out, before the seeming anguish of physical pain took over her voice again and she wailed.

Smoke rose from Maanik's left hand as a black spot spread across her skin. Hansa was trying to reach for it when suddenly Maanik spun and ran for the tall bedroom window. She slammed up the latch, flung open the sash, and with her bare hands struck and clawed at the screen beyond in an effort to shred it. Hansa shouted at her, grabbed at her, and struggled to keep a hold on her, but she didn't stop. Maanik punctured the black mesh and pulled at the ragged hole with both hands, making a large opening. Hansa screamed for Kamala's help as five black patches opened on the back of Maanik's coat, smoke coiling toward the ceiling. Then just as suddenly, Maanik thrust her hand onto the upper frame of the window and, searching with her foot for the lower frame, hoisted herself up.

Hansa felt a surge of power and adrenaline unlike anything she had ever experienced. Vaulting forward, she grabbed Maanik around the waist and wrenched her from the open window. They tumbled to the floor. She quickly pulled the lower edge of Maanik's coat up over her daughter's back and head and yanked it down so that her head and arms were encased. Hugging Maanik firmly, she dragged her across the bedroom to the doorway. Maanik struggled and kicked and Hansa could hear her screaming—once more in the language she did not understand. The woman wanted to vomit from fear but the noxious odor from her daughter's hair and the impossible heat of her body kept her focused. Kamala finally arrived in the room with scratches evident from a struggle with the dog. Together they manhandled Maanik down the hall to the small bathroom with a stand-up shower. Dragging the young woman into the tiny cubicle, Hansa slammed her hand on the water lever and cold water flooded down on them. While Kamala peeled the girl's clothes from her struggling body, Hansa maneuvered a hand into the mêlée, pinched the girl's ear, and shouted, "Blackberries!"

Maanik went limp.

CHAPTER 29

Maryam walked Caitlin to her Iran Air departure gate. It was a surprisingly emotional parting, given how little time the women had spent together, but what they had witnessed had altered them both.

Caitlin stepped into the queue for boarding. Almost immediately she got a text from Ben: *M deteriorating. Fire a real hazard.*

The person behind her clucked her tongue; the queue had moved but she had not. Caitlin stepped to the side.

Juggling her phone, ticket, passport, and a letter from the Iranian ambassador providing clearance to go home, she typed back: *I have new info. I'll come straight from airport.*

She waited; no response. She considered calling Ben but knew the explanations would not make a short conversation. Final boarding was called. Caitlin, last in line, hurriedly presented her ticket and was waved in.

Iran Air, it turned out, did not allow its passengers to use their cell phones or access the Internet during flights. That was frustrating; Caitlin knew that for thirteen hours she would wonder what Ben meant by "real hazard." Had Maanik tried to set herself on fire like Atash? Negotiations be damned: if Maanik had harmed herself beyond scraping her forearms, Mrs. Pawar wouldn't have waited. The girl would already be in the hospital—she would at this moment be drugged into an overmedicated automaton, and that would be the end of the exploration into what was truly happening to her.

Hold on, Caitlin urged Maanik in her head. *Hold on till I'm back.*

Of course she didn't believe Maanik would hear that, and yet the impulse did not seem so crazy after all she had experienced.

What if Vahin is right? If Maanik's mind was open to this "transpersonal plane," and Caitlin herself had some access to it as well, wasn't it conceivable that a message *could* pass from her to Maanik? Vahin had speculated that Caitlin may have acquired access because she had placed herself in such close psychic proximity to the affected young adults.

"Vibrations," he had said to her, pressing pamphlets and booklets into her hands before she left. "Each of us is like a tuning fork that does not stop. Like the tea, the soul vibrates and survives outside the body, outside of time. In life, we change pitch and resonate with each other, sometimes in pairs, sometimes in groups. Why should the soul be different?" He added in parting, "There are those of us who believe it is the purpose of all life to achieve a complete resonance—all of us as one."

"Make me one with everything." Caitlin found herself muttering the oft-mocked phrase of Eastern mystics.

"New-agey" was the expression that came to mind. Yet everything she had seen, the gestures and words, the shared symbol, the reactions of the animals, was exactly that: new-agey, mystical, quasireligious, fantastic. Choose the outré word that fit. But she could not disavow any of it, from the floating hair and fabric to the shock waves to the visions. Those were a part of that strange reality Vahin advocated. What made his explanation less valid than any other?

Caitlin mentally reviewed the signs along the road to this point.

The shared symbol drawn by both Gaelle and Maanik seemed a good place to begin. If Atash had been able to use his hands, might he have drawn it too? Caitlin still found the triangles made of crescents to be inexplicable. They were slightly Celtic yet not. They vaguely resembled a radioactive symbol—but that could be a time-biased comparison, looking back from the present instead of looking *toward* the present. If this symbol were really as old as a habitable Antarctica, perhaps it had been the unconscious inspiration for the modern symbol?

Habitable Antarctica. The thought had occurred to her so easily. She remembered the apparent map Maanik had drawn. When they reviewed its shape and topography, it linked closely to a map of Antarctica as though surveyed from the air. Could people have flown that long ago? Caitlin had seen ice in the vision with Atash—was that *also* Antarctica? Perhaps an ancient someone had traveled above it by balloon? She thought back to one of Jacob's science experiments. All that would have required were thermal currents somehow directed into a big sheath of—what? Pelts? Leather?

Too heavy.

Animal tissue? In the past, whales had been harvested for nearly every part of their body. Thin tissue, sinew, skin—was *that* possible?

The word "fantastic" came back to her. Maybe she was making leaps—but nothing else came close to making sense.

Antarctica. A different time, a different climate. With *people*? Humans? A society, a civilization? What else could it be? There was a sophisticated language of words and gestures. She thought of all the stories and fables she had heard in her life, from Noah and the flood to the Greek myth of Icarus. Even scholars had always said there was probably a foundation to our most exotic tales.

The first thing she would do when she had Internet again would be to search for any cataclysms that had occurred at the South Pole over the millennia, right back to Pangaea if necessary. The patients had mentioned fire from the sky and something about a wave. There had to be some connection. Her mind might be arguing against it, but that's what minds did. Her gut was telling her this was the right direction.

The plane banked left and Caitlin watched through her window as the Caspian Sea tilted back into view, sparkling in the late afternoon sun. She closed her eyes and recalled her conversation with Ben in the park in Turtle Bay. Her breath fluttered at the thought of him. She decided to talk to him, to ask to start over when the immediate crises subsided.

If they subsided.

She thought of poor Maanik wobbling through the hallways of a psych ward, drugged to oblivion. She contemplated the larger populace struggling thirty thousand feet below, constantly at war or at the mercy of an unstable climate and formidable geology. What if Vahin was correct? What if some *ancient race* was correct: that the vibration of souls, their continuation out of the body, was the way to truly survive? What if, in some ancient theology, there lay the common, long-lost origins of Valhalla and the Elysian Fields and Heaven?

The transpersonal plane.

Caitlin focused again. More than anything else, she wanted to communicate with Maanik, tell her *I'm still with you, distance be damned.* Vahin said they were connected. Could she send a thought to Maanik? How? What kind of wave could she make that would touch the girl?

She tried to relax her thoughts. She recalled the park, with Ben. Sunshine, unbuttoning their coats. Ben exuberantly describing the words he had deciphered from Maanik's gibberish. "Fire," of course, and "sky," but also "water."

Big water.

And then, suddenly, Caitlin had it. Atash had tried to form the superlative when she entered his hospital room—left hand angling away from the body, right hand crossing up the body on a diagonal. She didn't remember the spoken word that went with it but she didn't need to. The gesture had to be enough.

She closed her eyes and calmed herself as completely as if she were about to guide a client into hypnosis. She thought of Jack London first, the beagle barometer, remembered him sleeping and snoring. Then she thought of Maanik. She sifted through their moments together, remembered when Maanik had made a face for her, when she had seemed most like her normal teenage self. When she saw the girl clearly, when she felt the laugh they'd shared, Caitlin gently angled her left hand away from her torso and crossed her right hand up toward her left shoulder. Unexpectedly her lungs took a deep inhale and then exhaled—it felt as though she had pushed a physical weight away from her sternum, off her left shoulder. She kept her mind on Maanik and thought to her:

Ocean . . . big water . . . you and me together . . . hold on . . .

Suddenly Caitlin heard Maanik in her head, heard the girl say: *"I will."*

Caitlin opened her eyes, shocked. She hadn't imagined that voice. That had been *real*.

She looked around, at the quiet passengers in the plane, at the empty aisle seat beside her. Everything was normal—but not. She felt closer to Maanik here, now, than she did to the window beside her. In that moment, the familiar sights and sounds of life were no longer a reliable foundation. Like the sea far below, they were just the surface of something greater. Perhaps *that* was the comprehensive explanation.

Caitlin was startled to feel the effects of that realization in her body. It was as though she were energized from her feet all the way up. Her torso felt bright, almost radiant; her mind was clear as the tone of a tuning fork; and she was ravenous. She rang for the hostess and asked for the menu.

Something had clicked into place, though Caitlin didn't know what.

Over dinner, she devoured the materials Vahin had given her. She read about the combined power of souls, of prayer. Connected in the transpersonal plane, souls could form a powerful group spirit capable of ascending even higher, outside the reach of time, space . . . and death.

A cataclysm, she thought. Fire, ice, floods. A city or civilization beset by a volcano, an earthquake, a tsunami, encroaching ice. Caitlin remembered Maanik crying in their first session over an arm that had been ripped off and her dead pet that was not Jack London. Maybe that had happened to Maanik's counterpart in some ancient place— before that counterpart had died, burned to pieces by volcanic fire or an inferno caused by tremors.

But Maanik had said that she also became pieces first and *then* burned. What pieces? And how?

Okay, we'll come back to that, Caitlin thought, forcing herself to stay focused despite the mental lull caused by her full stomach.

She thought about Atash's vision. Other residents of the city seemed not only prepared for the cataclysm but eager for it. Instead of running away from an erupting volcano, these people in robes gathered in a courtyard of columns, apparently waiting to die. Eager to die? Robes that were soaked in oil; a reference to *cazh*; a word and gesture meaning what? Some kind of transformation.

Those residents—Caitlin had seen them. They had a ritual they were determined to complete. Whether that rite was done to thwart the volcano or honor it in the hope of pacifying it, she wasn't sure. But if Vahin was correct, perhaps the ritual had transported their souls to the transpersonal plane, whatever it was. Their souls left as their physical bodies burned to fine ash. Maanik's consciousness split into fragments and lifted up as her physical body burned.

Presumably then, the souls that reached the transpersonal plane were ensured not a life after death, but life beyond the reach of death.

But why have Maanik and Gaelle and Atash connected with that? Shared trauma here and now cannot be the only reason.

Those prayerful residents in robes had denied help to Atash's counterpart. Why had they excluded him? They had accused him of placing faith in "things without true power" and said that he had crafted his own fate. She thought of people she had seen in war zones, those who had tried to leave and those who had gathered in a place of worship and perished—difficult choices made under duress, but with the same goal.

Escape.

Then there was her father and the Norse-style longboat. Caitlin remembered Maanik talking about a dragon, perhaps a carved dragon head on a ship? Some residents may have taken to the sea, trying desperately to sail away as fire fell on an ocean already lashing them with steep waves. Atash's counterpart may have quailed at that choice. So he had begged the robed man to save his brother through *cazh* instead, turning to religion as a last resort. Rebuffed by the priest, Atash's counterpart had done the ritual without the help or sanction of the priests—and it seemed to have worked. Thousands of years later, with Antarctica long buried under ice, he had found Atash's soul, exposed by the trauma of his brother's execution, and somehow made his way in.

But why would that cause Atash to set himself alight? Had the soul given him the wrong message? Or—and the thought made Caitlin choke up—had that soul been trapped in that traumatic moment like some prehistoric insect preserved in amber, all this time.

Too many broad strokes, she thought, *but a start. A place to go with Maanik.*

Caitlin leaned back, shut her exhausted eyes, and tried not to think of Atash locked in a burning body for millennia. She thought of the animals instead. What was their role in this? Jack London had to be aware of the presence of something unseen. What about his avoiding his mistress's right hand? One of Vahin's booklets said that energy from the world around us entered through the left hand, the heart hand. Then, filtered by the body and soul, negative, unwanted energy exited through the right hand. Maanik's left hand on Jack London would have safely received his loving energy. But her right hand would have been emitting all the suffering her counterpart felt in the transpersonal plane. No wonder the dog had avoided it.

As animals had avoided Washington Square—Caitlin suddenly re-membered the news reports just after the rats stampeded. A resident of the area had been briefly interviewed about how her black Lab would no longer enter the dog run in Washington Square Park, and neither would anyone else's dogs. Yet there had been no mention of the dogs avoiding their owners, only the location, and the behavior of the rats certainly didn't resemble Jack London's reactions. If there was a connection here, it was not apparent.

Some possible answers—more seemingly impossible questions. But at the very least, they all seemed to be pointing in the same direc-tion. Her mind didn't tell her this in isolation, the way it usually did—her whole self told her. She felt again the bright radiance in her sternum.

Her meal finished and cleared, Caitlin turned off her light, lifted her window shade, and leaned her head against the seat. Her eyes rested on the clouds, the deepening dusk.

Shared souls, shared trauma, she thought. *If this is happening to other young people around the world, that might explain why Kashmir is rippling through those of us who don't even know where it is. But is Kashmir causing this?*

That didn't seem likely. Yet a connection was possible. Kashmir: a locus of frustration and pain touching all the ends of the earth. The transpersonal plane: a locus of ancient pain touching all the ends of the earth.

It no longer seemed possible to her to accept one and deny the other.

CHAPTER 30

When the call came in from Mikel, Flora Davies was sound asleep on the chair in her office. Weary in mind, body, and soul, she had surrendered herself to the black leather.

Still jet-lagged despite a long rest, Mikel had wandered back to the club at four in the morning to take another look at the new artifact. He found Arni's body in a pool of unsightly fluid and immediately called upstairs for Flora. They had at least three hours to erase the problem before any other Group members or staff came in for the day, and before anyone was likely to report Arni to Missing Persons. Friends and family knew that he was inclined to work late, especially when there was a problem to be solved.

The Group had never dealt with a dead body at the club. Not human bodies at least. Unusual creatures had occasionally found their way into the lab for study, all deceased and partial specimens hauled from the south polar waters—part of a giant squid, a ten-thousand-year-old coelacanth perfectly preserved in frozen mud, the body of a baby megalodon locked in ancient ice. They were rare, but Flora stayed in contact with a man equipped to deal with their remains. She located the contact on her phone and within minutes Casey Skett was literally running over from his walk-up in the East Village.

After hanging up, Flora went back downstairs and paced near Arni's head while Mikel looked for clues about his death. She was cursing the Group through the disposable medical mask she had put on, angry that they did not have the equipment or personnel suitable to perform a fast autopsy.

"And look at that—Arni wasn't even wearing his lab coat," she railed. "God only knows what contaminants his body is adding to the environment."

"You mean apart from liquefied brain tissue?" Mikel asked. He was also masked and kneeling beside the corpse.

She stopped pacing. "Is that what you think that is?"

"Judging by the color and small lumps of solid mass, I'd say so."

"Lovely," Flora said. "Nothing else unusual?"

"Not that I can see. Only the brain is where it shouldn't be."

She snatched latex gloves from a box on a shelf and began pawing over Arni's table—an insufferable mess—until she found a glass stirring rod. Then, squatting beside the corpse's head, she inserted the end of the rod into his left nostril.

"It looks like he was about to be mummified," Mikel muttered. "Brain out, organs next."

"His other organs still appear to be inside," she observed.

"Maybe I scared off whoever was doing this."

"This liquid has a film forming on top," she said, referring to the pool that spread like a halo from Arni's head. "He's been this way for a while."

"But you didn't hear anything?"

"Soundproofing," she said, while paying acute attention to the shape of Arni's nasal cavity. Flora twisted and turned the glass rod until all but the half inch she was holding had disappeared up his nose into his skull.

"My god," she said, marveling, "there's no sinus wall, no sphenoid bone. Mikel, there is *nothing* up there."

"Are you saying everything in his skull came out of his nose?" he said in a tone of total disbelief.

"Would you like to feel it?" She motioned with the end of the glass rod.

"No," he said, wincing slightly. "What would do that to some of his cranial bones but not the whole skull?"

"Perhaps we haven't seen it all," Flora replied, setting the rod on the table. She touched Arni's head with the toe of her boot, half-expecting it to cave under the pressure. It did not. "Damn it," she said. "I hate a mystery without enough time to solve it."

As if on cue, Casey Skett arrived, still as skinny and slack-eyed as he had been a decade earlier when Flora first found him. Mikel went upstairs to admit him and they rode down in the elevator. Casey worked for the Department of Sanitation, "DAR" division—dead animal removal. He was good at his job, but Flora also appreciated his discretion and his connection to the shelters—specifically, the ones with incinerators. He lifted Arni's body into a refrigerator on wheels with its contents and shelves removed. If anyone happened to notice Casey wandering around the shelter before dawn, he would say he was cleaning up more of the dead, decaying rats that had been in the news—did they want to take a look inside?

Flora and Mikel then spent forty-five minutes triple-washing the floor and two agonizing hours scrutinizing every inch of the laboratory and the locker room for anything that might catch the eye of a police officer. Then Flora went ahead and scuffed and dirtied things up, so the lab didn't look too scrubbed.

When they were done, Mikel went about seeking a potential cause. He'd noticed hours ago that his carved meteorite was sitting on the table and the Geiger counter was out. He approached the object cautiously and waved the wand over it for several minutes but nothing happened. Finally, he picked it up, wrapped it in cloth, and strode to the safe to stow it.

"Not there," Flora said. "We're putting all the relics in the deep freezer."

"For what?"

"As a precaution," she replied.

"Don't you think you're overreacting?" Mikel asked.

"As my great-uncle Commander Hunt said during the Blitz, 'One cannot overreact to this.' Anyway, it's my prerogative."

"But we don't know that this or any of them had anything to do with Arni's death."

"We don't know they didn't."

"That argument is ridiculous," he said. "We have to try and reconstruct what he was doing—"

"And we will, after we've had a pause and a good think. I've read your report about the trip. There isn't a damned thing in this building that we know as little about."

His impatience evident, he held up his find. "Which is why we need this here, now. This has more writing than any of them. We can learn from it."

"We will," she said. "Please, Mikel—consider all that's happened already, the rats in Washington Square, the birds around your plane. Those phenomena all have artifact proximity and they began after this *thing* started its journey." She shook her head ruefully. "Arni was a synesthete. These objects may be connecting with animal and possibly human consciousness on some level. Perhaps there was something emitted by this rock at an inaudible frequency, triggered by a certain kind of light or sound, perhaps, for example, the electrical output of an airplane or a Geiger counter."

"The rats weren't anywhere near *my* artifact."

"They were not," she agreed. "But they came running here, to the collection. Which is why I want all the objects stowed and stabilized until we've examined this more thoroughly."

Mikel shook his head. "That's the reason we have to *keep* studying them *now*, Flora, *while* they are being influenced. And I mean, why freeze it? Why not superheat it?"

Flora snatched it from his hand.

"You're being a little extreme here," he said.

"Arni is dead!" she said, showing the first real sign of emotion.

"I'm sorry too but we have a bigger picture here," Mikel insisted, "a force we don't understand and that we haven't understood for a long damn time. Being able to read some of the symbols is one thing. We're getting pretty good at that. Understanding the mechanics of these objects is bigger."

"You don't think I know that?"

"Of course you do. Look, this thing has obviously been through tremendous heat before and survived. Arni didn't heat it—no burner. No cigarette lighter. I don't think we're going to know the full extent of its functionality until we start ruling things out."

Flora turned away. "It goes in the deep freezer with the rest, since we know that all of these artifacts have survived low temperatures for thousands of years without killing anyone, *and that's final.*"

"How do you know that?"

She half-turned. "What?"

"That they haven't killed anyone before?"

She hesitated for the briefest moment. "You're right. I don't know. All the more reason for caution." Then, without another word, she went to the locker, loaded all the objects onto a tray, and navigated to a room down the hall. She packed each item in a plastic bag and put them away. When she returned, Mikel was leaning on the wall outside the lab, pouting. She flicked off the light, slammed the door shut, and followed him up the stairs.

"Go home," she said. "Get some rest."

"I'm rested. I want to work."

"Then go to the library and read. Finish watching the videos Erika collected."

"Why are you being like this?"

"Like what?" she asked. "Thinking?"

Mikel said nothing as they neared the landing. The old stairs creaked as they ascended in the near-darkness. Upstairs the phone was already ringing. Mikel fielded the first call from the police. Arni had been reported missing at seven a.m. by a friend he was supposed to meet the night before, and the floodgates opened. Flora was glad she had put the artifacts away: only now it occurred to her that they may have been seized as evidence.

The rest of that day was filled with exhaustive questioning by an ill-tempered detective and with open and measurable concern for Arni while police inspected every corner of the laboratory space and locker room. Flora's mind was on the deep freezer but they only checked it and did not violate its contents.

Finally, at midnight she summoned Mikel from home and ordered him back to the Falklands.

"For what?" he asked, not displeased but surprised.

"I've thought," she announced. "Do whatever you have to do to get access to the crew of the *Captain Fallow*. Find out where they located your artifact. Where there was one, there may be more."

"We've been down that road before with other artifacts," he said.

"That's true," she agreed. "But as far as we know, they never caused any brains to melt. I think your artifact is too small to generate power on its own. So a theoretical external power source, the cause of this phenomenon, would likely be on the other end, where the artifact is from. It may still be connected with that source, if there is one, still charged somehow."

He agreed with her decision. Favors were called in, arrangements made. Thankfully, Flora's sleepless night and her genuine tears the following morning had convinced the detective on his second visit that she was worried sick about Arni.

And now here she was, alone with a cup of tea . . . and, literally, for now, at a cold, dead end to their quest. She lifted her teacup and hurled it at the wall, her mind burning with frustration and rage.

Goddamn it. Enough! she said to the mysterious race she had spent half her life pursuing. *If you have anything to say to me, say it bloody faster.*

CHAPTER 31

It was midnight. Outside Caitlin's cab the cloudy sky reflected orange from the lights of the city—a sight that had always struck her as ominous. It seemed more so now: danger felt imminent. The rattling of the taxi's undercarriage was like the world itself, barely holding itself together as it hurtled onward.

Or this could just be jet lag, she told herself.

She'd called her father while she waded through customs, but Jacob was asleep and she didn't want to wake him. As she waited in line at the curb, chilly and impatient, she read two texts Ben had sent while she was in the air. The first was sent at 7:41 p.m.: *Found possible Viking Mongolian connection.*

And then at 11:11 p.m.: *Am with Maanik. Stopped them from medicating her.*

She called and he picked up on the first ring. Whatever tension there was between them when she left for Iran was gone, at least from his voice.

"Tell me you're back—"

"I'm back," she said. "What happened?"

He hesitated.

"Ben, if anyone's listening—we're beyond that."

"Right. She lost it," Ben said. "She just went wild and tried to throw herself from the window. Mrs. Pawar said she started to *burn*. They put her in the shower. She slept for a while and then it was more talk and gesturing, your blackberries cue, sleep—and then the same all over again. The ambassador stepped out of negotiations again to be with her; I basically invented meetings to keep the delegates in the building. I just got here at ten. They're keeping her out of her bedroom and that seems to be calming her."

"Have you been in there?"

"I'm at the apartment—"

"No, the bedroom."

Another hesitation. "Yeah. Cai, it's strange."

"What is?"

"The room is dead," he said. "When I'm in there I don't hear the pipes in the ceiling, air traffic outside the window. The air is motionless, thin."

"Where's the dog?"

"In the hall outside the bedroom." Ben said. "Facing the door."

"Is he quiet?"

"Yes, but he's definitely on alert," Ben said. "What do you know?"

"I think that room has connected, through Maanik, to another time and place. They're sharing a space like twins sharing a womb, and the older one is feeding on the younger. The room is mirroring what's happening to Maanik's mind, almost like a portal."

"Caitlin, that's—"

"A leap, I know. But I'm going to work on that assumption until someone comes up with a better explanation."

"Do you know why these locations are . . . colliding?"

"Not yet," she admitted. "Don't let the Pawars give Maanik anything except water, if she'll take it."

"I'll try but Mrs. Pawar is pretty desperate. Cai, there's one more thing." He hesitated again.

"Just blurt it out."

"Okay. Maanik seems to be emitting . . . something."

"Something?"

"It's thermal, I guess, but it seems to have substance too. A constant, steady flow from her right hand. Cold, like mist. Please don't tell me it's her soul or something."

"I don't think it's her soul," Caitlin said. She did not add, *But I don't know what it might be.* She looked out the window. "We're on the expressway now, traffic's not so bad. I'll be there in about forty-five minutes." She hesitated. "Are *you* okay? What's happening in Kashmir?"

She noticed the cab driver's face tweak, turn slightly toward her. She looked at the name on his license, Shri Kapoor. Their eyes met for a moment in the rearview mirror.

"The UN sent a small force over there but not in the way we hoped," Ben said. "We wanted a protectorate but this is playing out like martial law. The allied countries are starting to grandstand big-time, like the Allies after World War II. Everyone is jockeying for post-crisis influence even though we're not past the crisis yet. Russia was first, on behalf of India. China guaranteed loans for Pakistan. That's all I can say but it feels like we're flinging farther away from any kind of sane, predictable political process." He paused. "Like us," he said tiredly. "I mean, flinging farther away from each other. Not the politics."

She smiled, then promised, "We're going to fix that."

"There's the old college Cai with the old college try," he said.

"Rah," she said. "But first crisis first. Tell me about the Vikings."

"A story in runes," he joked. There was a flash of the old Ben as he dove in, the enthusiastic kid scholar. It made her laugh, and she could imagine his answering grin. "In the ninth century, the trade route between the Baltic Sea and the Caspian Sea was essentially conquered and controlled for two hundred years by people called the Rus."

"Rus as in Russian?"

"Exactly, but that came later, after they intermingled with the Slavs to the point of absorption." He was racing, as if he was trying to get it all on the table before she reached him in the cab. "In the early days they were specifically the Varangian Rus—'Varangian' is from an Old Norse word—and they came down from Scandinavia. They mostly stuck to the trade-and-raid routes, shopping in Baghdad, periodically attacking Constantinople, as pretty much everyone did for thousands of years—"

"Three Vikings walk into a bar in Constantinople . . . ," she said slowly.

Ben chuckled and sucked down a breath. He realized he was rushing.

"Okay," he continued, more slowly. "The Varangian Rus *also* traveled east beyond Constantinople, to the city of Bolghar on the Volga. The Silk Road was fully active—"

"But that trade route connecting the West to the East was much more recent than an ice-free Antarctica. What's this got to do with us?"

"The fact that it *happened*," he said. "This all occurred between the ninth and eleventh centuries. It was written about, mapped, charted. But it could have happened before, any number of times, and if no one wrote about it, or we haven't found the writings—"

"Or we haven't *deciphered* the writings—"

"Exactly. And how do we know that in your 'other time' things were even written? We've witnessed these words and gestures. Maybe there were people who just memorized things, like human computers."

And communicated those thoughts en masse, at death, to another brain? Caitlin wondered. *Was that also part of the transpersonal plane?* She was getting ahead of herself.

"Ben, we're coming to the Triborough Bridge and I need a minute to just absorb—"

"Of course. I'll see you in a few."

"Wait. Do you have your equipment?"

"After all these years, do you really have to ask?"

"Thank you, Ben, so much."

"You're welcome."

She ended the call, sat back, and took a deep breath.

Under the portentous skies, her mind returned to the task at hand, to Maanik. She had to figure out how to approach her; this could well be her last chance. Without really thinking about it, she reached out with her left hand and touched the frame of the taxi just above her window. At first she felt only the rumble of the road through the steel, but after a second she felt something deeper. She could *feel* a path extending far beyond the shape of the cab, the traffic outside, even beyond the towers of the city and the angry sky.

It reminded her of her first day in Central Park, decades ago, when she had walked toward scattered elm trees, then among them—and suddenly the trees aligned in long, straight rows. The feeling of alignment had been almost as audible as a click. Now, here in the cab, her perspective had shifted and extended again. The expansion was clear and energetic and familiar. She had felt this on the airplane in that moment of full physical acceptance of truth. Again she felt radiance in her sternum, and took a long inhale and exhale. She continued to breathe steadily and kept her eyes open, pinging from one visual cue to another: streetlamp to car to fire hydrant to pedestrian.

Arriving at the Pawars' apartment, passing through their door, the atmosphere was so heavy it threatened to unbalance her. All was quiet and dead around her, yet there was also turmoil.

Gales of madness, she thought, flashing back to the experiences with Atash and Gaelle. *Is that what Jack London feels?*

"Dr. O'Hara," the ambassador said with a formal nod.

"Ambassador Pawar," she replied. She did not want to get into a conversation with him. Maanik was stretched out on a sofa, covered in a quilt, her mother by her head, stroking her hair. Caitlin took one look at the girl's drained face and turned to Ben, standing well to the side.

"Please set up the camera in Maanik's bedroom."

Ben reached for his bag but hesitated, waiting for the Pawars' approval.

"No, *not* there!" Hansa blurted. "She is much worse in her room!"

"That's why we have to be there."

"But she nearly jumped from the—"

"I know. We will not let her anywhere near the window. Please, both of you, I *know* your daughter is still fighting this and I also know that medicine isn't the answer and that institutionalizing her will do no good. This is our last chance. We can't possibly succeed with a diluted version of the experience. It has to be vivid and I have to be in there with her."

"What do you mean, 'in there'?" the ambassador asked.

"I am going to hypnotize us together. I'm not going to listen and analyze like before, I'm going to experience everything that she is experiencing." She looked at Hansa. "Mrs. Pawar, please put Jack London somewhere else. On the other side of the apartment."

"I'll get him," Ambassador Pawar said. "He has not been inclined to leave that spot."

Caitlin knelt beside Maanik. *Left hand, heart hand, spiritual intake,* she thought. *Right hand, spiritual provider.*

Placing her left hand on her own chest, settling herself, Caitlin placed her right hand in Maanik's left. Something softened behind the girl's closed eyes and Caitlin felt a small squeeze of her hand.

"It's time now, Maanik," she said quietly. "Can you come with me?"

The girl struggled a moment, then nodded. Hansa made way as her daughter rose with an almost ethereal delicacy, as if she were weightless. Caitlin waited while Mr. Pawar slipped by with Jack London. The dog struggled but the ambassador held him tightly against his chest.

Caitlin led the girl down the hall. As they walked, she felt Maanik begin to stiffen.

"The room is safe," Caitlin said.

"No—"

"We are not going back to the moment of crisis. We are going to a time an hour or two earlier."

"*Sho*," she said.

Caitlin glanced at Ben, who was filming from the other side of the doorway. She didn't know what the word meant but Ben must have encountered it before because he held up a finger, meaning "one." One hour before the crisis. Maanik was already on her way back, if indeed she had ever left.

Maanik took a step into the bedroom and Caitlin felt her try to withdraw. She put the girl's left hand to her own chest. She could feel her heart throbbing through the fabric of her coat, through Maanik's hand. She took a deep breath. Maanik took one as well. They stepped into the room together and moved slowly until they reached the center. Then Caitlin took up the girl's right hand.

The polarity of Caitlin and Maanik vanished in a swirl. A different place appeared before Caitlin's eyes, the bedroom a dim backdrop fading with every beat of her heart. She was staring at a low building made of the same dark blocks with curved edges that she had seen in the courtyard. There were trees by a wooden door and Maanik—no, it was no longer Maanik—was moving to sit on a doorstep of stone. Caitlin remembered Maanik had described these trees before as part of her home. The girl held her chin in one hand and petted a white and gray seal by her feet with the other as the animal rubbed its whiskers back and forth along her calf. The girl seemed to be staring at Caitlin while engaging in conversation with an older woman who sat on the step beside her. Both were dressed in thick coats made of a kind of fur. The older woman was addressing the girl, shaking her head.

"You must not be distressed."

"But when it comes, anything could go wrong," the young girl replied.

"That is why we must leave before it begins," the old woman continued. "The power the Technologists are unleashing is potentially deadly."

"And the Priests?" asked a third voice, a young man's voice. Caitlin recognized it as her own, but not her own at the same time—and not the same voice she had spoken with in Atash's vision. The girl looked at Caitlin, as did the old woman, but they were seeing him.

The old woman hesitated. "I was once a Believer, but I'm not sure anymore," she finally said. "In any case, I would rather live now than ascend. Please save seats for us on your ship."

"You will leave early though? Otherwise, there may not be time."

"You anticipate panic," the old woman said.

"When the time comes? I do. Ascent through the *cazh* requires faith," the young man replied. "Strong faith. Most people will suddenly discover they want our strong hulls instead. I'll keep seats for you as long as I can."

The old woman looked up, gazed at a full moon brightening in a sky nearing sunset. Caitlin thought perhaps the woman would have made a different decision if it were just herself, without her granddaughter to consider.

The grandmother rose slowly to her feet and turned to go into the house behind them but kept her eyes on Caitlin's young man for a second—and suddenly Caitlin felt she was looking at *her*. "I know you care for her as I do," she said. "That is where I must put my trust."

Unnerved, Caitlin broke the gaze and glanced at the girl, who was flashing a smile, then coyly turning her face to look down at her seal.

Caitlin felt the young man start to move toward the girl. She felt a gust of cool air, only now realizing how pleasantly warm the evening had been. The boy took the girl's hands and Caitlin felt their connection. She realized then, with certainty, that Maanik and this girl had been merged ever since the visions started. And if this girl's soul, or transpersonal identity, or whatever it was, was connected to Maanik, then the girl was not going to leave with the boy on his ship. Something else had happened.

Caitlin let go and the boy let go and suddenly she was back in Maanik's bedroom, with Maanik staring at her. Caitlin quickly took both of the girl's hands, not to reconnect but to make sure she didn't get away.

"Maanik?"

The girl seemed confused. She tried to let go of Caitlin's hands but Caitlin held hers tightly.

"No. Stay with me."

"I have to go," the girl said frantically. "I don't belong here."

"Where?"

"Alive."

Horrified, Caitlin almost let go of her. This wasn't Maanik. This was the merged identity, some strange hybrid—part Maanik, part the other. It was not a split personality, not post-traumatic stress as anyone understood it, not even "possession." It was something else, something new. More importantly, she suddenly understood *why* they were merged.

"Listen to me," Caitlin said. The girl tried to withdraw her left hand. Caitlin gripped it and focused. "Listen. I know you're trying to complete the ritual, and I know you're trying to join the others and transcend. But something goes wrong each time your people—"

Suddenly her grip broke and cold wind blew against the back of Caitlin's head. She felt her hair rising, heard shouts and screams from every side. She saw a sky turning red with fire that was shot from the earth to heights she could not imagine.

The girl before her was heaving sobs. Her hands were trying to lift into the air, not in the gestures of the strange language but with drooping wrists, with the awful helplessness of a child crying inconsolably. Caitlin was crying too now, feeling the girl's gasping, choking cries in her own body.

The young man was not present. The grandmother was not present. There was just the girl in the midst of chaos. Clearly the crisis had come early. People had not been prepared. The well-planned exodus the young man had spoken of had not taken place.

But this was not Caitlin's concern. It was not something she could repair. She had only one objective.

"Maanik!" Caitlin called, hoping to reach her. "What you see around you is not happening. It already *happened*. You are not there."

The girl shook her head as embers fell and scorched her bare arms. "I . . . *am*. I must . . . transcend."

"No, you must not!"

"It is already being done," she said through tears.

This wasn't working; Caitlin would have to go through this girl to get to Maanik. "Tell me your name."

"Bayarmii," the girl wept.

"Bayarmii, you must listen. The ritual is not going to work. I know you want to join with the others, but something is going wrong."

"Why?" she wailed.

"I don't know yet. But I do know that this isn't working. You have to stop taking Maanik back with you."

"No, I need her."

"But you're *killing* her!"

"Yes," the girl said, rubbing at her face, trying to see through her tears. "If she dies, we will go together. That is what we were told."

"You've been told a lie," Caitlin said. "Bayarmii, you *will* ascend through your own private prayer. This ritual—what you're doing now, the *cazh*—it's something else. Please, let go."

The girl looked around. "I can't!" Her face was twisted, tortured, terrified.

Then there was silence. Maanik's bedroom began to waver back into Caitlin's vision.

"Bayarmii?" There was no response. Then, hopefully, Caitlin looked at the girl standing before her and said, "Maanik?"

"Yes," Maanik said, trembling.

Caitlin knew that something was still terribly wrong—the bedroom would not steady around them. The other place was still flashing in and through it.

"Maanik, do you understand what Bayarmii said?"

"Yes." Maanik was shaking hard. Caitlin took her hands again. "She's not letting go of me, though," Maanik said. "She's so scared. She wants to come with me."

"You must tell her *no*."

"But . . . she says she'll die if she remains. She says she has to come with me!"

She is already dead, Caitlin wanted to tell her. "Maanik, Bayarmii is very frightened and very confused but that's not *your* responsibility. It's not your job." Caitlin held her hands tightly as words spilled out of her. "Just like it wasn't your job to save your father. That was up to the bodyguard and he did it, he protected your papa." Maanik was weeping again. "You did what *you* were supposed to do. You kept yourself safe and that's exactly what you have to do here. You have to tell her no. Helping her is my job, and I will do it. But you have to come back to me first."

Maanik shuddered, sobbing.

"Listen to me. Your parents love you. Stay here for them and stay here for you."

"I *can't*," she choked out, trying to pull her hands away.

Caitlin held fast. "You can. Listen to my voice. Follow it."

"I'm lost—"

"You're here, with me, with your family, your mother and your father who love you dearly."

"Papa . . ."

"That's it," Caitlin encouraged her.

"Papa . . . papa . . . *papa!*"

CHAPTER 32

Maanik's final cry seemed to empty her. She collapsed and then they were both on the floor. The bedroom stabilized around them and the other place disappeared. Caitlin put her arms around Maanik and held on to her tightly as the girl wept into her neck. Caitlin could see the Pawars standing behind Ben, tears coursing down their faces. Caitlin beckoned them with a nod and then moved aside so the family could fall into each other's arms.

"Is she . . . ?" the ambassador asked.

"For the moment," Caitlin told him. "But we're not done. You must keep her here."

"Of course."

"No, I mean here in this time and place," Caitlin said. "I'm sorry, I don't have time to explain more fully."

She instructed the ambassador to help his daughter to stand, then led the family back to the living room and had Maanik lie down on the couch again. She placed the ambassador's right hand on his daughter's left. "Don't let go of this hand. Talk to her—about anything, it doesn't matter. Send good energy through your right hand and she'll absorb it through her left. Hopefully she'll keep shifting any bad energy out through her right."

The ambassador was confused but he didn't move his hand, and Caitlin quickly walked over to Ben. "I have to find a way to make this permanent."

"How?"

But Caitlin was already hurrying away. "Mrs. Pawar, please get Jack London and keep him with Maanik, close. I believe that will help. And would you mind if I borrowed something from your kitchen?"

Mrs. Pawar nodded and Caitlin searched through the kitchen cabinets until she found what she was looking for: jasmine tea.

"Ben, can you come with me?" Caitlin asked. "I need your help."

"Of course," he said, moving to her side.

As they returned to the living room Ambassador Pawar asked, "Where are you going, Dr. O'Hara?"

"Not too far," Caitlin said evasively. "Does Maanik's bedroom door lock?"

"Not from the outside."

"All right, can you please figure out how to obstruct the door, maybe with furniture or duct tape, or both? But make sure someone is always holding Maanik's left hand."

"Yes, yes," he said. "And if the flames start again?"

"If it comes to that, do what your wife did last time and put her in the shower. But Maanik should sleep now and hopefully I'll be back soon."

The ambassador nodded wearily but with a grateful look in his eyes.

As Caitlin and Ben walked briskly to the door, Caitlin asked, "Do you feel it, smell it?"

"Faintly," he replied. "I mean, there *was* a fire—"

"No," Caitlin shook her head. "Death."

"Jesus—no, Cai."

Caitlin did not bother to elaborate. She and the other place were still joined, somehow; the dead and dying were not far away.

Waiting for the elevator, Caitlin pushed the tin of tea into Ben's hands. "If I start to disappear or burn or god knows what, and you want to bring me back, open this and hold it under my nose."

"Mystic smelling salts?" he asked, sincerely confused.

"It's a little more aggressive than that," she said. "This is my 'black-berries,' a connection to a place that made a strong impression in the present."

"I see," he said, but didn't.

The elevator arrived and they stepped inside. Both were silent until Ben reached for her. She started to respond but stopped herself, kept her distance.

"Sorry," Ben said. "I only—"

"I know, it's just—whatever happens, don't touch me and don't let me touch you."

"Am I that irresistible?" he joked.

She smiled. "It's not that. There's just an energy balancing act going on inside me and I don't want to upset it."

"Can you explain?"

"Then and now. There and here. I'm holding them both. I don't want any outside energy to distract me."

He looked at her. "Was that meant to clarify?"

The door opened at the lobby and they hurried toward the street.

"It's like hypnagogia," she told him. "Half-wakefulness. Like when you're wrenched from a nightmare but you still feel partly trapped in it."

Ben held open the front door for her. "You don't seem half-asleep to me, Cai—girl with rivets—"

"Right, like the big strong ocean liner that ran into an iceberg," she said.

"But you're alert."

"Guarded," she corrected him. Under the entrance canopy she hesitated, peering around at the soft rain. "It's back," she said. "The feeling I had here before."

"Of being watched?"

"Yes." She closed her eyes, shutting out the glistening blackness of the street, seeing the high columns of that strange other place, the black pillars covered with misty sea spray.

"So where *are* we going?" Ben asked.

She snapped her eyes open. "I need to go to the United Nations."

"Okay. You want a cab?"

She shook her head and quickly started walking the few blocks to the Secretariat Building, silent the entire way, Ben's fingers hovering near Caitlin's elbow. She felt his energy, his care.

The rain intensified. The asphalt of the streets shone more and more like polished black stone and it was difficult to stay present here, now. Caitlin focused on the white lights of the thirty-nine-story oblong United Nations tower; they read like lines of Braille through the darkness. She did not speak until Ben had flashed his ID to the guard and brought her to the elevators.

"My office?" he asked.

"No. I want to go to the room where the Kashmir negotiations are taking place."

Ben froze. "The guard will want to know why," he said, anxiety in his face. "So do I."

"Trauma."

"I don't follow."

"You saw how Maanik's room was a magnet, a nexus?"

"You lost me. I thought *she's* the conduit, not the place."

"She is, but once that horror was out, it stayed. Jack London sensed it. I'm not a direct conduit the way Maanik is, so I can't go back without something that will act like a bellows, fanning the fire. I need more trauma, pain and fear."

"You know how that sounds?" Ben asked.

"Yeah. Sad, masochistic—and necessary."

"Rewind. You said 'go back.' To do what, exactly?"

"To work with them," she said, "the entities from Antarctica millions of years ago."

"Are you loopy? Assuming you *can* get there, this goes beyond racial memory, Cai, beyond Jung. I mean, *way* beyond."

"I know. Crazy as it sounds, I believe their souls were in the middle of something that locked them there, in that state, before some force from inside the earth vaporized their physical bodies."

"And they've been doing *what* in limbo for all these millennia? Trying to get back?"

"It's the transpersonal plane, not limbo, and yes, I think so. Maybe some of them have succeeded, cases that have been misdiagnosed as everything from demonic possession to severe schizophrenia."

"You got all this from a *vision* that may not be real, that may *never* have been real."

"That and a Hindu cleric."

"Oh, that makes it all right," Ben said.

"Damn it, Ben. Maanik catching fire was very real. We have to discuss this later, we're wasting time."

"No. You want in, you're going to have to tell me what you're planning," Ben said. "I'm worried about you too."

Caitlin sighed. She would have done the same thing if the roles were reversed. "What I think I saw were the souls of many individuals melding into one. They want to be joined in the transpersonal plane, in their afterlife, for some reason. And they can only do that as they are in the process of transitioning."

"You mean, the ultimate group hug before death? Or else your soul flies solo?"

"That's my general understanding," Caitlin said. "If they go individually, like the ancient girl struggling to take Maanik, it'll derail the purpose of the ceremony. I bought us some time by bargaining with that girl, Bayarmii, on her own. That weakens the ancient ritual but it's not going to hold. They'll pull Bayarmii back in and she will try and get to Maanik again. That's what's been happening, over and over. I think I have to encounter *all* the individuals while they're in the process of transitioning into their group soul, and try to stop the transformation."

"How?"

"I'm not entirely sure, but I'm going to try doing what people do at séances: turn on the light, break the spell. I can self-hypnotize but to go back and interact with them I need power, Ben, and trauma seems to be a key. Right now, the most traumatic event taking place near me is the struggle over Kashmir." *The locus of frustration and pain touching all the ends of the earth.*

"Cai . . . I hear you, but this is crazy talk."

"I prefer to call it a big leap of faith." She smiled a little. "Two agnostics walk into a bar . . ."

He couldn't even manage a nervous laugh. He stared at her a long moment, saw the resolve in her eyes. And punched button 38 on the elevator bank.

When they reached the floor Ben showed the guard his ID, introduced Caitlin as a special consultant from Geneva—she showed her WHO credentials—and they were escorted down the hall and admitted to an empty conference room. The guard returned to his post at the end of the long corridor.

Caitlin stopped Ben from turning on the lights of the room. She could already feel the buzzing of energy in the air. She felt high emotion in her lungs, her belly, the small of her back. She removed her coat and scarf, began to walk through the room, moving with a flow she couldn't see, only feel. Ben followed protectively, but at a distance.

Ambient light from the city glowed through a wall of exterior windows at the far end of the room. Caitlin bumped into the first of a couple dozen wide, golden leather chairs. There was only room for one person to comfortably walk around the table at a time, and nowhere to shove the chairs other than into their stations at the table. She considered standing on the table so there would be room to move if she needed it, but diffuser panels were slung low beneath the lights.

She was sure her head would come too close to them for comfort. Navigating to the end of the table, she found she had about four feet of space to the windows. It would have to be enough.

"What can I do to help?" Ben asked softly.

She shook her head slightly, gazed outside. "How strong are those windows?"

"Very. The recent renovations replaced all five thousand windows with the latest blast-proof panes. In a hurricane, this is one of the safest places you could be."

"What about a volcano?" she asked.

He didn't know if she was kidding. He didn't answer.

The city seemed small compared to the immensity of the time and distance she was beginning to feel. Caitlin was scared. She stopped moving and placed a hand on a conference room chair to steady herself.

Immediately she saw a vision of a human body on fire. The vision was slightly unclear, juddering back and forth as if seen with a hand-held camera. She realized that was exactly what was happening. This was the video of the woman who had self-immolated over her dead son, the few seconds of footage Caitlin had seen on her tablet. She heard voices shouting across the table, all around her, and then the people shouting . . .

. . . were there, in the courtyard, just beyond her fingertips. Suddenly she was one of many. Many voices, some chanting the *cazh*, some crying, some screaming. A few were just beginning to express the wonder of transcendence. Their bodies moved like reeds in a pond in their white and yellow robes. Then, as though the air and energy left them in a rush, their bodies dropped to the paving stones of the courtyard, across the huge crescents carved into the flat, black rocks.

Above their heads a pulsing force drew Caitlin's attention. She could not see it but she could feel it, and the presence grew as the bodies fell to the ground.

•   •   •

Ben watched every tendril of Caitlin's hair lift in a breeze he didn't feel. She opened her mouth and exhaled, but it was not the sigh of a single soul. It was the combined sound of multitudes.

Ben stepped back, reached for the tin of tea he had placed on the table. He stopped himself.

Not yet. But he was ready.

Now Caitlin was breathing heavily. Her arms were moving. Ben heard words, identified a few, combined them with the gestures to understand the superlatives. It was too late to set up his camera but he took out his cell phone and began recording.

"The fire!" she said. "So much death. The end is here!"

•   •   •

All around her, Caitlin could see the destruction of a civilization, and she was part of it, part of this place—Galderkhaan. She knew its name now, only as it was dying. Standing here by the temple, the Hall of the Priests, she could see the volcano to the east, blowing the center of the earth into the sky.

A towering, sulfurous wave of glaring orange and gold lava spewed from the volcano's mouth, knocking down the first of a long line of tall, glowing columns that led from the volcano to the sea. *Connecting yin and yang, the left hand to the right hand*, Caitlin thought with sudden realization. The Technologists had built the array, which gathered energy and passed it from column to column, like tuning forks growing exponentially more powerful. Was this some kind of technological response to the *cazh*? If so, something had gone wrong with this process as well. One by one, the pillars collapsed beneath the juggernaut of lava rolling toward the city. Clouds of red and black, fire and cinders, fell on the courtyard and buildings. Heaps of hot ash piled onto white and yellow robes that once held souls and were now just incendiary masses of flesh.

The wave of lava would overwhelm the courtyard soon. Caitlin had to find Bayarmii. She followed the sightline of tall columns away from the courtyard to the west, where the columns pierced the sea, shining green from their capstones. A full moon was gasping for breath between breaks in the clouds, strobing its blue-white light across the roiling ocean. The sea was flinging itself at the sky, hunching its back in titanic waves and bucking and kicking at the columns and the shore . . .

And at ships. Ships with long, graceful dragon's heads, each carved with a symbol of crescents entwined, the symbol that appeared on the capstones of the columns and in the paving stones of the courtyard— the sole remnant of a time before the rise of conflicting factions, chaos that helped bring a civilization to this precipice.

Focus, Caitlin, remember why you're here, she told herself. She remembered a young man, a granddaughter, a seal, and felt her mind suddenly fuse with the grandmother's. She was holding Bayarmii's hand—

Then the earth shifted as a huge sea wave struck hard, and she fell. When she clambered upright Bayarmii was gone. Caitlin looked back, peering through smoke and mist, ash and flame. She saw that Bayarmii had run back to the white and gray seal, who was mad with fear inside the house. The trees burned outside the front door. It was too late. Too late to join the boy on the boat.

"The *cazh*!" screamed the grandmother. "It's our last chance to ascend together!"

The girl obeyed. One of the burning trees fell against the door, trapping the girl and seal inside. A flaming branch cracked on impact, slashed toward her, simultaneously shearing and cauterizing her arm. The words of the prayer became more powerful and immediate and the spirit of the girl rose . . .

Caitlin could only hope that Maanik was not experiencing this, that Bayarmii was subsumed in the moment. But her hope was overwhelmed by the grandmother's willpower. She would not abandon her granddaughter. She, too, knew the words. She had been a devotee of the Priests in her youth. She spoke the *cazh*; she focused on the pulsing energy gathered above the dead and dying in the temple courtyard. Even as waves ran toward her and hot ash sizzled on her bare neck and arms, she spoke . . .

• • •

Ben saw Caitlin smile. Her expression was almost euphoric. She spoke with gestures: "Hundreds of feet in the air! I want to rise with the sea, with the wind, in a great swell! I want to look down at the white ice cliffs and the black columns . . ."

The conference room was vibrating as though a subway train were passing underneath, but it wasn't *moving*. Ben glanced outside. Through the driving rain and wind he thought he saw the East River rising in fifteen-foot waves. It had to be a trick of the thick glass, the rain, the mist.

He turned back to Caitlin. Her head was upraised, her arms in a pose he had seen when Maanik was at her most distressed, just before they used the blackberries cue. Caitlin's left fingers were spreading and reaching farther, seeking or pointing, he couldn't tell. There was a rippling above her, like rising heat.

"It's everywhere!" Caitlin cried out in English.

Where is the guard? Ben thought. *Isn't he hearing any of this?*

He could feel something building in the room, but it was ephemeral, invisible. A hot wind coiled around him. Was he experiencing what Caitlin felt with Maanik, a spillover of some ancient energy, hovering unseen like the air itself?

"What is everywhere?" he called.

"The transpersonal plane!" she cried. "Souls are rising! My god, it is *powerful*! I am ascendant! But there's more . . . I can't see . . ."

• • •

Other minds brushed past her, transcending spirits interlacing with each other as they departed one realm and entered another, unified in a churning mass soul. Yet everywhere, too, bodies were perishing before the ritual could be completed, before they could link with the group soul. Those souls were rising alone.

She could still question, she could still think: *Is that the key? But how can I stop so many from completing the* cazh *at once?*

But she threw the questions away, wanting only to be here and now, with them. One spirit turned from the group and looked into Caitlin's eyes.

Not you, the grandmother told her. *You are not one of us.*

Though Caitlin longed to complete the transcendence with them, see what was out there, she obeyed.

I am still Caitlin, she told herself.

She held back, then withdrew. She focused on the conference room floor beneath her feet, heard the pounding rain on the windows.

I must remain myself.

She thought of the people in the park in Tehran, the men and women doing Tai Chi, moving with sublime balance. She pressed her left foot hard against the conference room floor, like a sprinter pushing her foot into a starting block. This reality, coming in through her left, would hold her here a little longer.

I am still me.

She felt stabilized, literally with one foot in each world. But she still had to stop the mass soul that was forming around her, above her, in Galderkhaan. The souls that were seeking other traumatized souls in Caitlin's present.

•   •   •

Ben saw Caitlin's smile vanish. He noticed the change in her position. She was speaking again but he was finding it harder to hear her. He realized suddenly that it wasn't her voice that was changing; there was a pressure increasing in his head, and his eardrums were throbbing, as though he were in an airplane that had depressurized. He opened his mouth wide, worked his jaw, swallowed; it succeeded for an instant and then the pressure returned. With one eye on Caitlin he moved to the windows, trying to locate the source of the pressure. A vent . . . an ill-fitting window . . . a gap in the ceiling . . . ?

There was nothing. The wind threw rain at the windows like stones.

He set his cell phone on the table and ventured closer to Caitlin, staggering against the pressure in his head. Caitlin's hair was still floating. Her eyes were shut, her mouth was moving, her arms helping to fashion unfamiliar words. He fought against his brutal headache, to make his feet move toward the tin of tea.

"What do I do?" he whispered, half-praying for an answer.

• • •

Caitlin did not hear. Everywhere she looked, she could see the dead or dying. Beyond the trees she could see the same young man from Atash's vision, performing the *cazh*. Across the water she watched as a boat smashed into one of the largest pillars, coming to pieces, its inhabitants clawing at the waves, or raising their hands in supplication even as they drowned. *Gaelle*, Caitlin thought helplessly. There was nothing she could do to save them from their deaths. She had to press on, had to stop the rising group soul and protect others in the present . . .

• • •

Ben saw smoke rising from her flesh.

"Caitlin!"

"Don't . . . touch . . . me!"

There was a decanter of water on the conference table. He would use it if he had to. He did not understand very much but he knew this: they might never have this chance again. He had to let it play out.

• • •

Caitlin had no time left to think and not much of a rational mind to think with. Instead, she *felt* herself rise from the temple, rise from the conference room, beyond the ash and beyond the rain, into a cloud that was thunder and darkness, that was the coldness of the grave multiplied by eternity. Despite the grandmother's warning, Caitlin allowed herself to ascend, carried by the older woman's soul. Caitlin's grip on her own living body grew weaker.

Two worlds were merging violently. The storm seemed to roil above Manhattan as Galderkhaan was pulled into the sea with the roaring hiss of dying flames. The innumerable souls of the ascended were everywhere.

Caitlin clung single-mindedly to one thought, one objective: the group soul trying to form and cross the barrier of time. She thought of the young people she knew and did not know in her own world, others like Maanik and Gaelle and Atash who were made vulnerable by trauma and were probably being assaulted, their own souls being dragged painfully upward along with those of these ancient beings, for reasons still unknown. She had to stop them.

Below her, she saw the entire city, the roads and streets, the line of columns that ran from the volcano to the sea, glowing green with their strange energy—but also, in the capstone of the tallest column in the sea, a symbol. A triangle made of crescents within crescents. It was the same symbol she had seen Gaelle draw. The same one Maanik had drawn.

Caitlin glanced at the powerful, rising group soul, and then she knew what she had to do. She turned and plunged across the sky toward the largest column. There was no sense of weight or weightlessness, no sense of motion, only a sensation of sudden, lightning-like extension—point to point to point. Arms outstretched, she grabbed at the energy around the column as if it were tangible.

And it was. She felt it writhe in her embrace, become one with her, like the power she'd received from the snake but exponentially more. She wrenched her body around and with a long sweep of her arms, she cast the power toward the courtyard. It flew through and away from her, as in Haiti when, out of control, Caitlin had thrown Gaelle against a wall.

But this time she directed it.

The tsunami of lava was perilously close to the city as the energy reached the courtyard and infused it. The paving stones erupted in light from beneath, a brilliant glow that blazed through the huge triangle carved into them, the crescents within crescents.

Those who were still standing and chanting the *cazh*, those shocked Galderkhaani, screamed as the fusion of earth, fire, water, and light swept over them. Their movements changed from swaying to lurching tremors as their souls were yanked one from the other from the other, unlinked. Abruptly, their mortal screams stopped as their right and left brains ceased to function together. Their mouths remained frozen for a moment; an instant later the right sides of their bodies crumpled. They fell heavily to the stones where they died. Thick, bloody liquid flowed from their noses and mouths onto their burning white and yellow robes.

And Caitlin saw that once more their souls rose, invisible yet somehow tangible. But with this death, a death without the *cazh*, they were ascending as individuals. The group soul was no more. Whatever its purpose had been, that goal was unrealized. Whatever power had allowed the bonded souls to reach through time, that was gone.

The mammoth wave of lava broke over the city and destroyed it. There was nothing epic or prolonged about its demise: one moment Galderkhaan struggled, then it was gone. Caitlin felt the ecstasy of the energy depart from her; no longer immaterial, she plummeted into the sea . . .

And dropped to the floor of the conference room. Ben broke her fall.

There was a quiet hiss as the smoke rising from her body was suddenly doused. Ben stroked her hair back. Her eyes were closed, her mouth relaxed.

"Cai?"

There was no response. He flipped the top from the tin, brought the jasmine tea to her nose, and held her tightly with his free arm. After a moment he heard her very quietly inhale.

"Cai? Are you . . . here?"

She opened her eyes, struggled to focus. Then, finding his face, she smiled.

"Yeah," she said. "I'm here."

CHAPTER 33

Caitlin woke the next morning to see Jacob, fully dressed, leaning over her, smoothing her hair from her face. Caitlin blinked at the light shining from the hall through the open door, the tall figure of her father in the frame. Weak sunlight was filtering around the corners of her curtains.

"I'm going to school with Grandpa," Jacob signed, then pasted himself to her for a hug and a kiss. Smiling, she watched the bedroom door shut quietly behind them.

Her eyes closed and she suddenly felt achingly alone, lonelier than she'd ever felt in her life. She had been bonded in a group the night before, in a still-unimaginable way, and now that was gone. She ran a hand through her hair; it felt too fine and unfamiliar.

Knowing it was four a.m. in Santa Monica, she phoned her sister anyway. Abby sounded wide awake.

"Whoa . . . I was *just* thinking about you."

Caitlin was silent, staring at the ceiling. There was no way to tell her about any of it.

"Cai? Are you there? Did you butt-dial me?"

"Abby, do you think souls are real?"

"That's . . . unexpected."

"I know, I'm just—I don't know. You've been around death. I mean, person-to-person. Much more than I have."

"Too much of it," Abby said. "Too much of it young, sudden, *needless*. Drugs, drinking, texting while driving, hit by cars, shot in malls."

"And?"

"And, yeah, I do. This may sound nutty but sometimes when people die—only for an instant, the kind of moment that's so fast you wonder if it happened—I can feel them. Not always, but briefly, after the life signs are gone, it's very clear to me that I'm not the only person in the room. The feeling is stronger if I'm holding their hand." Abby waited a moment. "Why are you asking?"

Caitlin had expected the question; there was no easy answer. "Just soul searching," she joked.

"Cute," Abby groaned. "Dad says you've been traveling."

"Oh yeah," Caitlin said. "That I have. Call you later?"

"Sure. I've got to go anyway."

"Wait—you were just *thinking* about me? What are you doing up at this hour?"

"Got an early surgery," Abby said.

"Ah. Good luck."

"Thanks. Burn victim."

When Abby said "burn victim," Caitlin felt herself tense. She wondered if that would always happen, going forward.

Their call ended and she lay back. Her eyes closed, her mind closed, and she was asleep again.

Three hours later, when Caitlin was fully awake and caffeinated, the tabby Arfa draped across her lap, she opened her computer and her e-mail. At the top of the list was one from Ben, subject line: *2.5M hits in 4 hrs*. Caitlin clicked on the attached video—and she was watching brightly painted trucks full of men and lumber driving into something like a shopping center in India, but a wrecked, distressed shopping center. It looked as if it had been through a hurricane. The men piled out of the trucks and hurried to greet the few people who were edging cautiously toward them from nearby houses. Then the video jumped to show construction—men repairing domed roofs—and people setting up long tables with lunch.

Caitlin called Ben and he picked up immediately.

"What am I watching?" she said, smiling as she saw little kids helping to drag planks toward a blasted shop front.

"The solution to all our problems," he said. "This video was posted at around noon Jammu time and it went viral faster than any video in history. This shopping center saw a showdown between armed forces with guns, bombs, you name it. That's what I was watching the night after we—after I stayed over. Apparently, truck-loads of Pakistanis and Indians just converged on the city and now they're rebuilding everything, the temple, the stores, the cinema. When the video went viral there was an international outcry calling for reconciliation. Both delegations showed up this morning to make a deal. It was—actually, it was very strange, like they'd all woken from a fever or something."

"That's amazing," Caitlin said. "It's too . . ."

"Impossible?" Ben asked. "Nevertheless, that was all it took. Supposed enemies treating each other as people, with dignity. Cooperation. Kindness."

"And the governments listened," she mused.

"Listened? This was just the face-saving grassroots stuff they were praying for."

"What does that mean for Kashmir?"

"We're not sure," Ben said. "Both governments agreed to pull their troops from the region. It'll take some effort before they actually *do* it, but the ambassador and his counterpart are hard at work on that now. He has a second wind, I'll tell you that." Ben chuckled. "Actually, I guess I don't have to tell you that."

"How is Maanik?"

"The ambassador said she's herself again."

"Specifics?"

"She has her energy back, her joy, her enthusiasm, and she's been on the phone with her friends nonstop."

"Does she remember anything?"

"Honestly, Cai, nobody wants to ask her. She was told she had a very bad lung infection and she didn't question it."

"What about the dog?"

"He's fine too," Ben said. "That was the third thing I asked: how's the world, how's Maanik, how's Jack London."

"He's a part of this somehow," Caitlin said. "Like the snake in Haiti, possibly even those rats that massed downtown."

"Odd grouping, wouldn't you say?"

"I would."

"Any idea how they're connected?"

"None," she admitted. But the claw tips of the crescent symbol flashed through her brain.

"Speaking of which, you and the snake showed up in a YouTube video," Ben said.

"What?"

"Yeah. I'll send you the link. Don't worry. Only a couple hundred hits. You haven't gone viral."

"Am I identified?" she asked.

"Not by name," he replied. "Now I have one more question before I head back into the conference room. How are *you*?"

She chuckled mirthlessly. "Honestly? I have no idea. My brain is present and accounted for but . . . there's been a shift of some kind." She extended a hand toward the little sliver of Hudson River she could see outside the window. "There's something . . . different. I can't explain it."

"You self-hypnotized into quite a state," Ben said. "I'm not surprised you're a little disoriented."

"Disoriented but connected."

"To what?"

"I don't know that either." She let her hand drop. "To something."

There was more to say, a lot more, but Caitlin let it go. Everything she'd experienced would require a great deal more reflection and investigation.

"Can I assume that whatever it was, whatever *they* were, they're gone now?" Ben asked.

"I'm not sure. I'm not sure they were ever *here*."

"If by 'here' you mean 'on earth,' the linguistic evidence certainly supports their existence," Ben said. "You and Maanik didn't make that up."

"No," Caitlin agreed. "But a civilization that may have existed before we began recording history . . . a civilization that still seems to have active moving parts, probably *did* make it up."

"And—group hug—a civilization you and I seem to have discovered," he added proudly.

"That too. It's a very big idea to process."

"One which I'm thrilled to investigate," he said. "I was looking at the data from yesterday. There are a lot of new words and two of them kept repeating, something about 'those of spirit' and 'those of mechanism.'"

"Priests and Technologists," Caitlin said.

"Yes, that's about right." He hesitated. "You want to talk about it?"

"I'm still unclear about what the Technologists were doing. The Priests were attempting to escape their physical bodies and ascend, but they were also trying to unite."

"You mean join hands, like that kid's game, Ring Around the Rosie?"

"No, more like what I said before, a séance. A ritual where the whole is much greater than the sum of the parts. A joining that was very powerful and getting stronger, that was fishing for souls here, now. That's why I did what I did. I felt that if I could interfere with their ceremony, they would be unable to rise as a group."

"What was the point of their joining?"

"I don't know."

Ben was silent.

"Go ahead," Caitlin said. "Say it."

"Cai, do you actually believe any of that? Especially the part about going into the past? Not physically, obviously, but out-of-body?"

"I must have," she said. "I mean, reverse-engineer it, Ben. Maanik is okay."

"Yes . . ."

"The things I just described fit with the words you translated."

"Also true," Ben agreed.

"So how else do you explain it?"

Ben was quiet again.

Caitlin fell silent too, sifted through scraps of memory. "Ben, did anything happen with my hair?"

"Why do you ask?"

"It's acting . . . unruly today."

"Yes," he said, and she heard reluctance. "It was standing on end."

"Moving as if in a wind or water?"

"No, standing as if it got zapped with static electricity," Ben answered thoughtfully. "A charge built up by the storm, I figured."

"A charge I felt through those blast-proof windows? That you didn't feel?"

Again, Ben was silent.

"Well, one puzzle at a time," she said. "Something changed Maanik after the assassination attempt, and something yesterday changed her back. The world is a little saner today. Maybe that's enough for now."

"Not for me," Ben admitted. "I'm still stuck on the simple, non-metaphysical question of how Galderkhaan could have existed at all."

She started at that. "You know its name?"

"Yeah, you said it last night."

"Galderkhaan," she repeated.

Ben continued. "And it fits the rest of the language, vaguely Mongolian. How could modern humans—they were modern, weren't they?"

"They appeared to be," she answered. "Shorter, maybe? A golden tinge, though that may have been the play of light and smoke."

"Okay, but not Neanderthal or an early hominid," Ben said. "How could they have thrived when our species was supposedly still lemurs in the trees?"

"I don't know." She was silent for a moment. "There is one thing I do know, though."

"What's that?"

"I've got to get going. A psychiatrist walks into her office—"

"Okay, go," Ben said.

They ended the call and Caitlin gazed at the bright world outside, petted the purring cat. She noticed she was petting with her right hand. She switched to petting with her left hand and felt a flow of *something* roll up through her fingers to her heart, settling her, calming her. Arfa purred louder.

"What do you have to do with this?" she asked the cat. She gazed at pigeons on the ledge. "All of you?"

But even as Caitlin felt herself calm, a part of her stood back, apart, wondering what life was going to be like now.

She sighed and set the cat aside, returned to common ground between the old self and the new—her e-mail. She noticed near the top a message from Gaelle Anglade. There was something in the subject line that never would have been there just a few days before.

A smiley face.

EPILOGUE

Mikel Jasso peered over the starboard-side railing of the *Captain Fallow*. The soft fringe of his hood blew against his cheek, protecting it from the sharp wind. The ship was running along the eastern stretch of the Weddell Sea, prevented by the ice pack from approaching the north coast of Antarctica. Presently they were skirting a blocky iceberg that towered hundreds of feet above their heads, gleaming the purest white except where it blushed turquoise blue at its base—but no one was admiring the pale giant. Like the other crew members and scientists crowded along the rail, Jasso was watching the mass of emperor penguins swimming north across the sea.

The number in the migration was unprecedented, as far as veterans of these seas could remember, and it was a month before the penguins' breeding season was supposed to finish. And there was something else, several crew members noted. There was no playfulness in the movements of the penguins, no cautious reconnaissance along their flanks; they did not even bother to swim around the ship, simply propelling themselves beneath it to the other side. Mikel observed them with a careful eye, remembering the flight of the albatrosses. There was the same kind of urgency here, not the haste to get somewhere but a kind of single-minded need to get away from something.

Why now? Jasso wondered.

The question of the albatrosses and the rats had not been far from his mind when he arrived back in the Falklands and saw an unusual number of vessels heading out to sea.

"A lot of fish heading north," a seaman had explained to Mikel.

So now it's fish, Mikel had thought as he tracked down the *Captain Fallow* and financially induced her captain to welcome him aboard. Mikel's forged geology credentials would not bear intense scrutiny, but they held up under the general disinterest of a captain all too happy to receive a surprise "bonus" this year.

The ship had sailed east past the ancient submerged volcanoes of the Scotia Sea, curving south when the ice pack allowed, and the trip had been singularly uneventful with few stops. Mikel spent a great deal of time with the geologist he'd robbed weeks ago while the man slept. Together they watched the fathometer, the GPS, the seismometer, and other equipment. He'd had plenty of time to wonder why the stone he'd acquired had killed Arni now when other stones had been in the Group's possession for over two years. And then, an hour before the penguins began their strange exodus, Mikel had checked his e-mail on one of the ship's computers. Flora had sent two messages, the first a query about a woman in some handheld video from Haiti.

Who is this? Flora asked.

But Mikel had neither the bandwidth nor the patience to inspect the video. He told her he would have to watch it some other time.

Flora's second e-mail was much more interesting—and immediate.

The stones melted the ice in the freezer, she wrote. *I transferred them to another freezer; same thing.*

That, too, was new and presently inexplicable.

What is happening? And why now?

As the penguins continued their departure, Mikel noticed a change in the wind. But it wasn't the wind that had shifted. He pushed from the railing and shouldered his way to the bridge. As he entered the warm, cramped room he asked, "Where are we going?"

"We're following the penguins," the captain snapped in his thick Maine accent.

"Why?"

"Because we just picked up transmissions from research stations McMurdo and Dumont d'Urville," he replied. "It sounds like every damned penguin in Antarctica is checking out. No one knows why. I'm putting some space between us and the continent."

"What do the brain trusts think?"

"The same thing us nonbrains think—that something's scaring them. My guess? Could be some kind of massive ice calving. No one knows."

Mikel was about to ask if the satellites showed any preliminary breakage when a massive crack echoed across the ship.

He grabbed a pair of binoculars from a locker and raced back to the railing. Another crack turned his knees to water but he steadied himself and fixed the binoculars on the iceberg. He felt bodies press around him as the sightseers switched their attention from the penguins to the block of ice—which was splitting in half. But as the awed cries of the veteran sailors suggested, it was like no phenomenon any of them had ever witnessed.

Seawater surged around an ice tower newly separated from its mother berg, swirling like an inverted whirlpool and in slow motion. Mikel swore and shoved his face harder against the binoculars, struggling to accept what he was seeing. It was there for only a moment before that side of the new iceberg turned away from the ship.

The sheared face of the massive chunk of ice had not been purely white or blue. It had held something no living person had seen in Antarctica, an object that would make sense only to someone who had seen it before—and Mikel had.

"What the hell?" he heard someone murmur. "Was something out there?"

"I don't know," said another as the vessel chugged away.

A third person tried bravely to take a video but Mikel artfully inserted himself between the passenger and the object, pretending to slip on the icy deck. By the time the phone was turned back to the calving iceberg, there was nothing to shoot.

Mikel didn't listen to any of the speculations. He had seen the vast brown ovoid marked with black crescents, and below its lowest curve, a smaller, rectangular projection. He had already formed his own hypothesis, rejected it as impossible, then embraced it again—for Mikel had seen this image on a shard of barnacle-crusted pottery.

It was an airship from the lost world of Galderkhaan.

ACKNOWLEDGMENTS

The authors wish to express their gratitude to agent Doug Grad; to Steve Burkow, Sally Wilcox, and Aaron Anderson; to editor Brit Hvide and the team at Simon & Schuster; and most especially to Clare Kent, who managed the flow of pretty much everything.

Gillian Anderson

Gillian Anderson is an award-winning film, television, and theatre actress whose credits include the roles of Special Agent Dana Scully in the long-running and critically acclaimed drama series, *The X-Files*, ill-fated socialite Lily Bart in *The House of Mirth*, Lady Dedlock and Miss Haversham in the BBC productions of Charles Dickens's *Bleak House* and *Great Expectations*, respectively.

Anderson is currently playing the role of DSI Stella Gibson in the critically acclaimed BBC 2 series *The Fall*, Dr. Bedelia Du Maurier in *Hannibal* and is starring in the Young Vic's production of Tennessee Williams' *A Streetcar Named Desire* as Blanche du Bois, directed by Benedict Andrews. She currently lives in the UK with her daughter and two sons.

Jeff Rovin

Jeff Rovin is the author of more than 100 books, fiction and nonfiction, both under his own name, under various pseudonyms, or as a ghostwriter, including numerous *New York Times* bestsellers. He has written over a dozen Op-Center novels for the late Tom Clancy. Rovin has also written for television and has had numerous celebrity interviews published in magazines under his byline. He is a member of the Author's Guild, the Science Fiction Writers of America, and the Horror Writers of America, among others.

Gillian Anderson's Favourite Books

A Visit from the Goon Squad
by Jennifer Egan

The Hare with Amber Eyes
by Edmund de Waal

Olive Kitteridge
by Elizabeth Strout

The Kitchen House
by Kathleen Grissom

Shantaram
by Gregory David Roberts

The Elegance of the Hedgehog
by Muriel Barbery

The Giving Tree
by Shel Silverstein

The Late Hector Kipling
by David Thewlis

The Time Traveler's Wife
by Audrey Niffenegger

The God of Small Things
by Arundhati Roy

Anil's Ghost
by Michael Ondaatje

She's Come Undone
by Wally Lamb

The Last King of Scotland
by Giles Foden

A Million Little Pieces
By James Frey

Bel Canto
by Ann Patchett

A Hologram for the King
by Dave Eggers

Be Near Me
by Andrew O'Hagan

State of Wonder
by Ann Patchett

The White Tiger
by Aravind Adiga

A Fine Balance
by Rohinton Mistry

The Sense of an Ending
by Julian Barnes

In the Forest
by Marie Hall Ets

On Beauty
by Zadie Smith

The Magician's Assistant
by Ann Patchett

The Known World
by Edward P. Jones

The Corrections
by Jonathan Franzen

A Map of the World
by Jane Hamilton

The Kite Runner
by Khaled Hosseini

Saturday
by Ian McEwan

The Burgess Boys
by Elizabeth Strout